THE F WORDS

A NOVEL

THE F WORDS

A NOVEL

BARBARA GREGORICH

A City of Light imprint

Cross Your Heart
A City of Light imprint

City of Light Publishing
266 Elmwood Ave. Suite 407
Buffalo, New York 14222

info@CityofLightPublishing.com
www.CityofLightPublishing.com

Book design by Ana Cristina Ochoa

ISBN 978-1-952536-26-7 (softcover)
ISBN 978-1-952536-27-4 (eBook)

Printed in the U.S.A.
10 9 8 7 6 5 4 3 2 1

Library of Congress Cataloging-in-Publication Data
Names: Gregorich, Barbara, author.
Title: The F words : a novel / Barbara Gregorich.
Description: Buffalo, New York : Cross Your Heart, a City of Light
    Publishing imprint, [2021] | Audience: Ages 12-18. | Audience: Grades
    10-12. | Summary: Caught spray-painting the F word on his Chicago high
    school after his community activist father's arrest, sophomore Cole
    Renner is sentenced to write two poems a week and uses his words to
    fight for justice for his father, for himself, for his best friend, and
    for his fellow students.
Identifiers: LCCN 2021012299 (print) | LCCN 2021012300 (ebook) | ISBN
    9781952536267 (paperback) | ISBN 9781952536274 (adobe pdf) | ISBN
    9781952536274 (ebook) | ISBN 9781952536274 (epub) | ISBN 9781952536274
    (kindle edition) | ISBN 9781952536274 (mobi) | ISBN 9781952536274 (pdf)
Subjects: CYAC: Social justice--Fiction. | HIgh schools--Fiction. |
    Schools--Fiction.
Classification: LCC PZ7.G8613 Faah 2021 (print) | LCC PZ7.G8613 (ebook) |
    DDC [Fic]--dc23
LC record available at https://lccn.loc.gov/2021012299
LC ebook record available at https://lccn.loc.gov/2021012300

CONTENTS

SEPTEMBER   1

OCTOBER   101

NOVEMBER   179

DECEMBER   321

JANUARY   359

For Linda and Guy,
who would march with Cole

CHAPTER 1

 BALANCE ON THE CHAIN LINK fence in the growing darkness, tilting into my work, finishing the last word. Fifteen of them. Fifteen of the F word, stacked one on top of the other like a long stretch into forever. Some of them red, some black. I stash the red can in my pocket next to the black can, let go of the brick wall, and jump down from the fence—right against Mr. Nachman, my English teacher.

"Holy shit!" I shout. And then I dodge to the left, positive I'll get away. I'm on the cross-country team and Nachman isn't a jock.

But it turns out he has fast reflexes or maybe just knows which direction to move in, because he grabs me by my collar and pins me against the fence.

"Cole," he says, "spray painting the school won't solve anything."

"I don't know what you're talking about."

He shakes his head. He's wearing a Cubs baseball cap, the dark blue kind with the old 1908 logo, a bear holding a bat. My favorite of all the Cubs hats. "Why the school?" he asks. "Why not the police station? Or the courthouse?"

In class Nachman's always asking questions like that— penetrating questions my mother calls them whenever I tell her. Questions that show he knows what you're thinking, and that he wants you to go further.

I want to tell him about the injustice of injustice, 'cause I know he'll appreciate that. I want to tell him I don't know what he means about the courthouse or police station. But he knows about Dad. The whole school knows. All of Chicago knows.

So I tell him the truth. "The courthouse has lights all around it. So does the police station."

He nods at this and studies the words on the wall.

Or maybe he's admiring my tagging skills.

"It's not easy to fight against injustice," he says.

Is he talking about me?

Or about Dad?

"There are effectual ways and ineffectual ways," he continues. "Legal ways and illegal ways. Solitary ways and group ways."

He stares hard at me, like we're in class and he wants his point to sink in.

"Dad didn't incite people to violence. It was a peaceful sit-in. Until the cops came. He shouldn't be in jail for fighting against injustice."

Nachman nods and keeps looking at the words on the wall. Technically just one word, fifteen times. He's dressed in jeans and a long-sleeved T-shirt. I'm dressed pretty much the same way. Except for the two cans of paint in my pocket.

"Why red and black?" he asks.

Why red and black?! Man, how am I supposed to know why red and black?

"They look good together?"

He studies the words. Or the wall. Or maybe the night sky.

"Lots of politics there," he says. "Red, the color of workers' revolution. Black, the color of anarchy. Which, maybe, spray painting the walls of a public building might qualify as."

Hardly, I think.

Still pinning me against the fence with one hand, Nachman pulls out his cell phone.

"No!" I shout, grabbing for it. "Who are you calling?!"

"Relax," he says. "I'm calling Ms. Delaney to—"

"No!" I struggle to get free, but he plants one of his feet on top of mine and increases the weight against me. Nachman's stronger than I would have guessed.

"Please don't report me," I say. Okay, beg. "I can't get kicked out of school." Ever since I took part in the student boycott of state testing last spring, Delaney's had it in for me. Every time she sees me in the hallway—which I make sure isn't often—she scowls.

"Trust me, Cole. I'm calling Ms. Delaney to tell her there's graffiti on the school wall and she needs to call someone to cover it up before school starts in the morning." He glances up at the F words.

"But— but she'll ask you who did it."

"I saw you standing near the school, Cole, but I didn't see any spray paint in your hands or on your clothes. Proximity doesn't prove guilt."

Is this the truth? I run the scene through my head at rapid speed, like the finish line is just ahead. The cans were in my pocket before I jumped off the fence. I glance at my clothes. Clean.

I'm impressed.

With my cleanliness, yeah.

With Nachman's noticing it.

Most of all with his quick thinking.

"You'll have to clean this up," he says. "Here's the plan. I'll tell Ms. Delaney you and I think that spray-painting the school walls was somebody's immature act, and you volunteered to clean it up." He looks at me.

No way. "It was an angry act."

He gives a tiny smile about something, takes his foot off mine and moves back. "Anger is most useful when it's controlled and directed."

I move away from the fence. In case he wants to pin me against it again.

"So. You volunteered to clean up the spray painting." He waits.

I think about my position, almost like this is a cross-country meet. If Principal Delaney knew what I'd just done, she'd suspend me for sure. If I got a suspension, I couldn't run cross-country. Coach is totally strict about that. And Mom couldn't take my getting a suspension, not on top of Dad going to jail this morning.

"You aren't going to tell her I did it?"

"As long as you clean it up, starting tomorrow after school, and as long as you turn in an extra assignment every week."

"What?! What kind of extra assignment?"

Another tiny smile flits across Nachman's face. "Call it an F-word assignment. Every week from now until the end of the school year, I want you to look up two F words in the dictionary and write a poem about each."

"Two!" I shout. "Poems!" I shout. "Until the end of the school year! Man, you may as well turn me over to Delaney now."

Nachman doesn't say anything. He just waits.

After a while, I try again, "There aren't that many F words, not as many as there are weeks from now until June."

"There are a lot of words that begin with F, Cole—*fair, fight, family, fear, false, foe, futile, final.*" He looks at me with his assignment face. "Get a dictionary and pick any two words. Every week, from now until the end of the year."

"But why do I have to write them in a poem? Can't I just copy out the definition each week?"

"Anybody can copy. I want you to think and I want you to create. When we were writing poetry last year, yours were very good. I think you have a knack for it."

A knack for it, yeah, sure. It's just my luck to have Nachman as my English teacher two years in a row. Why they moved him from ninth grade to tenth is a mystery. Not that

I mind him, though—he's fair. And he usually has interesting stuff to say. In class, that is. But what's he doing out here in the dark, on the grounds of August Mersy High School?

I let out a big sigh. Not the kind like when I win a race and am happy and trying to get my breath back all at once, but the kind like when I'm waiting for the gun to go off. The nervous kind you let out when you know you're in for a long, bad, pain-filled time of it, but you can do it because… because you can. "Yeah," I mutter. "Okay."

"Okay what?"

That's just like Nachman, too.

"Okay, you'll tell Ms. Delaney I volunteered to clean the spray paint off the wall. Okay, I'll start cleaning it off the wall tomorrow."

He waits.

"Okay, okay! I'll turn in two F-word poems a week."

"Good," he says, adjusting the brim of his cap. "Tonight is Thursday, which means that this week's assignment is due tomorrow. Ms. Delaney will arrange for you to start cleaning."

And then he punches a button on his phone and puts the phone to his ear. He turns and leaves me there and walks off to wherever he was going or whatever he was doing.

The number 74 bus lurches to a stop just as I make it to Fullerton Avenue. I hop on and ride to California. That's avenue, not state. There I catch the number 52 heading south.

I hop off at Bloomingdale Avenue and walk back west, the same direction I came from, and jog home in the dark.

Mom asks if I was working late at Mrs. Green's. I tell her I was moving pots of sumac around, shifting the mums and asters to a new spot. That part is true. I leave out the part about my tagging the school wall. She's tired, I can see, because last week, when Dad knew he'd be going to jail for sure, Mom started working a second job. I heard them talking about it, saying we needed the money for the mortgage payments. And for Dad's legal defense.

She's sitting at the kitchen table, staring at Dad's new battery-powered megaphone. He bought it last spring, after his old one died. I stare at the megaphone, too. "Take care of it for me," Dad told me this morning.

And then he left to meet his lawyer and report to Cook County Jail.

I tell Mom I have an English assignment and she says good night. I go to my room to write two poems. Two F-word poems.

I think about texting Felipe to tell him what happened. We've been best friends since first grade. But Felipe likes to talk all night long—even if the talk is texting—and I need to write two poems. I'll tell him tomorrow.

A long shelf is screwed to the wall above my desk. I keep my baseball mitt on it, and the trophy I won in cross-country last year, Freshman All-City. And the dictionary Mom gave me as a present last Christmas. Dad gave me a new pair of cross-country shoes, but I keep them in the closet.

I open my tablet, and suddenly I'm sleepy.

Running cross-country does that to you.

Spray-painting in the September night probably does that to you, too. I try to remember what Nachman told us about poetry last year. I try to remember what kind of poems I wrote last year. I can't.

Far. That's the first word that comes to me. I write:

FAR

**is not here
it is there
far is the opposite
of near**

I look at the poem.

Kind of simple.

Quick, though.

Last year Nachman told us not to be afraid of quick poems. He said quick could mean perceptive. And something about quick meaning the most important part of a person, a person's core.

Nachman wants assignments handed in on paper, so I hit Print, insert Page Break, and think about a second poem.

My elbow's resting on the dictionary. I open the book, find *far* and read the definition, just to be sure. To, from, or at a considerable distance. I think about that a while and it makes me sad.

After a while I glance across to the next page and my eye lands on *fart*.

No. That would be pushing it.

But there, just a couple of words away, is fartlek. Yeah, I know *fartlek*, which is all about training. For running, but maybe for other things, too.

I copy the dictionary definition, breaking up the lines so that it looks like a poem… but then I figure I better add something of my own or Nachman might not count it as a poem. This is what I end up with:

FARTLEK

from fart, Swedish for speed
and lek,
Old Norse for play, play speed,
a training
technique for runners,
alternating intense
time
with less intense
time,
all in one continuous workout.

But whoever called it play speed
never
had to
do it.

I look it over and the words *intense time* bother me so much I want to delete them. But I can't, because that would mean writing a third poem. I print out the poem, put it with the first one, and go to sleep.

CHAPTER 2

"**ID YOU SPRAY PAINT THOSE** words on the school wall, Cole?" Ms. Delaney sits behind her desk, giving me a fierce stare. *Fierce*: an F word. Nachman is messing with my mind, even though he's not here.

My Mom and Dad aren't like most parents, at least not like the parents of my friends. I mean, how many other parents do you think teach their kids about the right to remain silent? None that I know of. Mom and Dad taught me that in some places around the world, including England, where it might have all started 500 years ago, an accused person has the right to remain silent. Dad says the right was fought for, as a defense against the ruling class, which could take away your land. Or your life.

Maybe people like Ms. Delaney.

I prefer telling the truth. But if I tell the truth here, I'll get a suspension or maybe even an expulsion. I wasn't the only kid who refused to take the state tests last spring, but Delaney sometimes acts like I was.

I don't say anything.

"Answer me, Cole," she says in her principal's voice.

"I have the right to remain silent."

"Which means you did it," she shoots back.

I guess it does.

Sometimes.

Like now.

"Not always," I answer, because I realize silence doesn't always mean guilt. "I might be protecting somebody," I say, to throw her off track.

She jumps on that. "So you know who did it. Give me their name."

I sit there amazed at how we jumped from I did it to somebody else did it, and I see how easy it is to mislead a person who's looking to punish someone. I stare at my feet and keep silent.

"It's your duty to tell me, Cole."

I shake my head. No way. It's not my duty to incriminate myself. Not my duty to get a suspension.

"I could expel you for not telling me."

My head jerks up. Could she? We stare at each other, then I just shake my head again. I don't think so.

"If it was you, Cole, it's a sign. A bad sign."

A sign?

"Your first mistake was participating in the ill-advised boycott of state-wide testing. You and the others, each of you misguided, created a situation in which August Mersy High School failed to make the required 95-percent-participation. You made our school look bad. You made me look bad."

Man, that was, like, five months ago.

And I think we made our school look good, not bad. We showed people that we can think about what's happening to us in school each day. We can analyze. We can reach decisions. We can act.

"What you don't understand, Cole, is that I'm trying to help you. I have many more years of experience than you do, and I'm a better judge of what's good for the school and its students."

She goes on like this, and just when I think she's forgotten all about the words on the wall, she jumps on them. "Tell me, Cole: did you spray paint the school wall?"

"I have the right to remain silent." And man, am I ever glad I do—Ms. Delaney is tricky to argue with.

Now that she's back on topic, she keeps up her tell-me-who-did-it question and I keep up my silence and it feels like five weeks go by, but the wall clock says it's only five minutes.

I'm not paying much attention to her. I keep thinking of Dad, wondering if there's some way he can get out. For good behavior or something. Except that his jail time just started yesterday. Jillian dumped me the day before—the day the court sentenced Dad to four months in jail. She didn't want to "be associated with somebody whose father is a criminal." That's how she put it. At least five of the F words I spray-painted were for Jillian.

I squirm just thinking about Dad in Cook County Jail.

Finally, Ms. Delaney stands up and opens the door to her office. A sign I can leave, and I jump up. Maybe a bit too eagerly.

"You've always been a good student, Cole. Don't turn into a troublemaker. You don't have to end up like your father."

I stumble when she says this but catch myself from falling. I can't believe she just said what she said.

Man, that's cold.

So cold I don't know what to say. So I just walk out and don't look back.

———

Seven hours later I'm standing on a ladder scrubbing solvent into my red and black graffiti, listening to Felipe. I'm scrubbing F words off the wall and running F words through my head, wondering which might make good poems.

Felipe is standing on another ladder next to mine. He doesn't have to be here helping me, but he is. He walked into Ms. Delaney's office and told her he heard that I had volunteered to scrub words off the north wall and that he wanted to volunteer, too.

I wish he hadn't done that—I'll bet Ms. Delaney now suspects him of spraying the graffiti.

But I have to admit, the work feels easier because he's here.

"Your name starts with F," I tell him, "You probably count as an F word."

"*¡Sí!* I'm a capitalized F word."

I think about that for a while, wondering what I can do with a capitalized F word.

"Be careful you don't get solvent in your eyes," shouts Mr. Cafasso from below. He's the school janitor, and Ms. Delaney told him to supervise Felipe and me. I think he's just making sure we don't fall off the ladders.

"Cole," he sort of shouts up to me. "How's your father doing?"

I stop spraying and look down at him. "Uh. I don't know. Okay, I hope. We get to visit him tomorrow."

Felipe looks down, too. "Tio Hank is strong," he tells Mr. Cafasso. "And he will return stronger than ever."

I sure hope that's true.

"Tell your father I said Hi," says Mr. Cafasso. "I went to grade school with him."

That's kind of cool. "You went to Euclid Grade School?" I ask him.

"You bet. I've lived in Logan Square all my life. So has my wife. Hey! Watch it! The solvent is dripping!" He jumps out of the way.

"Sorry!" I turn back to the wall and pay more attention to what I'm doing.

Logan Square is one of Chicago's community areas, which are bigger than neighborhoods. In fifth grade Felipe and

Fatima Assaf and I did a social studies report on the seventy-seven community areas and the two hundred neighborhoods. Fatima painted the community areas on a large piece of cloth, and Felipe and I wrote the names of each area. The teacher gave us an A-plus.

Dad grew up in Logan Square.

"Spray it well," Mr. Cafasso calls up to us. "Then we'll let it sit for twenty minutes."

I feel bad that Mr. Cafasso has to spend his time supervising us, all because I spray-painted the wall. This is probably what Nachman wants me to learn—think first, spray-paint later.

Or not at all.

I study the solvent label, hoping it might say something like toxic. I could point that out to Mr. Cafasso and he might let Felipe and me go.

Fat chance.

Fat. An F word. Just three letters, too, probably easy to make a poem out of that. Nothing comes to mind, though. Nachman read my two poems as soon as I handed them in this morning.

"Fine, Cole," he said. "Fine work." He kind of grinned when he said it. He was probably using an F word just to show me they're everywhere.

I must have slowed down on solvent spraying because Felipe nudges me. "Hey, Cole! No fair sniffing that stuff."

"*¿Cómo se ve?*" I ask, hoping he tells me it's looking good. "Is anything coming off?"

"Not yet," answers Mr. Cafasso from below. "The solvent has to saturate the paint. Finish applying it, then we'll wait twenty minutes. I wonder who did this."

I keep spraying.

And then Felipe asks me about Jillian. He wants to know if the breakup is *definitivo*. Yeah, I say, it's definite. I don't know if I want it to be definite, but Jillian sure does. I am absolutely gone from her life.

"She's running for class president again," I say. "Like ninth grade wasn't enough."

Felipe is quiet.

I glance over at him.

"What?" I ask.

He shrugs. "I wouldn't mind running for class president."

I turn too suddenly and the ladder sways.

"¡*Cuidado*! Careful!" shouts Mr. Cafasso, steadying the ladder.

"For real?" I ask.

Felipe scrubs extra hard for a while, the wire brush screeching against the faded brick. "For real," he says at last. "But I didn't put my name in because… you know…"

Because he thought I'd want Jillian to win.

"Man," I tell him, "I'd want you to run even if Jillian hadn't dumped me."

He grins. "But I would win, and she would be heartbroken."

Yeah, heartbroken. Not Jillian. "Whoever wins, wins." I spray more solvent and attack the bricks with the wire brush. "Is it too late to put your name in?"

"No. The deadline is noon tomorrow."

"Get off this ladder right now," I tell him.

"*¿Qué?*"

I point my brush at the school doors. "Go put your name in. Now." My brush drips solvent down the ladder.

"Careful up there," shouts Mr. Cafasso. "Pay attention to what you're doing, Cole."

Felipe stands on the ladder for a bit, thinking. "You sure?" he asks.

"*¡Totalmente!*"

"That's cool, Cole." He touches me on the shoulder and climbs down the ladder. "That's really cool."

"I'll be back!" he shouts, waving as he disappears through the school doors.

Like I'm going somewhere.

The first day of first grade was when Felipe and I met. Felipe Ramirez and Cole Renner. We always sat close together, at first because of the alphabet, then because we liked each other. And then we looked for each other wherever we were. We both love sports. Felipe plays soccer, I run cross-country and track.

Felipe didn't say anything when I told him how I'd sprayed the wall and how Nachman had caught me. When I told him about my assignment, he said just one word: "*¿Poemas*?!" and shook his head.

From where I'm standing on the ladder, I can almost touch the stone letters that form an arch over one of the side doors. AUGUST MERSY HIGH SCHOOL. If you read any of the information in the glass-enclosed hallway displays—which I like to do—you'll learn that August Mersy was a German immigrant who settled in Illinois and fought in the Civil War. He led a regiment of German-American Union soldiers at the Battle of Shiloh.

I keep spraying the solvent. Maybe one F word would have been sufficient. Fifteen might have been a bit excessive. After a few minutes I sense somebody below. I look down and see that Felipe's back. He's climbing up the second ladder again. Down on the ground is Hannah Iwata, holding a camera.

Taking pictures, actually.

Of Felipe.

Hannah's a junior, assistant editor of the student newspaper, *The Fire*. Probably its chief photographer.

Felipe reaches the top and grabs his can of solvent.

Hannah keeps taking pictures.

"What's happening?" I ask him.

"Photo opp. I'm now an official candidate for tenth grade class president. Hannah was there when I signed up and asked if she could take photos."

"She wants to photograph the loser?"

Felipe aims the can of solvent in my direction but doesn't push the button. "Opponents can be dissolved," he says.

We get back to work and finally climb down the ladders to wait for twenty minutes. Mr. Cafasso studies his wristwatch. Hannah gives us a wave and is about to disappear back into the school. But the door opens and Fatima, Hasna and Salma walk out together. They're dressed alike in jeans and long tops, but they wear different kinds of hijabs. Salma is from Sudan and always wears a bright hijab, like green or yellow or blue. Fatima and Hasna are Palestinian. They must go shopping together to buy matching headwear. Today they're both wearing black hijabs with swirls of purple, green, and rose.

Last year Amani was always with them. But not now. Felipe told me he heard ICE deported her whole family. ICE is Immigration and Customs Enforcement.

"Hey there," I say to them. "Wha's up?"

"*¡Hola!*" Felipe says.

"*Salaam*," the three of them say, almost in unison. And smile. Fatima's smile grows bigger as she looks at Felipe.

I realize that Hannah Iwata is still taking pictures. Of the five of us talking.

"Lookin' good, Felipe," Hannah says. "Good luck with the election!" And then she walks back into the school.

The five of us talk for a while, mostly about being sophomores this year and our classes and teachers. Then the three of them say bye and leave.

"So what's your plan?" I ask Felipe. He's standing there looking up at the wetness on the wall.

We watch the solvent conquer the paint, mixing the red and the black together, turning it into a gooey mess.

"Election plan?"

"Yeah. Election plan."

"I'm working on a campaign slogan," he tells me. "What about 'Lend a Helping Hand'?"

I stare at him. "Seriously?"

"No. It's lame. But I'll come up with something."

It had better be soon. Student elections are just two weeks away.

"Okay, boys, time to wipe things clean." Mr. Cafasso hands each of us a bunch of terrycloth rags and points to the ladders. "Put your elbows into it."

CHAPTER 3

UNDAY MORNING MOM AND I have breakfast and then get ready to visit Dad. I'm excited about seeing him. But scared, too, about what it's like in jail, and how Dad will feel.

Mom goes to her desk, which is really a long table that Dad built into one end of the dining room. Our house is small, but like Mom always says, efficient. The downstairs always smells good because Mom loves to bake. Right now the whole house smells like chocolate chip cookies, with just a touch of cinnamon. Mom baked them this morning, to take to Dad.

She logs onto the Cook County Department of Corrections site to check on visiting hours, me standing right behind her.

That's when we learn that we can't go.

It turns out Mom needed to fill out a visitor application.

"Didn't you know?" I blurt out. "Didn't they tell you?"

Mom doesn't make mistakes like this. I can't believe she made this mistake now. I want to see Dad.

She's scrolling up and down the page, too fast to find anything.

"You should've asked me, Mom—I would've done it." I'm bouncing on my toes. Hoping there's a mistake.

"Stop it, Cole. You're making me nervous. And I would have asked you if I had known we needed an application!" She pushes everything on the desk aside and puts her face close to the screen.

I kneel on the floor so I don't have to stoop so much. Over Mom's shoulder I read the computer page as she starts the application process. At almost the same moment we both see that it takes at least three days to approve the application.

"Three days! Mom!!!! How can they do that? Three days?!" I jump up off the floor.

"Cole, please sit down! They do it because they're uncaring and inefficient. And because they can. It's another way of punishing prisoners."

I pull up one of the dining room chairs and plop down on it. My cans of spray paint are upstairs, in my room. I wish I could use them on something. Or somebody. Like the people in charge of visitor applications. I don't know how Mom could have made a mistake like this. Dad is there in Cook County Jail, waiting for us to visit!

Dad's new megaphone is on Mom's desk. She must have put it there. She reaches out a hand and pulls the megaphone close. Like she's hugging it.

I take a deep breath. "I'm sorry, Mom. I know you didn't know."

She nods.

"Are there any, like… exceptions? An emergency pass? All kinds of people must forget that they have to do this."

She shakes her head.

What this means is, we can't visit Dad today.

Mom types furiously, the keys making small thunks as she pounds them. "I'm almost done," she says. "I'll hit send in a minute. Three days from now, they should approve the application."

I read over her shoulder. "Wait! It says I can't visit Dad!" I shout. "Visitors under 17 not allowed!"

"Unless accompanied by an adult," she tells me, pointing to more information. "You'll be with me, we'll be together."

"I can't go in the morning, before school." I point to the information which says visiting hours start at 10:00 a.m. and go to 9:00 p.m. "You said I could visit him every Thursday morning, before school starts!"

"I thought you could, Cole. I'm sorry. I thought you could."

She finishes the form and points out to me that I need to bring my school ID card with me and that it has to have a photo.

To get to see Dad.

In jail.

It feels like he's in jail on the inside, and we're in jail on the outside.

"When can we see him? It doesn't say."

Mom scrolls through pages of information, half of it in bold type. Like a warning.

It looks like the only time the two of us can see Dad is next Sunday. Which is good, I guess, because I have a meet all day Saturday. Running cross-country is a team sport, seven runners on a team, and the scores of the first five runners count. I came in fifth yesterday. Not fifth in the meet: fifth on our team. Usually I come in second or third. And sometimes first. I don't feel good about being fifth, even though I know it's the whole team effort that counts. Coach depends on each of us. And we depend on each other. To always be there and always run our best.

"Do we have to apply for the hours?" I ask. "Is there a line? What if they allow only a few people in at a time?"

"It's okay, Cole. We'll work it out."

"Look," I say, pointing at a list of contraband. Things you aren't allowed to bring.

I put my finger on the word.

Food.

Mom sees. She puts her head in her hands.

We can't bring Dad any of his favorite foods. No food at all.

No books, newspapers, or magazines.

Dad loves to read. He reads the newspaper every day. He reads books all the time. What's he going to do without something to read? I rock back and forth in my chair, angry and nervous and sad and mad all at the same time.

Mom still has her head in her hands.

I touch her shoulder. "It's okay, Mom. It's okay about the cookies. Dad will understand."

She puts her right hand on top of mine, then she straightens up and we keep reading the list of contraband.

No cell phones.

No drinks.

Mom and I aren't supposed to have anything on us but our keys and photo IDs.

I keep wondering what Dad will do all day long in jail, with no phone, no books, and no food that's any good. But Dad's attorney told us he'd be in Division Six, which is a minimum security division. So maybe he gets to move around and read and stuff.

Jail sucks.

This whole Sunday sucks.

Whenever anyone on the cross-country team says anything like "this sucks," Coach comes back with the same two words. "Mental toughness, boys. Mental toughness."

Mental toughness, I tell myself. Mental toughness.

I look at Mom, who's sitting there holding Dad's megaphone. "I'm going out for a run," I tell her. She nods, hugging the megaphone closer.

But I don't go on a *run* run, like a training run. No fartlek, no tempo, no hills. Just what we call junk miles— runs that count for weekly mileage but don't work on any particular skills.

What I do is run north half a block and zig into an alley, heading west. Some of Chicago's alleys are paved with brick, but lots of them are still dirt. I like running on the dirt alleys better than I like running on the streets. Chicago has more alleys than any other city in the country. Like, 1,900 miles of alleys! That's almost from here to San Francisco.

The alleys run behind houses and are lined with garages so people can turn into their alley and then into their garage. On weekends Mom opens our back gate while she's working in the garden, so neighbors can visit. Dad opens the garage door and works on a project at his workbench. Before he went to jail, he started building a new bookcase. Most of our neighbors do the same kind of things, some working on their cars, some just sitting outdoors on lawn chairs. Mom and Dad say that the alleys are the real world, where people act like friends and neighbors should.

Dad runs with me most Sundays. He doesn't let me call his part of it a junk run. I wonder if he's thinking about running right now, wishing he were here. I wave to people I know, some by name, some because I see them whenever I run the alleys. When I reach Mrs. Erickson's house I stop and pull out the key I have in my pocket.

Dad rents Mrs. Erickson's garage for his Suzuki motorcycle. He gave me a key to the garage a couple of years ago, and I'm supposed to get a key to the motorcycle when I turn sixteen, which is in February.

I unlock the side door to the garage, flip on the light switch, and close the door behind me. I take the cover off the

Suzuki. And then I sit on the bike, which is a deep purple color. I sit there a long time, not doing anything. Just wishing Dad wasn't in jail.

———

MONDAY.

Six days away from seeing Dad. I tell myself to take it one day at a time. Sort of like Coach tells us to take it one step at a time. Sort of like what Coach said to me on Saturday, when I finished fifth on our team. "One race at a time, Cole. One race at a time."

It helps that Monday is always an easy day at school—no track practice because we just ran a race on Saturday. And on Mondays I don't go to work.

Felipe and I toss a baseball around after school on the baseball diamond with a bunch of other kids, mostly sophomores like us. Just about all of us are wearing Cubs gear of one kind or another. I pull off my hoodie and toss it along the fence once we start playing. If the cub on my gear looked ferocious, I could write an F-word poem. But it doesn't. It is marching forward, though. Maybe *forward* will be a poem.

As we toss the ball around, Felipe lets everybody know he's running for class president. Naturally someone shouts "¡*El Presidente!*" and then everyone picks up the phrase. *El Presidente* gobbles up a grounder and tosses it underhand to second. I glove it on the run, tag the bag, spin, and toss to first.

Double play!

If it were a game, and if there were a runner on first.

It being Monday, Felipe comes home with me for dinner, just like he's been doing every year since first grade. I go to his house for breakfast every Wednesday, just like I've been doing since first grade.

Mom makes a huge meatloaf, Felipe's favorite. Dad's favorite, too. Then she grabs a sweater and heads out the door to Mrs. Green's. I work for Mrs. Green four nights a week. But now Mom works there, too, three nights a week plus all day Saturday. Mrs. Green offered her the job after Dad was sentenced. Mom's a painter. The kind who paints walls. She works wherever the painters' union sends her, but her favorite jobs are when she gets to stencil. That's her specialty: stenciling. Which she does in every room in the house. The wall outside my room says COLE'S ROOM. It's cool. The lettering is sort of cracked, like when a toon hints there's an earthquake coming.

Mom and Dad both have union jobs, with good wages and benefits. But she and Dad talked about missing four months of his wages, how high city property taxes are, the mortgage, and paying his defense lawyer. Dad didn't want Mom to take a second job, but Mom said she would feel better working.

I wash the dishes and Felipe dries. We go out on the back porch and talk. If Dad were home, the three of us would be talking about the Cubs and their chances of going to the World Series again. Mom would join us and talk about the White Sox, 'cause she's from Bridgeport, a neighborhood on the south side of Chicago.

After a while, Felipe says it's time for him to leave because he has an idea for the class elections. I ask what it is, but he's already off the porch and halfway down the walk. "*Mañana*," he shouts over his shoulder.

I stay out on the porch and open a lot of apps on my phone, one at a time, checking what's being posted where and who's saying anything worth reacting to. I stay away from anything to do with Jillian. My fingers twitch to visit the Cook County Jail website, but what good would that do? Mom and I just have to wait until the jail says yes to her application.

Finally, I go up to my room to write a poem, figuring I'll get one done today and one tomorrow, so I can forget about them for the rest of the week. There it is, another F word: *forget*. I add it to the growing list of F words I'm keeping on my tablet. And phone. And scraps of paper. There are F words everywhere. Somehow the list reminds me of the capital-F word, Felipe.

FELIPE

Friend
Energetic
Laughing
Intense
Proud
Everlasting

That last word surprises me 'cause I wasn't thinking it, it just came from out of nowhere. I didn't even know I knew the word *everlasting!* I decide I like it, though, and print the page. The dictionary's on my desk where I left it last week. Seeing it reminds me of something. *"Troublemaker."* I've been wanting to look that up ever since Ms. Delaney called Dad a troublemaker.

The dictionary is, like, no help at all. Troublemaker: one who causes trouble.

I look up *trouble.* Tons of definitions there, including difficulty, inconvenience, and bother. This makes me think Ms. Delaney doesn't want to be inconvenienced.

Then why is she a principal? I wonder.

I toss the dictionary on my bed, flop onto the bed after it, and grab the thin strip of paper I stuck in the F's. Unless Nachman changes his mind, I'm going to wear out these pages.

I flip the dictionary open and what do I see but a picture of a Ferris wheel. It reminds me of when Mom and Dad and I would go down to Navy Pier and all sit in one car and ride the Ferris wheel. I read the definition, which uses words like "upright wheel" and "rotating" and "suspended seats" and "horizontal position." I don't think I could work these words into a poem, not like I did with the definition of *fartlek.* Some guy named George Washington Gale Ferris, 1859-1896, an American engineer, invented the Ferris wheel. I didn't know they had Ferris wheels in the nineteenth century.

I begin to write words on a sheet of paper, like Nachman taught us last year, just anything that comes to mind. After a while I look them over and began to circle the ones that look like they can go the distance. Instead of waiting for tomorrow,

I write the poem now.

FERRIS WHEEL

We used to ride the Ferris Wheel
down at Navy Pier,
Mom and Dad with me
safe between them,
my hands gripping the bar
as we hung suspended
in the air,
waiting for the ride
to end.

Dad sits behind a different
kind of bar today.
He is not safe and
his sentence
is not

suspended.

CHAPTER 4

N TUESDAY I JOG UP Albany, through Palmer Square Park and to Fullerton, where I catch the number 74 bus. At Kimball I see Felipe standing by the bus stop sign. He's bouncing up and down on his toes. He waits until everybody else at the stop gets on, then jumps onto the bus steps: Clang! Clang!

He spots me and slips through all the people still trying to decide where they want to sit.

"Tenth grade—*Mi Familia.*" He raises both eyebrows. "Wake up, Cole! My campaign slogan!"

Familia. A Spanish F word. Almost identical to the English one.

Scooting in next to me, he bumps me toward the windows. "Last night I posted it on the school's web site, right under my picture on the election page. Perfect, right?"

I put up my hand and we high-five. "I like it. A lot."

What I like best is how Felipe's slogan says we're all family. The whole human race. Not just the narrow mom-dad-kids thing.

"Papa loves it," Felipe tells me. "And Mama is so proud of me running for class president she even"—he punches me in the arm—"forgot to warn me about You. Know. Who."

He means ICE, Immigration and Customs Enforcement. Ever since I can remember, Felipe's mother has always said the same thing as he goes out the door: Beware the Cold Ones. I don't know why she says that to him. Felipe was born here, so ICE can't grab him and deport him to Mexico.

"What can I do to help with the campaign?" I ask.

"*Nada.* We can't pass out leaflets or anything like that, the rules say we have to do everything on the election web site. But you can tell everyone you know to vote for me."

"I will," I say.

The bus takes longer than usual, and when we get off at August Mersy we have to hustle to history class.

Yesterday Mr. Ortiz talked about what he called "the extension of rights for Americans." None of us could figure out what that meant. Then he explained that the Nineteenth Amendment gave women the right to vote. In 1920. And that in 1924 Congress gave citizenship to all Native Americans.

Man.

Felipe asked Mr. Ortiz why these things were called "extension" of rights, when, really, the same people who "extended" the right had been suppressing the rights for hundreds of years. The whole class got into the topic, Felipe and me arguing that "extension of rights" is a lie, that the rights were won through protests. Others arguing that it's only a word, the important thing is that women and Indians now have these rights. Others not paying attention at all.

"Extension of rights is not my term," Mr. Ortiz told us. "It's the wording of the Illinois Board of Education."

The way he says it makes me think Mr. Ortiz understands that "extension of rights" isn't the right term. The rights were won by the people who fought for them. Just like the right to remain silent was won hundreds of years ago.

Today Mr. Ortiz is spending the whole fifty minutes going over questions that have been on state tests the last few years. No discussion like we had yesterday. Just memorization.

Mr. Ortiz keeps us past the bell and by the time he lets us go the hallways are practically empty. Felipe sprints one way to his next class and I sprint the other way to make it to Nachman's class on time. As I run down the corridor I keep an eye out for Ms. Delaney, who doesn't allow running.

Who do I see ahead of me but Jillian. She's dressed in pink, which she wears like four days of the week. She calls it her signature color. "Blondes own pink," she's always saying.

"Hey, Jillian," I say. "Hi."

She barely glances back at me. Keeps on walking.

I jog ahead and keep up with her easily. "How're things?" I ask.

She picks up her speed, but just for a second. Next thing I know, she stops and turns toward me.

"Hi, Cole." She smiles. "I'm glad you're still speaking to me. I want to be friends."

I make a sound something like Uh, not sure what to say. I register that *friends* is an F word. But I don't think Jillian is using it honestly.

"I was really surprised to see that Felipe is running for class president," she says. "He has no experience."

For a second I'm confused, trying to track how we got from her wanting to be friends to Felipe running for class president. Then I see none of this is about me. It's about the election.

"Experience? In running for class president?" When people say stupid things, I sometimes just say their words back to them.

"In representing the class." She rearranges the books she's carrying.

So Jillian was class president in ninth grade—so what? Like that gave her a world of experience.

"People have to start sometime," I say. "You seem to be saying that only students who won last year's election should run this year."

She ignores this. "His slogan is lame."

I shake my head. "It's strong. I like it."

"*Mi familia*," she mocks. "Lame."

I'm beginning to figure out Jillian is talking to me only because she wants to dis Felipe. Or win my vote. Which I can't believe—that she thinks she can dump me because Dad's in jail and that I'll vote for her?

I have no idea why I ran to catch up with her. Foolish, Cole. Foolish.

Normally I'd tell myself Dumb, Cole. Dumb. But I've been infected with some sort of F-word virus.

"What's your slogan?" I ask.

"Just Jillian."

Something like a snort explodes out of my mouth. I try to cover it up, but Jillian frowns. "What's wrong with my slogan?" she demands.

I'm thinking how Jillian is anything but just. How just was it that she dumped me because Dad was sentenced to jail? But I don't tell her that. "If you like it, good," I say.

She nods at this and rearranges her books again. That's when Jared Anderson walks by.

Stops next to Jillian.

And glares at me.

Jared is, first: a thief and a bully. When he was in fifth grade and Felipe and I were in third, he always tried to take our lunch money. Usually we could outrun him. Second: he's tackle on the football team. Third: he thinks he's hot stuff.

Jillian smiles at Jared.

Jared puts his hand on Jillian's shoulder.

I stand there thinking, that was fast.

Jillian glances at Jared, then at me. "Being elected class president two years in a row will look good on my college applications, Cole."

When I don't say anything, she adds more. "I really want this to happen. For me. And for the whole class. It's important."

I adjust my backpack. Fuming.

Me, not the backpack.

How dumb does she think I am?

Jillian takes my silence as a sign to leave.

Which it definitely is.

"I hope you vote for the right person," she says over her shoulder.

"You'd better vote for the right person, Renner." Jared stands and glares at me for a second or two, then leaves.

I can still run faster than him, so I'm not worried.

I watch Jillian walk into Nachman's classroom.

And that's when I notice something in my sideways vision.

Tall and straight, like a pillar.

Dressed in black, like the bad guy in a western.

Standing in the corner of the hall.

It's a girl, but I've never seen her before.

She's staring at Jillian's back. Then she turns to stare at me. Straight at me.

"Well," she says. "I know who I'm voting for."

I open my mouth to say something, I don't know what, but Nachman steps into the doorway, standing there between the jambs. "Cole," he orders, "get in here."

Then he says, "You, too, Treva."

I walk into Nachman's classroom.

The pillar follows me.

CHAPTER 5

MOVE TOWARD MY SEAT IN the back row. There's an empty chair right next to mine and the pillar follows me there, but before she can sit down, Nachman says, "Hold on a second, Treva."

She stops, and that stops me, too, though I don't know why.

"Class," says Nachman, "say hi to Treva Soldat from Oregon."

Treva gives an embarrassed smile and kind of waves her hand at all of us. Some of us say hi, some wave back. All of us stare at this new girl dressed in black. I realize then how tall she is, almost as tall as me. I wonder if she runs cross country, or plays basketball or volleyball. No basketball player I know dresses in black. Her long black duster looks like it would have been at home on Wyatt Earp.

The two of us sit down next to one another and take out our tablets. Nachman tells the rest of us to introduce ourselves to Treva, so we do a quick up one row, down the other recitation of names. When I tell her my name, her eyebrows go up.

I wonder what that means.

Nachman has us reading *Walden*, and for the last two weeks we've been learning about Thoreau, Emerson, and the Transcendentalists. Yesterday he told us the story about Thoreau refusing to pay taxes to a government that condoned the buying and selling of human beings as slaves. We learned about Thoreau's night in jail. When Emerson asked, "Henry, what are you doing in there?" Thoreau replied, "Waldo, the question is what are you doing out there?" It made me think of Dad. He's in jail just like Thoreau was, to protest an injustice. Thoreau refused to pay taxes. Dad refused to let a neighborhood school be closed.

Today we're on the first chapter of *Walden*, "Economy," which is more than fifty pages long. Not very economical, I think. But the other chapters are all short ones. And maybe we won't have to read them all.

For a while Nachman has us talk about a single sentence: *The greater part of what my neighbors call good I believe in my soul to be bad, and if I repent of anything, it is very likely to be my good behavior.* This makes me think of Dad, too: that's him to the max. People call our political system good. Dad doesn't. People call religion good. Dad doesn't. People call capitalism good. Dad doesn't.

I catch a glimpse of black to my left. It's the sleeve of Treva's coat as she shrugs it off. She's wearing a tight black sweater with a neckline that scoops down. Short black skirt. Black tights. Black boots. Her skin is white, but her hair is jet black. So are her eyebrows. And her skin's not exactly white, it's kind of cream colored.

I totally lose track of class.

Then I snap back. Better pay attention.

To Nachman.

Who's asking us when Thoreau moved into his cabin.

"The Fourth of July," Jillian answers.

The symbolism's pretty obvious. I think about Jillian. I open the F-Words file on my tablet and start a new poem. "Fickle." I type words like fickle, pickle, tickle. Nickel.

None of the words fly and I can't make them fly. This poem is going nowhere. I close the document.

And then I realize that Nachman's talking to me.

"What do you think of that, Cole?" he asks.

"What?" I ask.

He stands in front of the class and reads: *Most men appear never to have considered what a house is and are actually though needlessly poor all their lives because they think that they must have such a one as their neighbors have.*

I'm still trying to get my head around the sentence, thinking maybe Thoreau should have practiced writing poetry. Short lines.

"Do you think people are burdened by owning houses that far exceed their income level?" he translates.

"Yes," answers Jillian, even though Nachman was talking to me. But our class has a lot of back-and-forth and jumping in with opinions, so I don't mind. "Some people live in thousands of square feet and own three cars and work all the time," she says, "and worry about their huge mortgages every day. They buy beyond their means. They should wait until they can afford large houses and a lot of cars."

"The ruling class keeps wages low," says Treva. "And lower. The average person is never going to be able to afford to buy a house."

I give Treva a quick glance. She used the words *ruling class*, just like I do. Almost nobody talks that way.

Emerald Jackson is nodding her head up and down, up and down. "We the richest country in the world, not counting some of those little Arab emirates like Qatar. Everybody should have a huge house and three cars." Sometimes Emerald talks in Black dialect. Like now. I always like it when she does.

Jillian frowns at this but doesn't say anything. Probably wants Emerald to vote for her.

Salma gives a small smile, mostly to herself.

Nachman notices. "Salma?" he asks.

"Contentment and happiness can be achieved in small spaces," she says. "It is the spirit which should be immense. Not the dwelling."

Nachman taps her desk. "Well stated, Salma."

Then he looks at me. "What do you think, Cole?" he asks. "Big house? Small house? Rented rooms?"

I'm not thinking about big houses versus small houses. I'm thinking about having a house at all, and how if you don't have one, or the chance to have one, the argument doesn't matter.

Nachman is still waiting. "I guess I'm for small houses," I answer. And then I add, "With neighborhood schools that kids can walk to."

Treva nods. Emerald and Salma nod. Jillian frowns.

Nachman smiles.

"Why is 'Economy' the largest chapter in *Walden?*" he asks.

"Money rules our lives," answers Emerald. "We need to earn it to buy food and housing. And clothes. And go to college. He's saying we need to make decisions about what we'll spend our lives doing." Sometimes Emerald speaks in standard English. Like now.

Jillian nods. "That's why he wrote *Walden*," she says. "To help people see they could get by on less."

"Why should they get by on less?" Treva demands. "The ruling class gets by on more and more."

"Amen." That's Emerald.

I study Treva but try not to be obvious about it. She's wearing a black chain around her neck, and at the end of the chain is a pendant shaped like a raised fist. And then I notice a small tat on her wrist.

It's a black flag, waving on a long pole.

I know that flag.

It's the flag of anarchy.

Treva Soldat is an anarchist.

I wonder how long it'll be before Ms. Delaney calls her a troublemaker.

CHAPTER 6

HEN THE BELL RINGS WE grab our backpacks and start leaving the room. I'm looking at Jillian, who isn't looking at me. I move forward to talk to her, but Treva steps in front of me, blocking the way.

"Is your father Hank Renner?" she asks.

She didn't have to step in front of me to block me: her question stops me in my tracks. Where is she going with this question?

"Yeah," I answer. "He's my Dad, and I'm proud of it." I tell her that just in case she's anything like Jillian. Which I suspect an anarchist isn't.

"Your father is a hero," she says.

Did I hear her right?

"A hero," she repeats, looking me in the eyes.

Hers are gray. With tiny flecks of reddish brown.

"He fights for what's right," she says.

My head nods. Like it's making its own decision.

"He fights for the people."

My head nods again. And one more time. Then I realize all I'm doing is nodding and that makes me feel stupid. I stop nodding. The fact is, I'm speechless.

"Uh, how do you know about my father? I mean, you're from Oregon. And this is your first day here."

"My uncle sent me newspaper articles."

"Why would he do that?"

"Because I was active in the Boycott Standardized Testing movement out there. He thought I'd be interested in anything to do with school protests."

My head nods again. "Okay. Does your uncle know my dad?"

"I don't think so."

I wonder if Treva knows that I know she's an anarchist. Dad doesn't like anarchists. He says they believe the world can be changed by provocative actions. "We need to build a mass working-class movement," Mom and Dad are always saying.

"Dad is a hero," I say. That feels like it needs more, so I add something. "I'm glad you think so."

"Were you there?" she asks. "When he was arrested?"

My stomach gives a tiny lurch, like there's danger ahead. Why does she want to know this?

"Time to move," Nachman announces. "New class coming in."

I look around. He's talking to Treva and me.

And then I notice Jillian standing there, looking at us. So I guess he's talking to her, too.

The three of us move out of the aisle and through the door.

Treva taps Jillian on the shoulder, which annoys Jillian. "What's the name of the student newspaper?" Treva asks.

"*The Fire*," is all Jillian says as she moves away and walks down the hall. I watch as she stops to talk to other students, one by one. Probably saying "Just Jillian" to each of them. I'm kind of wondering what made me interested in Jillian in the first place.

Treva is smiling. "*The Fire*. Totally right."

She fishes a piece of paper out of her pocket and studies what's on it. Her coat has a lot of pockets. Six that I count. I wonder if anarchists need coats with lots of pockets. "Where's room 412?" she asks.

"Follow me," I say. "Yeah, I was there," I add.

"At the demonstration?"

"Yeah. The Committee called a demonstration because the Board of Education announced it was going to close Euclid Grade School. It already closed more than forty neighborhood schools last year."

"I read about that," she says, "in the articles my uncle sent me links to. Chicago has closed more public schools than any other city in the country. That's bad. Seriously bad."

I lead us down another corridor. "Dad's on the board of the CSPE, the Committee to Save Public Education. He was the main speaker at the demonstration."

We shoulder our way through other students. Now that I've started telling her about what happened, I find I want to describe the whole thing.

"A thousand or more people showed up in front of Euclid Grade School. My mother was there, Felipe was there—he's my best friend—most of our neighbors were there. Dad had his new megaphone."

Dad asked me to help him pick it out, online. We chose one with an 8-hour lithium battery and a 600-yard range. That's six football fields long. I remember the descriptions all said, "for speaking to large groups of students," which made me laugh. I guess they didn't want to say, "for speaking to large public demonstrations."

"What did he say?" Treva asks. "In his speech."

"He said that Chicago was selling its public schools to private buyers and selling out free public education. That privately owned public schools are run for profit. They pay teachers less and teach kids less. He said that the parents whose kids went to Euclid wanted the school open. Every time Dad made a point, the crowd shouted back: *Keep Euclid Grade School Open!* And *Defend Public Education!*"

"Cool," says Treva. "Did you shout, too?"

I give her a look, like it's a dumb question. "I can shout loud when I have to."

"Me, too," she says. Happily.

We reach geometry class, but we stand outside the door.

"Most people started showing up around seven in the evening," I tell her. "We were there maybe an hour. The crowd got bigger and bigger. I remember looking around and there were twice as many people behind me as there had been before. And then, I don't know how it happened, the whole crowd surged forward. Like a wave. There was no way to move in any direction except forward. It felt like we were being pushed by something big that wouldn't stop. We were all pushed through the doors of the school. Mom, me, Felipe, other people I know. Dad was pushed along, too. I could see his head over the crowd."

"That's exciting," says Treva.

I look at her.

"I mean, it's exciting that people were out demonstrating for what they need, don't you think?"

I'm wondering what Treva would have done if she'd been there. Shouted slogans? Or pushed forward through the school doors.

When I don't answer, she continues. "Tell me about the sit-in part."

I'm still wondering why she wants to know all this. But I want to tell it to somebody, so I continue.

"There's a huge entrance hall in Euclid. Whenever it rained, the school used to let us stand there before the bell went off."

"You went to Euclid Grade School?"

"Yeah. Me and Felipe. After the whole crowd was pushed inside, everybody just sat down in the entrance hall." As I'm talking, I'm remembering how cold the cement floor felt. That was back in April. "We sat there for an hour, maybe two. Dad walked through the crowd, talking to people about our right to stage a nonviolent protest like a sit-in."

I remember feeling really hungry and hearing people on their cell phones calling friends to bring food.

Which they did.

Food for hundreds.

It was like everybody for blocks and blocks ordered pizzas to be delivered to their friends sitting in at Euclid Grade School. Volunteers stood outside and passed the boxes inside, and Dad and a few others began to distribute all the food.

After everybody ate Dad assigned Felipe and me and a few others to collect the trash and pile it in a corner. Somebody volunteered to go buy boxes of thirty-gallon trash bags.

Felipe and I were still collecting empty pizza boxes, paper plates, napkins, and soda and water bottles when we heard what sounded like a thousand police sirens.

Flashing blue lights everywhere.

Cops with clubs bursting through the doors, grabbing people still half-seated, dragging them out the doors.

People yelling. Screaming.

Dad grabbed Mom and Felipe and me, pushed us through a classroom door, and opened two big, wide windows. He watched as we stepped over the sill and onto the grass. Then he turned to the people behind him and started helping them through the window.

I tell all this to Treva. "The last I saw Dad he was helping more people escape through the windows. When he didn't come home, Mom and I went down to the district police station. They told us Dad had been arrested and charged with inciting to violence. Which he didn't do."

"I want to help," she says.

"Help?" I manage.

She gives me an impatient look, like I'm a dolt.

I feel like one.

"Help with the fight."

"Against?"

"Everything. All the things that are wrong. War. Poverty. Racism. Global warming. Everything."

Part of me is in awe.

Part of me is wondering if Treva is trustworthy.

Most of me is wondering how we're going to do this.

The bell rings and we walk into geometry class. Together.

I spend the whole class dealing with what's racing through my brain. Thoreau, *Walden*, economy, houses, Dad, Treva, Jillian, anarchy. I feel like I've been picked up by the tornado and dropped in Oz.

I feel flustered.

Flustered.

The world is full of F words. If you had asked me before Nachman's assignment how many English words I could think of that began with F, I'd have said, Not many. Now it seems the opposite is true—there are F words everywhere, all the time.

Last week I googled the frequency of F in the English language. E is the most common letter used, appearing more than 12 percent of the time in any piece of writing. T is the second most common, showing up a little more than 9 percent of the time. F comes in at fifteenth most common—it's there a bit more than 2 percent of the time. Except for me: for me, F seems to be everywhere.

I make sure Mrs. Heneghan isn't looking, then I double click on my dictionary and look up *fluster*.

It turns out *fluster* has been part of English for four hundred years.

The dictionary doesn't know where the word comes from. I didn't know that dictionaries might not know where a word came from.

Its best guess is that the word comes from Iceland, which I find kinda cool, that words we use come from places like Iceland. The original meaning of *fluster* was to confuse with alcoholic drink, to render slightly intoxicated. Dad would like knowing that. He likes words and he likes beer. Now its meaning is more to flurry, confuse, make nervous. I look up flurry, and the noun is first: a number of things arriving or happening at the same time. The dictionary gives me an example—*a flurry of editorials hostile to the administration.*

I think: A flurry of articles demanding the release of Hank Renner.

Could something like that happen?

I don't think so.

But I can hope.

Mrs. Heneghan asks Hasna to draw a rhomboid on the board. Which Hasna totally aces. She wants to be a doctor or an artist, which are kind of opposite extremes. Hasna's art is all geometric shapes.

I sort of pay attention to what Mrs. Heneghan is saying about rhomboids, but I sort of pay attention to my tablet, too, where I'm writing another poem.

FLUSTER

unknown origin
   confused feeling
      rhymes with Custer

uncertain vibes
   make me ask—
      should I trust her?

CHAPTER 7

FELIPE'S HOUSE IS SIX BLOCKS from mine. Eight Chicago blocks equal one mile. I run the distance at an easy pace, an eight-minute mile, pulling the straps of my backpack forward, so it doesn't bounce against me. Coach might tell me to pick up the pace. But not at 6:30 in the morning.

Six minutes and I'm there, running down the alley behind Felipe's house. Juliana and Isabella are waiting for me at the back door.

"*¡Hola Coleto!*" they shout, jumping up and down.

"*Hola Juliana. Hola Isabella.*" I bend down and give the two of them one big hug. Juliana's in second grade and Isabella's in first.

We go indoors and I greet Felipe, his younger brother Benito, and Tía Veronica, who gives me a hug and motions for me to sit. "Ah, Coleto, I am so happy to see you. Sit down and we will eat."

I didn't always call her Tía, I started out calling her Mrs. Ramirez, but after a couple years of feeding me, she insisted I call her Tía. And I call Felipe's father, who's already at work, Tío Carlos. Felipe calls Mom and Dad Tía Stacey and Tío Hank. He doesn't like the sound of *aunt* and *uncle*.

Tía almost never calls me Cole. I think it was hard for her to say when she first met me. Felipe whispered to me that in Spanish a *col* is a cabbage. "You don't want to be a cabbage," he said. "A *coleto* is a jacket."

I wasn't sure I wanted to be a jacket, either. But it sounded better than a cabbage.

Juliana and Isabella always save me a seat between them. "*Coloso*," they say, then burst into giggles. They think I'm very tall.

Tía puts a plate of *huevos rancheros* in front of each of us, starting with me. The eggs are on top of salsa, which is on top of tortillas. With beans and avocado on the side. I wait until we all have our plates, then I dig in. The food is as delicious as its aroma. Tía's house always smells good, just like ours does. But in a spicier way, like there's a jalapeño waiting to let you know its power.

"I talked to your mother, Coleto." Tía puts her hand on my shoulder. "She has told me why you could not visit your father. I am so sorry. But it will be *mejor*. You will see."

I nod. It will be better. I don't see how it could be worse. "The *huevos rancheros* are delicious," I tell her.

She pats my shoulder. I can tell she knows I don't want to talk about Dad right now.

The table we're eating at is dark, stained oak with thick legs. Dad's probably eating off a plastic cafeteria table in the jail. If the jail has a cafeteria. The dark wood looks perfect in Tía's kitchen, which is painted in yellows, oranges, and turquoise. Dad's probably staring at dull greenish-gray walls that make you wish you were somewhere else.

Tía gives my shoulder a final pat, then moves to sit at the other side of the table. "Coleto," she says. "Felipe is running for class *presidente!*" Her smile is huge as she looks at Felipe.

I wipe up the last of my egg yolk and salsa with the last of my tortilla. "*Sí.*"

"Do you think he will win?" she asks.

"I am very popular, Mamá," Felipe says.

"*Sí,*" she says. "You are very *sociable.*" She pronounces it in Spanish: so-si-AH-blay. She looks at me. "That is why you brought Coleto home your first week of school."

Tía asks Felipe and me questions about what the class president does. I let him do most of the talking: I can tell he's excited about the whole thing.

Soon Tía looks at the clock and pushes herself away from the table. "*La escuela. La escuela.*"

School.

We all stand and help clear the table, and then we grab our backpacks and head out the back door. Tía stands and waves. "*Cuidado con las personas frías,*" she warns. Beware of the Cold Ones. ICE.

Benito, who's in sixth grade, takes charge of Juliana and Isabella, making sure their backpacks are on straight. Then he walks behind to make sure that all three of them get to Euclid Grade School on time. After the big demonstration and sit-in and arrests, the Chicago School Board announced that Euclid would remain open one more year. Thanks to Dad and the other protestors, Juliana and Isabella get to walk to a school four blocks away. I take out my phone to take a picture and text it to Dad… and then I realize I can't text Dad. But I can show him the photo when we see him on Sunday.

Felipe and I stand and watch Benito, Juliana, and Isabella until they turn the corner. Then we hustle down to Fullerton and catch the westbound #74 at Kedzie.

Felipe asks me if I wrote an F word poem about him. "Capital F," he reminds me.

I pull out my phone, find the poem, and show it to him. I watch as he reads it.

He grins. And then he sends the poem to himself.

"The p," he says. "It should be Proud *Presidente*."

"Nu-uh. Each letter gets one word only. You'll have to change the spelling of your name if you want two P words."

We arrive at August Mersy ten minutes early.

The day is warm and we don't want to go inside, so we lean against the chain link fence. The one I stood on to spray paint. I glance up at the bricks Felipe and I scrubbed last week. They're lighter than the rest of the building. Cleaner, too. I guess I'm lucky Nachman didn't make me clean the entire outside of August Mersy High School.

Felipe and I check our phones.

I guess we logged into the tenth grade election site at the same time.

"¿*Qué?*" he shouts. "¿*Qué?*"

Jillian's candidate page has a new slogan, in letters striped red, white, and blue.

VOTE AMERICAN TEAM,

VOTE AMERICAN DREAM

VOTE JUST JILLIAN

CHAPTER 8

HE'S SAYING I'M NOT AMERICAN." Felipe's words hiss like steam.

I'm wondering if maybe Jillian just chose the wrong words. By accident. Like maybe she didn't know what the words imply.

But I can't sell the idea to myself. Jillian knows what she's doing.

"Yeah," I say. "She's implying it."

"*Implicar es lo mismo que decirlo.*"

Yeah, I had to agree. Implying it is the same as saying it.

"This is war!" Felipe hits the top of the fence with a fist. The fence shakes.

"Maybe not war," I argue, "but definitely a battle. So we need a battle strategy."

That's when I notice Treva walking toward us, holding her cell phone.

"*La muchacha alta*," Felipe announces, also noticing her. It's hard not to notice somebody that tall, dressed in black, walking toward you in an I've-got-you-in-my-sights way.

"*Anarquista*," I remind him. "Dad says anarchists are unpredictable."

So far, though, I'm finding Treva more interesting than unpredictable.

Felipe nods.

"Hey," says Treva.

I hey her back.

"I'm Treva," she says to Felipe.

"Felipe," he replies.

"How do we fight back?" she asks.

Felipe and I look at each other.

"We?" he asks.

"Fight back?" I ask.

She waves her phone in front of our faces. We see Jillian's campaign slogan.

"Underhanded. Devious. Deceitful. Treacherous. Crafty. Crooked. Lowdown. Reactionary."

I'm pretty impressed with her vocabulary. No F words, though. "Stop," I say, holding up my hand. "We surrender."

She grins at this. Like I hoped she would.

"We fight back then," she says.

Felipe studies her a while. Finally he nods. "*Sí*."

"We fight to help Felipe win the election," I say, just to make sure we all agree on what we're fighting for.

"Totally," says Treva.

"No bombs," says Felipe. "No assassinations. Either one could get me in trouble."

He's kidding.

I think.

Treva tilts her head and gives him a serious look. "Old style. Vaporizing is more efficient."

She's kidding.

I hope.

"We could write a declaration of some kind," says Treva, "and pass it out to each student."

"No leaflets allowed," Felipe tells her. "Maybe I can talk to each tenth grader between now and next Tuesday, asking them to vote for me. Charisma always works."

"We could demand that Jillian be disqualified," I say. "She's being racist, implying that Mexican-Americans aren't Americans."

This riles Felipe again. "My ancestors were Americans before Jillian's ancestors came over on boats! The Americas extend from Tierra del Fuego to…" He looks at me.

I take a stab at it. "Ellesmere Island?"

"*Sí.* Some place very cold."

Treva frowns. "The principal isn't going to disqualify her."

"I know," I say. "Just brainstorming."

"Keep it up," she says. "We need to do something."

That very second, as Treva is telling me to keep brainstorming, I have an idea. I swear it comes from my swimming in F words. "*Familia,*" I say, straightening up from where I was very comfortable leaning against the fence. "Felipe's slogan is *Mi Familia*. We're all part of the same human family, and we can remind people of that by taking photos. Photos of different students posing with Felipe. *Familia* is everybody, and everybody loves photos."

Treva points her phone at Felipe and me. We automatically pose. She automatically clicks. "We're going to wage a photo campaign. I'm in!"

I turn to Felipe. "Treva and I can take photos of you with the other students. Two, three, four students at a time. In the hallway, on the baseball field, at this weekend's football game, in the cafeteria, in class. Everywhere!"

Felipe is there, totally. "We post them on the election site! *¡Inmediatamente!* Each one says *¡Familia!*"

"Uh," says Treva.

We look at her.

"*¿Qué?*"

"We can load the pix onto the election site, but we probably shouldn't run them *inmediatamente*. Probably not until Friday night."

I get it. She's right. "The election is Tuesday. If we started posting the photos today, Jillian might counter with something, who knows what."

Treva points a finger at me and smiles. "If we start posting Friday night, she won't have time to run her own photo campaign because we won't be back in school until Monday morning. I mean, she can come to school on Saturday if she wants to, but I doubt there will be anybody to take pictures of."

Felipe looks around, then motions for Treva and me to step closer.

We do.

"We run them on a random loop," he says, "so nobody knows when the photo they're in will come up. They'll be watching all day long, looking for themselves!"

"*Brilliantamente!*" says Treva, giving Felipe a high-five.

"*Brilliante,*" he corrects.

"Oh. Sorry."

The three of us look at each other. We each give a small nod.

We're a team.

A battle team.

"This is good," says Felipe. "*Gracias.*"

"We can start taking photos now," Treva suggests.

Felipe smiles at this and looks around for kids to pose with.

"Wait," I say. "We need the word *Familia* on each photo."

"I can do that," says Treva. "I'll add *Familia* in text over each jpeg."

I shake my head. "I'm thinking of something with more… participation. Something warmer. Something that the other students can be doing."

"Warm like me," says Felipe, grinning.

"I can borrow a flame-thrower," Treva says.

I really like her sense of humor.

Assuming she's kidding.

"I was thinking of three pieces of poster board," I explain, "with a syllable on each. *Fa mi lia*. Students who pose with Felipe could hold up the syllables."

"*¡Brilliante!*" shouts Treva, doing a little dance. "Syl-la-bles," she sings. "Harmless little syl-la-bles!"

"We need to move fast," says Felipe. "Who's going —"

And then he freezes.

I look to see what the problem is. So does Treva.

There's nobody around us.

I look where Felipe's looking, toward Pulaski Road, and then I see it. There's a woman standing across the street. She's dressed in blue pants and a blue jacket that says POLICE ICE. What are they doing here—looking for students to deport? Like they deported Amani last year?

"Two million people," mutters Felipe. "That's how many people ICE has deported in the last eight years. One of them was my Tío Julio, and one was my cousin Antonio."

Felipe doesn't usually talk about this with other students. He must feel good about Treva.

As we watch, another person gets out of the ICE car. The two of them leave their car right there on Pulaski and walk toward August Mersy High School. We watch until they're out of sight, heading toward the front doors.

When Felipe talks again, his voice isn't happy, like it was. "We need to move fast," he reminds us. "We need the posters by tomorrow morning."

"I'll make them tonight," I promise.

He grabs me by my hoodie sleeve and Treva by her coat sleeve. "Cole knows my class schedule. I'll text it to you, Treva, and the two of you work out who meets me when and where. You name the time and place. I'm ready."

El Presidente is serious about this.

By third period the news is all over school: ICE took Gi Pak out of his biology class and into their patrol car. Gi is a junior who came here from Korea three years ago. He's on the cross-country team.

Was.

"He's gone," Felipe says. "When ICE comes to get you, they don't bring you back."

"Deported?" Treva asks.

Felipe nods.

After school Felipe and Treva meet to take more photos while I go to cross-country practice. When I get there, Coach looks sad. He gathers us all around and tells us about Gi. Nobody says anything.

Somebody should say something.

"This is wrong," I say. "It's making people, like, disappear."

Coach looks at me. He pats me on the back, but he doesn't say anything.

After cross-country practice I take the Fullerton bus to a hardware store near home, to buy poster board. It takes me a while because I want the paper cut to a certain size.

Mom waves papers at me as soon as I walk in the door. "Permission arrived!" she cheers. "We can visit Dad this Sunday morning, ten o'clock."

I was feeling cold all over from ICE, but when Mom tells me this I feel warm, like I swallowed rays of sunshine. I can't wait to tell Dad what's happening in school. To sit down with him sitting across from me. "For how long?"

She makes her be-mature-about-this face at me. "Only fifteen minutes. But that's just for starters," she says before I can say anything. "The visits can increase to thirty minutes and sixty minutes."

Fifteen minutes? A week? That's cruel.

"And," she says, waving more papers at me, "I've filled out all the forms to get Dad phone privileges. We'll get to talk to him every Wednesday night."

"For how long?"

"The first one is just fifteen minutes. But later ones can be half an hour."

Part of me is dying to see Dad. Part of me believes it will never happen. Like he's been taken off Earth and can't come back. Sort of like Gi Pak and Amani.

"Mom… do you think Dad's okay?"

"Of course he is," she says, giving me a hug.

But I know she's saying that for both of us. Jail must be a horrible, horrible place. Anything can go wrong. I don't even want to think about prison movies I've seen. Somebody's always getting stabbed.

I need to see Dad, to know he's okay.

Mom needs to see him, too. For the same reason.

"What happened in school today?" she asks, changing the subject.

She motions for me to sit down, so I flop into Dad's La-Z-Boy and hang my legs over the arms. I tell her about ICE and Gi Pak. Then I tell her about Jillian's campaign slogan. Mom's eyebrows go up, but all she says is, "And?"

So I tell her about what Felipe and I are doing, and I tell her a new girl named Treva is helping. Mom likes our idea. I show her the poster board I bought. It came in orange, lime green, pink, or white. At first I considered buying pink, to show Jillian she doesn't own the color. But I ended up with white.

"Why so small?" she asks.

Mom's used to carrying protest posters stapled to pieces of wood. Those signs are usually two feet wide, sometimes more. The poster board I chose is letter-sized, eight-and-a-half by eleven inches.

I stack up the three poster boards and put them in the middle of my school books. I turn the whole stack sideways and exhibit it for Mom.

"Ah. You can walk down the hallways without the posters being seen. Very good, Cole!" She pauses. "You can tell Dad about this when we visit. It will make him happy."

"Yeah. I will. I'll even show him some of the pictures."

Mom shakes her head. "No phones allowed. We have to leave them behind when we check in."

Man, this sucks. And Dad's not a criminal, even.

But I guess he is, technically, because he was accused of a crime and convicted and sentenced.

I think the cops arrested Dad because he was the leader. The one who spoke to the crowds. With his new megaphone. Which Mom has moved from her desk to the kitchen table, in Dad's spot.

We talk some more and then I grab some cookies and go upstairs to my room.

I spread the boards out in front of me and wonder what color markers to use. Red and black, like I did on the school wall? No, better not use the same color scheme. Ms. Delaney might take it as proof.

Colors, colors, what colors? I tap the poster boards against one another, thinking.

And then Tía's kitchen colors fill my brain: orange, turquoise, yellow. Colors that look good together. Colors that are happy.

As I create the first poster, *Fa*, I make sure my handwriting is nothing like the style I tagged the school wall with.

I make all three posters and then go to sleep, wondering what tomorrow's first photo will be.

CHAPTER 9

THE NEXT MORNING, THE SCHOOLYARD'S covered with fallen leaves. Felipe and I crunch through them and meet Treva at the fence. I show them the three posters. FA MI LIA.

"Perfect!" says Treva.

"*¡Lindos colores!*" Felipe grins at me. Then he takes charge, looking around for where to start.

Emerald Jackson walks by, giving us a wave. Felipe and I have known Emerald since sixth grade. She's one of the smartest people I know. And she reads more than Dad, even. Emerald's wearing green, like she usually does. And a pin that says BLACK LIVES MATTER.

Felipe stops her and talks to her, and next thing I know Emerald reaches out and grabs the two nearest tenth graders, Rodney James and Kathleen Kowalski, one with each hand. Felipe reacts to this—he gives two posters to Rodney and one to Kathleen. He can't give one to Emerald because she has Rodney and Kathleen in fake headlocks. Nobody bothers to see if the syllables are in the right order. Felipe drops to one knee in front of them and Treva snaps off several photos.

Rodney and Kathleen look a bit dazed, but they're with it enough to hand the posters to Emerald and to point out more tenth graders. Emerald marches toward them. The bell rings, but neither Felipe nor Treva look ready to quit. I watch Treva taking photos, then I hurry off to history class in case Felipe's late and I have to invent an excuse for him.

But he makes it to class just in time.

In Nachman's class Treva slides into her seat just as the bell's going off. "My locker," she whispers. "Noon."

I'm there on the dot and she hands me the three posters.

"Afternoon shift to you," she says with a grin. "This is fun."

"How'd you do?"

She pulls out her phone and does some clicking. "I got Felipe in the hallways between classes, and I got him and other kids in study hall. One-hundred-and-eight photos, but I shot two of every group, so that makes fifty-four separate sets of people." She turns the phone toward me.

I'm impressed. "What're kids saying?"

"They're loving it! They love Felipe. He knows everyone! He spends time talking to them."

I smile at this. "Yeah."

"My Dad would be proud of me," she says. "Of what I'm doing."

Something about the way she says it makes everything inside me stop still.

I look at her.

She tries to say something, but no words come out. Finally they do. "He died three months ago."

"I'm sorry," I say.

"We moved here to live near my uncle."

I nod, not knowing what to say. Losing your father... I don't want to let myself think about something like that.

"Mom thought I should, you know, have a kind of father figure around."

All I can think to say is, "I'm glad you're here."

Treva gives a small smile. "Thanks."

I settle the three posters between my books. "We should meet up tonight. You and Felipe and me. To go over the photos."

"Okay. Where?"

"We can meet at my house, but I have to ask my mom first. I'll text you and Felipe. I get off work at 7:30 tonight. If Mom says fine, I'll text you the address."

The bell rings and Treva and I go to the cafeteria together, to find Felipe. So I can start taking photos.

After school Coach has us work on negative splits: running the second half of a distance faster than the first half. When practice is over I walk to the nearest hot dog stand and buy two Chicago style dogs, which means they're messy to eat because each is topped with mustard, onions, sweet pickle relish plus a dill pickle spear, tomato slices, pickled chili peppers, and lots of celery salt. I know this isn't the kind of meal Coach encourages us to eat. But Coach isn't here, and I figure hot dogs once a week can't hurt me.

I catch the #74 east, get off at California, and have to wait a while for the #52 southbound bus, but I make it on time to Mrs. Green's, where I do all the heavy lifting and moving that she wants me to. It's Mom's night off at Mrs. Green's.

When I get home Felipe and Treva are already there, eating Mom's cookies. Felipe's drinking coke and Treva's drinking coffee and Mom is looking happy. I sit next to Treva. Our arms brush. Bare skin against bare skin. Every hair on my arm tingles.

Mom stacks some cookies on a plate, pours herself a mug of coffee, and goes into another room, leaving us at the kitchen table. Where she stacked some pads and pencils.

I kind of laugh at the pads and pencils, but it turns out all three of us use them to doodle on and draw quick diagrams of how the photos should connect and fade in and out. Or flip in and out. Or flop over, or whatever. Lots of F words there, but none of them grab me.

When we're finished, we're happy with our work and with the decisions we made. I wish there was an F word that meant teamwork, because… because, I realize, I want to write a poem about it. Want to. For myself, not for Nachman's assignment.

That's kind of strange. I'm not a poet.

But Nachman said I'm good at poetry.

In the middle of the night, I'm in deep sleep one minute and wide awake the next. Join forces, my brain says. I sit up, confused. *Forces*, my brain insists. F-o-r-c-e-s.

I get it. An F word.

Groping for my tablet, I find it, open it, and tell my brain to start dictating.

Which of course it doesn't.

It's always me who does the work.

FORCE

Don't force your police
force on people,
people who ask for
better jobs
and homes
and schools

Don't force your
red-white-and-blue
thinking
on others

because

they will join forces
to force
you
out.

Huh.

What I wrote wasn't about joining forces, but about being forced. A poem can start out with one idea and end up with something totally different.

I go back to sleep.

Friday morning, I hand two F-word poems to Nachman. He reads the top one, "Flustered," and looks up at me. He shoots a glance down the aisle at Treva. Then he reads "Force." "I like the way you use *force* with a couple of different meanings," he tells me. Then he reaches into a beat-up canvas briefcase and pulls out a file folder. He opens it and puts my two poems inside.

A file folder?

For my poems?

File. Folder. F words are coming at me from every direction. Like a... I can't come up with the word for a bombardment of stuff.

Nachman will know.

"Mr. Nachman, what's the word—the F word—for a bombardment of things? Like a whole slew of bullets coming all at once. Or a whole slew of something, all at once."

"Fusillade," he suggests. "Good word."

That's it. That's the word. I thank him and go to my seat.

Treva flashes me a thumbs-up. Jillian looks at us. Probably wondering what we're up to. Jillian is going to experience a fusillade.

At five-fifteen today.

Which is Friday.

F words all around us.

———

Friday's a busy night at Mrs. Green's, so I don't have time to check the school's web site on my phone. But Felipe and Treva keep pinging me with texts all night long, telling me the photo campaign was a great idea. Telling me that Fatima is at the computer lab, too, and offered to help. I wish they'd send me some photos along with the texts, but I guess they're too busy putting things together.

I leave my phone on a nearby flower cart in the back of the greenhouse and make sure that just about every one of my jobs takes me in that direction.

Mom's pruning kalanchoe plants and sweeping away dead leaves. Mrs. Green likes things neat. "Interesting seedlings in the back?" Mom asks with a laugh.

She's on to me.

"Felipe and Treva keep texting what's happening with the photos."

"And?"

"Everyone's loving them. I can't wait to see them!"

When work is done we help Mrs. Green close things up, tell her goodnight, and go to our favorite pizza place.

It makes me sad when we walk in, that Dad isn't with us. The morning he went to jail, Dad told us not to worry, that he could do 120 days of time. But I do worry.

My phone pings. And this time, at last, it's the photos, one after another.

While we wait for the pizza, Mom and I scroll through them.

They. Are. Awesome!

Way, way better than I thought, thanks to the kids in them. And I gotta admit, thanks to *Fa mi lia*. Kids are holding the three posters frontwards, backwards, balanced on their fingers, in order, out of order, one kid holding all three posters, three kids holding one poster, kids holding posters sideways, kids holding other kids sideways, one kid holding all three posters with his bare feet.

And Felipe in every single photo.

He knows everyone. They know him.

I pull out my tablet and write a poem.

FUSILLADE

Low-blow shots
won't win the battle,

won't even win
the election.

Low-blow shots
can be vaporized
by a fusillade

of friendship
fotos.

CHAPTER 10

"LET'S GO." MOM HOLDS THE front door open and I duck through it, testing the porch railing on the way out. Solid. Dad and I built the new cedar porch—more like a stoop—last summer.

I can tell Mom's nervous about getting to the jail on time because it's Sunday and the bus schedules are different. I'm nervous, too, but not because of transportation. I'm nervous about what Dad will look like. All locked up. Will he look... defeated?

I can't stand thinking that. Maybe Mom is right: concentrate on bus schedules.

Except for us, the bus stop is empty, wet leaves from last night's rain plastered everywhere. The rain's down to a drizzle. Mom opens her umbrella, I pull up my hood.

Eventually the almost-empty California Avenue bus wheezes to a stop in front of us, like an exhausted elephant.

Yesterday's race was wet, but if it rains all week like it's supposed to, next Saturday's will be a mud bath. Coach will be counting on me if there's mud. He says I'm a natural in the elements, which is his word for rain, mud, snow, and ice. Just plain grass and dry land don't count as elements. "Brave the elements, boys," he likes to say.

"Brave the elements," I tell Mom as I slide my CTA permit against the scanner.

"The elements aren't my enemy," she answers back.

We sit together in the back. I watch water from the street spin up and hit the windows, then veer off into the wind. The bus is going to take us all the way down to 2700 South California, the location of Cook County Jail. I've never been that far south on this bus route. I study the route map above me. The bus is going to switch from California to Kedzie. Mom and I will get off at 2700 South Kedzie and walk two blocks east to the jail.

"Cole, I have to talk to you about something."

I look at Mom, afraid there's something wrong. Something more than Dad being in jail. Which is as wrong as wrong can be, so what could be worse?

"When we talk to Dad, there might be places in the conversation where we have to use code."

"Code?" I ask, not sure I heard her right.

"Most likely everything that prisoners say and do is heard and watched."

"Like, when we talk to Dad somebody's listening in?"

"We don't know. There could be electronic bugs, there could be a guard standing nearby listening and reporting, there could be another prisoner who listens and barters any information. It could be there are no bugs at all. But it's best to act as if they're there."

Dad being in jail is injustice. But that's not enough? They have to listen in on his conversations? Man. Totalitarian state.

"It's mainly names and actions we need to be careful about," Mom explains. "Like the names of people who urged the crowd forward, into the school. The cops keep asking for names."

"They do? Have they asked you?"

"They offered Dad a bargain—if he gave them names, they'd go after those people and let Dad off with a lighter sentence."

"When?"

Mom shrugs. "Always. Before the trial, during the trial, and probably now, while he's in jail."

I don't have to ask if Dad took up the city's offer. Dad wouldn't give them the names of other protestors. "All this over a grade school!" I shake my head.

"You know it's about more than that, Cole."

Yeah. I do. Mom and Dad have talked about it. Felipe and I have talked about it. A few kids at school talk about it. The people who run the country want us to be under-educated.

"McJobs or the military," Felipe always says. "That's what they want."

They don't want us to think, at least not think deeply. Or critically. Multiple choice questions on standardized tests— that's about as far as they want us to stretch.

But they're wrong. We do think. Teens think all the time. About everything. Sex. Money. Jobs. War. Peace. Equality. Sickness. Health. Everything. We think, and we talk to each other.

I twist in my seat. I don't want a minimum wage job. Nobody does. And I especially don't want to join the armed forces and help the ruling class conquer the world. Because I know there is a ruling class and I know it doesn't care about the billions of people who make up the world.

We ride in silence a while, the bus lurching to stops along the way, picking up a person here and there. The closer we get to Cook County Jail, the more people get on board.

Mom leans toward me. "If you don't know whether or not to say something, look at me. One tap of my finger on the counter means say it, two taps mean say it in code."

I sit there processing this. Not only do I have to write F-word poems, I have to learn how to talk in code.

Which might be kinda cool.

If I wasn't so scared of saying the wrong thing.

When we reach 2700 South Kedzie, we get off the bus.

So does everybody else who's on it.

The neighborhood is, like, empty. As if nothing wants to live or grow around the jail.

You can't miss the jail. Its buildings—a whole bunch of them—loom ahead. Almost no windows, and what windows there are, dirty.

The complex is huge.

Gigantic. The buildings sprawl out for six or seven blocks east and south.

It's a mega-jail, like something out of an apocalypse film. Barbed wire everywhere. My breath comes hard, like somebody's pressing heavy stones on my chest. I feel sick to my stomach.

"Largest jail in the United States," says Mom, watching me. "Ninety-six acres."

I guess maybe I'm standing there with my mouth open or something.

How is Dad going to survive in this huge, dark prison? How are we even going to find him?

Mom nudges me. "Roughly 3,000 square feet in a Chicago lot, roughly 43,000 square feet in an acre. How many houses could be built on the land occupied by the Cook County Jail?"

I'm used to this kind of challenge from Mom. Or Dad. He's probably going to ask me how many prisoners are inside the jail. I have no idea.

I think Mom wants to keep me from worrying.

Which is impossible when you're standing in front of a tyrannosaurus-sized fortress. F-word. My mouth is dry and my stomach feels like I'm going to throw up.

Maybe Mom's right: doing math will help. I take out my phone, but Mom tsk-tsks me. "Head work," she says.

I do the head work and come up with an answer. "About 1,350 houses."

Wow. That's a lot of houses that could be sitting here. And a lot of jobs people could have building those houses.

Mom nods. She puts her arm around my waist for a second. "It's not going to be easy, Cole. But we have to be strong for Dad. And ourselves."

I nod, but the barbed wire makes me swallow. Strong chain link fences, backed up by loops and loops of barbed wire, coiled so tight you'd bleed to death trying to escape.

Mom links her arm through mine and we follow the crowds, and when we see a sign for the division Dad's in, we follow it.

And then we stand in line with lots of other people. Several lines, actually.

Most of the people are poor, wearing worn-out clothes and worn-out shoes. I feel out of place in my new Cubs hoodie, and I wish I'd worn something not so new.

There are other white people in line, but most of the people here are Black or Latinx or Native American. A lot of really old people, and a lot of young people. Babies. Toddlers. Kids of all ages. Women who are pregnant.

The lines aren't moving. We're all just standing there, waiting. Every fifteen or twenty minutes, guards come out and let maybe twenty visitors in. Then they slam the doors shut and the rest of us keep standing.

I'm looking at the crowd but trying not to stare, when I sense that I'm being stared at. I look around, trying to figure out where the vibe is coming from. And then I see Emerald Jackson, standing one line over, staring at me. Naturally she's dressed in green. But Emerald's not like Jillian—Emerald never says she owns green.

I wonder how long she's been looking at me, and why she didn't say something. Maybe she's waiting to see if I'll say something to her. So I walk over to her line.

"Hey, Emerald!"

She raises her hand and I hit it with mine. Strong, because Emerald would be insulted if I didn't.

"You here to see your father," she says.

"Yeah. We couldn't see him last week because Mom didn't know about the application process."

Emerald turns to the woman she's with. "This my mother," she says to me. "This Cole Renner from school. His father's a political prisoner."

I say hello to Mrs. Jackson, but what I'm concentrating on are Emerald's words: *political prisoner*.

Yeah, I think. That's right. Dad led a political protest, and the city government arrested him.

"Who are you here to see?" I ask Emerald, wondering if it's okay to ask something like that.

"My brother," she says.

"I didn't know you had a brother."

"He older than me. Smarter, too."

"Nobody's smarter than you, Emerald."

Mrs. Jackson smiles at this.

"Ms. Delaney doesn't think I'm smart," says Emerald. "She thinks I'm a troublemaker."

I look at Emerald. "That's what she called me, too. A troublemaker."

She nods, sort of like we're in this together. Which we are.

"My brother's a political prisoner, too," Emerald tells me.

"All black people are political prisoners," Mrs. Jackson adds.

"My dad says that, too," I say.

"We're all in the same fight," Emerald says. "Black people know it. Most white people don't."

I look around to see if the line Mom is in has moved. It hasn't.

"Wanna come meet my mother?" I ask Emerald.

"Of course I do," she says. And marches ahead of me.

"Hey!" says Mom as Emerald approaches. "Green Girl! I know you!"

Huh?

"Backpack Woman! So you're Cole Renner's momma."

"You guys know each other?" I ask.

Mom sticks out her hand and Emerald shakes it. "I'm Stacey Renner," she tells Emerald, who introduces herself.

"Black Lives Matter," Emerald tells me over her shoulder.

Now I get it. Mom and Dad go to some of the Black Lives Matter demonstrations. And Mom almost always carries a backpack when she goes off to a demonstration or rally. I'm almost always at cross-country practice when the demonstrations are called, most of them in the early evening.

Mom asks Emerald who she's there to see, and then she asks her how long before her brother gets out.

"The week before Thanksgiving. Momma's planning the celebration menu already."

Mom's about to say something, but Mrs. Jackson shouts over that they're going in, so Emerald leaves and Mom and I watch a small group move into the building.

And then our line moves, too.

CHAPTER 11

NSIDE, THE GUARDS ORDER US to take our shoes off. Everybody else is already doing it, kind of automatically, but Mom and I are a bit slow. Neither of us was expecting it.

We line our shoes up on a dirty plastic tray, the kind you use to drain boots on. Then we hand over everything in our pockets, including our cell phones. They're put into a plastic zip lock bag and the guards give us each a number. I wonder how many cell phones are ripped off while the owners are visiting somebody inside.

Still in our socks, we follow the guard down a long hallway, then into a long, wide room. Strong cleaning fluid smells hit me. Just like the hallways at school. Only worse. All down the length of the room are visiting booths, with glass partitions between them.

Each booth has one metal stool in front of it. The stool is bolted to the floor.

"Mom. Is Dad going to be on the other side of that window? We can't touch him?"

Mom brushes my arm and points her finger at the guard in front of us. "Be strong," she mouths.

I straighten up, like I'm going to run a race I can't possibly win, but I don't want to telegraph defeat.

Because—maybe—I could win.

"You're racing against yourself," Coach always says. "Know yourself."

What I know is, I have to be strong for Dad, so he doesn't worry about Mom and me. I tell myself to hang tough.

Check, says Self.

The guard, who's wearing a gun, takes us to one of the partitions. Mom sits on the stool. I stand. The glass isn't glass, it's a thick plastic. With thousands of handprints all over it.

After about a minute a door on the other side opens and Dad walks through. He's looking for us right away, and when he sees us his face lights up.

I swallow hard. Rub my eyes.

"Stacey," Dad says, and touches his hand to the plastic. I can't hear him, but I can see what he said. Mom touches hers so that if there were no plastic, they'd be touching each other.

Then Dad puts his other hand on the plastic.

For me.

I put my hand against his, adding to the number of sad handprints. I feel warmth where I'm touching Dad's hand.

But that's an illusion, I know.

It's me, sending out energy, wanting to touch Dad himself. And Dad sending out his own energy.

He's wearing a dark gray t-shirt with DOC in black letters on front. It looks worn, like maybe hundreds of people before him have used it. But at least it looks clean.

"Are you okay?" Mom asks him as he sits down.

But he can't hear her.

He bends down, toward the bottom of the glass, where there's some kind of long strip of metal, with perforations built into it.

On our end, Mom bends down, too, and repeats what she said, this time into the perforation.

I squat, so I can hear what Dad's saying.

"Dying of boredom, but otherwise fine. Dying for home cooking, too."

"They won't let us bring you anything," says Mom.

"I know. It's okay."

Dad unbends and sits up. Mom does the same. I stand. We just look at each other for a while.

I study Dad to see if he's okay. He's big, taller than me, with lots of muscles that come from working as a carpenter. And from lifting weights in our basement exercise room. Just two more inches, though, and I'll be as tall as Dad. He kids me about it all the time, calling me Short Stuff just to get a laugh.

He looks okay. I don't see any bruises or scars. I guess I was worried about fights, though I don't know why.

I do know why: because of the pressure people in prison are under. Dad looks paler than he did two weeks ago, like he hasn't seen sunlight for a while.

I squat again and tell Dad that Mr. Cafasso asked about him. "Tell him I say Hi," Dad's voice says. We can't see each other when we talk because we're both bent down.

"How's cross-country coming?"

"We placed third a week ago," I say. "And fourth yesterday."

Dad unbends to look at me. Mom bends down and speaks. "Cole will be running in mud this week."

"More mud, longer spikes," Dad says. "Be prepared."

"I will be." It's easy for me to talk because I'm in a squat.

"How're F and F doing?" Dad asks into the perforation, then straightens up.

What?

I look at Mom. She nods her head. Then she looks down at her fingers. I glance at them. She taps two times on the counter.

This is code.

And then I get the first F—Felipe.

But what's the second?

Dad looks at me.

Mom looks at me. She points at Dad, then herself, then me. She makes a little circle in the air, including all three of us.

Then I get it.

Family.

F and F is Felipe and Family.

"Fine," I say into the speaker. "One of them is running for class president.

Dad's bent down to hear more, but he comes part way up to give me a grin. "Hope the one wins."

Mom bends forward. "Hank, I petitioned for phone permission for you, and it came through. The three of us can do a phone call or live chat every week. Our time is 7:30 Wednesday night."

"Starting this Wednesday?" he asks.

"Yes."

Dad straightens and nods. And gives us a thumbs-up.

Mom and Dad both bend. "Cole is helping with the class elections," Mom tells him.

Dad sits up to look at me. "How?" he mouths.

I lean forward, into the perforation. "Uh, I'm helping… my friend. By taking pictures of him with other… classmates."

Dad nods and kind of grins. Probably at my feeble code. *Feeble.*

"We can tell you more Wednesday," Mom says.

"Okay," he mouths. I think he'd rather look at us than hear us.

Nobody says anything for maybe two seconds, then Dad asks how the Euclid Grade School cases are coming along.

Mom tells him the lawyer's working hard to get all the charges dropped against everybody. "And if we're successful with that," she says, "then she'll ask that your conviction be overturned."

"That would be great," says Dad. "But let's not count on it, okay?"

They straighten up.

Mom nods.

Dad looks at me.

I really want Dad home. But I know I need to show him we'll be okay while we wait for him. I want to say something funny for him. It comes to me. I lean forward and he bends down. "I'll use the time to grow two more inches," I say.

"Dream on, Short Stuff." He straightens and puts his hand against the plastic again. I do the same. Mom puts her hand on top of mine.

My eyes start to water. I squeeze them tight and turn away for just a second. When I turn back, I see Dad doing the same thing. Mom's hand squeezes hard on mine.

The fifteen-minute visit seems like thirty seconds. A guard comes to take Dad away, and another comes to take Mom and me away. Dad turns to wave before he disappears through a heavy metal door.

Our phones are okay, our shoes are okay. But next week I'm dressing in my oldest clothes, wearing my rattiest shoes, and leaving my phone at home.

Mom and I walk to the bus stop and wait.

She looks sad.

"Are you okay?" I ask her.

She nods. "I'm okay. I'll just be more okay once Dad is home."

Me too.

We get on the bus, which plods its way back up Kedzie and California.

Mom sits there.

"You want to talk?" I ask.

"No. You?"

"Those speak-through things, built down so low—that's on purpose, isn't it?"

"Most likely," she answers. "The ruling class is cruel." She looks at me. "But we are strong."

She means us, the working class. Mom, Dad, me, Felipe, Tía and Tío. And millions of others. Around the world, billions of others.

Thinking about the way prisoners—and their visitors— are treated makes me sad.

But however bad it is for Mom and me, it's far worse for Dad, who's inside.

"I think I'm going to work on an assignment," I say.

"For which class?"

"It's for Mr. Nachman," I tell her.

She nods and I pull out my phone and type a poem.

FACE TIME

is a
life line
when you
face time.

My poem's about Dad. But I can see it's also about Mom and me.

I realize something else, too.

The poem isn't for Nachman. I don't mind if he sees inside me, the way he's always telling us poetry allows people to do. But it's not right to let him see inside Dad. Not unless Dad wants him to.

And then I think—does this mean I'm writing F-word poems not just for Nachman, but for myself, too?

Maybe for other people to read some day?

I can't answer that because another poem comes to me and I work on it. It's not for Nachman, either.

FAZE

He pretends that
incarceration
doesn't faze
him, that it's just
a bad break
in life.

But when I see
his outdoor skin
losing color and
when I see how
he hangs
on every word we say,
his imprisonment
fazes
me.

CHAPTER 12

ELIPE, TREVA, AND I MEET at the fence. Sooner or later, *fence* is going to be a poem.

Treva and I try, a couple of times, to talk about the photos and whether they'll help Felipe win—but talking isn't possible, because Felipe's being congratulated and high-fived and fist-bumped every few seconds, by just about everybody in tenth grade. *¡Fantástico!* is a frequent remark. An F-word remark. But the most common greeting is *El Presidente*.

"So," I say to Treva, "I'm thinking the photos worked."

"My photography skills are superb," she says.

"So are my syllabication skills."

"Whoa!" She laughs. "Syl-lab-i-ca-tion? Not sure I could top that, even if I wanted to."

Inside, I'm grinning. Because I made Treva laugh.

"Seriously," she says. "It was a great idea. Looks like the tenth grade wants Felipe to win."

We hang around watching Felipe's supporters until the bell rings.

He's surrounded by a bunch of kids, so Treva and I leave him behind and walk down the hallway together. We glance at each other and kind of smile at the same time. Treva raises her hand in a give-me-five gesture. I slap it.

"I'm on my way to history," I tell her.

"That depends on what you accomplish."

Huh?

Then I get it and laugh. "History class."

"Biology for me," she says, slipping off her backpack and shrugging out of her long black coat.

I'm blinded by red.

Treva's red tee, her red vest, her red scarf.

Black jeans and black boots, though, just like before.

She sees me staring, so I gotta either say something or look like a dork. "I didn't know anarchists wore red."

"Who says I'm an anarchist?" she demands, slinging the backpack over one shoulder.

"Your tat," I shoot back. "Black flag. Left wrist."

Treva looks at her wrist. She nods, then sticks her arm straight out, so that her wrist is almost in my face.

I stop, mostly so I don't walk into her arm.

She stops, too.

"Temp," she says.

I can see that now. The edges are starting to fade out.

"In case you change your mind?"

"Totally. I've been rethinking things. "

That's interesting. "How?"

"I've been talking to people," says Treva. "About political struggle. Anarchists are great. They're against authority and they act. But maybe they aren't so interested in organizing everybody else to act."

Just what Dad's always saying. "Who have you been talking to?"

She smiles. "It's best to not name names."

What?

"I talk to my Mom and Dad about things like that all the time," I tell her. "Protests. Social struggle. Felipe and I talk. There's nothing wrong with talking."

Treva nods. "Right. But I don't want to name names."

I decide not to push it. "Okay."

"Changing your mind about a thing is okay," says Treva. "Like, you know where we stand by the fence each morning? If you look up at the school wall, you can see that somebody tagged the wall. And somebody cleaned it off. My first day here, I thought that was really cool—that somebody tagged the wall. It was like a comment on herd education, standardized testing, being trapped inside school all day long."

It was about injustice. But I don't say anything.

"But now, I don't know," she says. "I think tagging the wall like that, whoever did it was acting like an anarchist."

"You mean he wasn't organizing others to act," I say.

"Right."

I don't want to be talking about who tagged the school wall. I look at Treva's clothes again. "I like the red," I tell her.

"Red and black," she says. "Socialism and anarchism."

"My mom and dad are socialists," I say.

"So they know more than most parents about what's going on in the world." She raises her eyebrows as she says this, asking me if what she just said was true.

I nod. "Was your dad an anarchist?" I ask. "Or your mom?"

All of a sudden she looks sad. I shouldn't have asked about her dad. "I'm sorry about your dad," I say, too late. It sounds lame.

"I miss him," she says. "I wish he was alive. You know what's so hard to accept?"

I shake my head.

"That it's forever."

A wave of sadness washes over me. For Treva. For the absoluteness of that F word. *Forever*.

Another bell goes off. Two minutes to class time.

"Which way's your locker?" she asks. She still hasn't got the layout of August Mersy down.

I point sideways with my thumb.

Treva heads in that direction. I follow her, open my locker, toss my backpack in, pull my tablet out.

Out of nowhere, Jillian is standing there. Dressed in pink.

Treva looks at her without saying anything. I manage a "Hi, Jillian."

"I'd like to talk to Cole," Jillian says. Announces, actually, as if she's speaking to a crowd. "Alone."

"So find him when he's alone," Treva says.

Wow!

I want to give Treva a fist bump or high-five or something for standing up to Jillian like that. But I don't. Even though Jillian deserves it.

Jillian walks away.

"She's not going to like losing," says Treva.

"Definitely not."

Treva heads off to biology and I go to history. Class.

———

Today Mr. Ortiz quizzes us on questions that will be—or might be, or were—on the standardized state tests. Boring.

I spend the time thinking about Treva. About how she didn't back down to Jillian. About her not having a father anymore. Which is so much harder than having a father who's in jail.

I think about everything except memorizing answers to test questions. The answers to which we've gone over three times already this year.

When class is over Mr. Ortiz tells me that the principal wants to see me.

What?

He waits until after class to tell me this?

I don't know which is worse, sitting through the test questions or going to see Delaney again.

He writes me out a pass and sends me on my way. Felipe gives me a questioning look. I give him an I-have-no-idea shrug.

Nikki Zurlo is sitting behind the wooden counter in the outer office. She's a good friend of Mom and Dad's.

"You can see Ms. Delaney now, Cole," she says, buzzing me through the low wooden gate. It's so low I could probably step over it if I tried, so I wonder how much good it does. Not that any student really wants to see the principal.

"Sit down, Cole," says Ms. Delaney.

I grab the same chair I sat in a couple of weeks ago.

"I've called you in on a very serious matter, Cole."

My mouth feels dry already.

Delaney looks at me. "I've called you in, Cole, because you have influence over Felipe Ramirez."

Man, I don't like this. I don't like the way this is going. "We're friends," I say. "The influence goes both ways."

"Felipe's decision to run for class president was kind of a last minute decision," she says.

It's not a question, so I don't say anything. What's she up to?

"I wonder what made him do this?" Delaney says. Asks. Leads.

"Have you asked him?"

"I'm asking you."

"I don't feel right talking about Felipe when he's not here."

She looks at her desk. She writes something. "Last year, Jillian was an excellent class president, wouldn't you agree?"

I shrug.

This annoys Delaney. "She organized three freshman dances. Built freshman attendance at football games. Acted as liaison to the yearbook staff. And those were only the visible things. She saw to it that I received minutes of all meetings, for example. She kept me informed about the freshman class."

"Informed?" I ask. "What do you mean?"

Delaney brushes something away from her face.

Or maybe it's my question she's erasing.

"Cole, I'm wondering if perhaps Felipe could be persuaded—considering his last-minute candidacy—to step down. To withdraw from the election." She looks at me. "There are already three candidates besides Jillian. Felipe makes five, which is a bit much, don't you think?"

I blink. Because I had no idea this was coming.

"What are you saying?" I ask. "That you want Jillian to be class president? Or that you don't want Felipe to be class president?"

Delaney sighs. Leans back in her chair. "The class presidency is very important to a girl like Jillian, who will go to college."

Man, I feel like I'm about to lose it. I put my hands under my thighs. Take a deep breath. "You think Felipe's not going to college?" I ask. "Is that because he's Latino, or is it because he's working class?"

The loud smack of a ruler on Delaney's desk makes me jump. "Do not talk to me in that insolent tone, Cole Renner."

"You dissed my best friend."

"Jillian is the better candidate. Jillian is not a troublemaker."

Whoa!

Troublemaker.

That's what Delaney called me—when she said she didn't want to see me turn into a troublemaker like Dad. And now Felipe's a troublemaker, too.

"What's a troublemaker?"

She glares at me. "A troublemaker is what I don't want you or Felipe to be. I don't want disturbances in my school. Do you understand?"

Sure.

I understand.

But I don't agree.

"I'm very disappointed in you, Cole. This is the second time you've been in my office this month."

What she means is, it's the second time she's called me into her office. It's not like I'd come here voluntarily. And I'm thinking it's the last day of September, and if she had just waited a day, I wouldn't have been in her office twice in one month.

Delaney stands up. A big hint. So I stand up, too.

She walks to the door and opens it. "I am death on troublemakers, Cole. Tell that to your best friend."

Delaney closes the door again, her on one side and me on the other.

FENCE

Too much fence
makes me tense

Breaking loose
makes good sense

CHAPTER 13

THE MORNING OF CLASS ELECTIONS, Felipe is pacing up and down along the fence, stopping every few seconds to greet somebody.

"Nervous," Treva whispers to me.

"I won't win," he announces when his pacing brings him our way.

We tell him we think he will win.

"I'll win," he announces the next time he reaches us. "I know I'll win."

We nod.

"I couldn't eat a single bite of breakfast this morning," he says. "Not even *una sola tortilla*."

I feel bad for him.

Treva offers him a granola bar. He stares at it, then stuffs it into his pocket. He forgets to thank her, which pretty much means an alien life form is inhabiting Felipe's body. Something from a planet where they never say thanks or *gracias*.

Yesterday, when I told Felipe about Delaney calling me into her office, he listened without interrupting. When I finished, he nodded. "She's afraid of me."

During first period Ms. Delaney makes an announcement over the PA system, reminding all sophomores, juniors, and seniors to vote for who they want to be their class president. We can vote in-person or from our phones or tablets.

"Voting closes at noon," she reminds us. "Your vote counts."

All morning long, whenever I see any sophomore on their tablet, I wonder if they're voting. I tell everyone I can that Felipe will make a good class president.

I guess there are a lot of votes to count: Ms. Delaney doesn't make the first announcement until 1:00, letting everyone know that Turner Blevins is now the senior class president. Felipe and I look at each other and grin. We know Turner, who's on the baseball team, and we like him.

Another hour goes by before Ms. Delaney speaks on the PA system again, this time to tell us that Petra Lindquist is the new junior class president.

Felipe squirms in his seat. "She and Jillian are friends," he whispers.

By the time we walk into Mrs. Gluckman's eighth period biology class, the tenth grade vote still hasn't been announced.

Some students look at Felipe and give him thumbs up. Some look at him without any expression.

Felipe's rubbing his palms up and down his pant legs.

"Nervous?"

"Itchy."

"Right."

We both laugh.

We go to our usual seats: four students around each small sink. I sit next to Felipe, as usual. Hasna sits across from me, and Ethan Ralis, who runs cross-country, sits across from Felipe. Hasna's kind of the leader at our table because she knows biology so well. I can hear Felipe breathing, like he's in a race.

Then I realize he is. Not a cross-country race. But a race to represent tenth graders. To argue for what he believes in.

The period's almost over. Mrs. Gluckman is talking about plant parts: roots, stems, flowers. What's taking Delaney so long?

We have five minutes to go. Mrs. Gluckman's explaining our homework assignment. Felipe and I look at each other. We're both wondering what the problem is.

And then we hear the PA system click on.

"The tenth grade results are in," announces Ms. Delaney. "Sophomores now have a new class president. One we hope will represent the class well." She pauses.

Felipe stares at the speaker on the wall.

"The new class president for tenth grade is Felipe Ramirez."

We hear the click of the PA system being shut off a micro-second before the whole room cheers and claps.

Well, most of the room.

A big, happy feeling washes over me as I look at Felipe.

He's blinking hard and looking down.

Reaching over, I touch him on the back and keep my hand there, hoping that will help him out. "*Victoria,*" I say quietly. "*Coraje.*" Victory. Courage.

That makes him grin. He wipes his eyes quickly and comes up smiling at everyone. "Thank you," he says. "I will try to be a good class president, fair to each of us. I will even try to be fair to juniors and seniors!"

That makes us all laugh, even Mrs. Gluckman. She congratulates Felipe and then tells us we're dismissed.

Out in the hallway Felipe is mobbed. I wait for so long that I'm afraid I'll be late for track practice, so I catch his eye, point to my watch, and set off.

But he comes running after me.

"Mamá and Papá are having a party tonight, to celebrate. We want you and Tía Stacey to come. And Treva. Can you text Treva and tell her? Eight o'clock, because I know you work at Mrs. Green's tonight."

"You just got the results a couple of minutes ago. How can there be a party tonight?"

Felipe grins. "Mamá started cooking Sunday night."

"Good thing you won," I say as we slap palms.

I turn toward the locker room, but Felipe stops me again. "Nobody in my family has ever been chosen for something like this," he says. "I'm the first."

I nod. "Tía and Tío will be very proud of you. They're proud of you already, but this is special."

"I wish Tío Hank could be there tonight."

That chokes me up, but I swallow hard and tell Felipe I'll take lots of pictures, and tomorrow night, when we have our video visit with Dad, I'll hold the photos up to the screen.

Then I hurry to the locker room to change clothes and get to practice without Coach calling me out. I run so fast and change so quickly that I even have time to text Treva about the party.

I hope she can come.

One whole side of Mrs. Green's Greenhouse is lined with bags of potting soil, perlite, and cow manure. Every single bag I lift has a hole in it somewhere, and the dirt finds its way down the inside of my t-shirt. By the time Mom and I get home, we both need showers.

"I'll bet Felipe's happy," Mom says as we leave our house.

"Super excited. But serious, too. And he says Tía has been cooking since Sunday."

"Can't wait to taste everything. I wish…"

I know what she means. She wishes Dad were here. I put my arm around Mom and give her a hug.

We reach the block Felipe lives on. Treva's standing on the corner, looking around. Man, she looks hot! Like sexy hot. She's wearing a black dress with red lace tights and black shoes.

"You're on the right block," I tell her. Then I introduce her to Mom.

"I think I see the target house," says Treva, pointing at Felipe's house.

People are gathered on the front lawn and porch, and the front door is wide open.

"Awesome deduction, Sherlock."

"Hey," she answers, "could be two parties on the same block."

We make our way through the crowd and finally get inside. The rooms are strung with *pancartas* in every color you can think of. The one across the dining room says *¡Felicitaciones, Felipe!* Others are cutouts of birds and flowers and skeletons.

Rice, beans, tortillas, tamales, and salsas fill every table. Mom goes off to find Tía Veronica. I say hello to Bianca, Felipe's cousin. She's eight years older than us. Bianca used to go to August Mersy High, but she was expelled and ended up graduating from another school. We hug, then I introduce Bianca to Treva. Then I say hello to all of Felipe's other aunts, uncles, and cousins, introducing Treva to everyone.

Treva and I pile our plates with food and edge our way through the crowd toward Felipe, who's standing at the end of the living room, wearing a white shirt and black pants, surrounded by Benito and a bunch of tenth graders. I see Ethan, who I saw just hours ago in cross-country. I see the whole soccer team. I see Emerald, who's listening and nodding her head. And I see two girls wearing different colored hijabs. Fatima's in red and Hasna's in blue. Salma isn't here.

"Congratulations, Felipe," Treva says. "I knew you'd win."

He smiles at this, then high-fives Treva. "Not without you, my official photographer."

"Hey, I took pictures, too," I say.

"Out of focus," he jokes. Then he looks at Fatima. "Fatima helped Treva and me in the computer lab all day Saturday. When we were adding more photos and working on how to do the random loop."

Fatima gives a big smile.

"Your photos with Felipe were great" I tell Fatima and Hasna. "The way you draped hijabs over the syllables was super-cool."

They both smile big time.

"Do you always carry extra hijabs with you?" I ask.

"Some students pull off our hijabs," Fatima answers.

"So we always have an extra one with us," Hasna explains, opening her purse and giving us a look inside. A black piece of cloth covers everything. I guess it's her hijab.

Ethan must be wiped out from today's practice, 'cause he's not saying much. He does look deep into Hasna's purse, though.

"Or an extra two with us," adds Fatima. She's more into literature than into biology and tells everyone she wants to be a college professor.

I wonder how some kids know what they want to be, and then go ahead and become it. And others, like Felipe and me, have no idea what we want to study when we go to college. Assuming we go to college.

Fatima asks us if we know how many votes Felipe got. I look at Treva. She looks at me. I guess neither of us know. In the excitement of Felipe winning, I never stopped to ask by how much. We shake our heads.

"Four-hundred-and-fifty-six votes," Fatima says. "That's an awesome sixty-eight percent!"

"Point six seven nine five," Hasna tells us.

We stare at her.

"That's great!" she says. "I was just being precise."

"More than two-thirds of the vote," says Treva. "Totally awesome!"

Felipe doesn't know where to look. He's embarrassed.

"Wow, Felipe, that's incredible!" says Ethan, high-fiving him.

We talk about all kinds of things, and soon it's ten o'clock and time to go. Not just because all the kids have classes the next morning, but also because Chicago has a 10:00 p.m. weekday curfew for anyone under the age of seventeen.

Mom asks Treva where she lives. It turns out to be three blocks south of August Mersy High, so Mom and I walk with her to the bus stop. So does Ethan, who lives in that direction.

"All around us people are fighting for everything that's denied them," Treva says as we walk. "But nobody fights for us."

Mom looks at her. "Teens, you mean?"

Treva nods. "We're a source of cheap labor. We're herded into schools all day long and taught subjects we have no choice over, made to take stupid multiple-choice tests we have no say about. And we're subject to a stupid curfew."

"Would you like me to organize a pro-youth demonstration?" Mom asks her. "I have poster board, mailing lists, and a megaphone."

What?

Ethan looks startled. "Can you do that, Mrs. Renner?" he asks.

Mom just grins.

Treva looks as surprised as I do. "You're not serious, are you?" she asks Mom.

"You answer my question, then I'll answer yours," Mom says.

Treva thinks about this for a few seconds. "No," she says at last. "I don't want you to organize a demonstration for our rights. We should do it. When the time comes."

Mom smiles.

Treva smiles.

I grin, thinking Mom's a great teacher.

Ethan looks at me, then at Treva. "Count me in," he says. "If it ever happens."

The westbound #74 bus comes. Treva and Ethan board it, and Mom and I wave goodnight to them. Then we turn around and walk home.

In my room I think about maybe writing a *feliz* poem. It's Spanish for happy, and everybody at tonight's party was happy. Then I think about curfew and wonder if maybe Nachman would count a word that has an F somewhere inside. Probably not.

But I look it up anyway, and learn that it comes from *cuvrir*, which is French for cover, and *feu*, which is French for fire. A curfew was a law to cover fire at night. I guess so the fire wouldn't burn the town down.

That makes me wonder if teens are like fire. And the law wants to smother us.

FIRE

Fire flicks,
flares, twitches,
flames. Fire's fury
will not be tamed.
Not be tamed.

CHAPTER 14

HEN I REACH FELIPE'S HOUSE on Wednesday morning it seems like the party is still going on. The decorations are still up, and so is the *¡Felicitaciones Felipe!* banner. But the dishes have all been washed and put away, and everything is neat, like it always is. Tío Carlos is just finishing his breakfast, drinking coffee so strong I can smell it. Felipe looks like he needs something strong, too. Or an extra night of sleep.

"Coleto," Tío says as he stands and gives me a hug. "Thank you for everything you did to help Felipe win the election."

I shrug. "I didn't do much. Felipe won because everyone likes him. And they know he'll do a good job for us."

Tía motions for me to sit, so I take my place between Isabella and Juliana.

Tío is almost never there for Wednesday breakfast, and when he is, he has to rush or he'll be late for work. He rushes now, taking a thermos of coffee with him.

"What time did you get to sleep last night?" I ask Felipe as we eat.

"Never!" shouts Benito.

"Really?"

"I stayed until everybody left," Felipe tells me. "It is the polite thing to do when the party is in your honor."

Tía stretches and yawns. "The last guest left at three o'clock," she says. "And then I put everything in order. Bianca stayed to help me."

I hope Tía can take a nap after we all leave for school.

"*Mamá*," says Felipe as we gather our things. "*Por favor, un cafecito para mí.*"

She pours some strong-looking stuff into a thermal cup and hands it to Felipe.

"For you, too, Coleto?" she asks.

I shake my head.

Felipe sips the coffee all the way to school, and by the time we meet Treva at the fence, he looks awake. Pretty much.

We talk about last night's party and we talk about the election and it seems like a hundred kids come over to congratulate Felipe. When there's a lull in the action, Treva asks him what student issues he plans to tackle. Those are her words: *student issues* and *tackle*.

He thinks before he answers. "I don't know," he says, "but important ones. Bullying? Being forced to study for the state tests? Teaching respect for all the different nationalities in our student body? The bleak future of working menial jobs?"

I'm thinking about this when I notice an ICE car going down Pulaski.

Slowly.

Felipe's back is to the street, so he can't see it. So is Treva's. I watch the car, thinking it's going to stop and another student's going to be grabbed. My fists are clenched.

The car slowly rolls out of sight.

"All important issues," Treva is saying.

Felipe sips some coffee, then tilts the thermal mug upside down to his mouth.

All gone.

"Opposing standardized testing is good 'cause we've done it before and kids will remember," I say. "Last year almost a quarter of the students boycotted the standardized tests."

They nod.

"But bullying is everywhere. We should fight that, too," I say.

"And hatred of Muslims," Treva adds.

"Every hour we spend learning the answers to those dumb state tests is an hour we could be learning about the world," I say. My eyes are on the street. The ICE car hasn't come back. "How are we supposed to deal with the world?" I ask. "Give everybody a multiple choice test?" Sometimes I think there's going to be another world war and we'll all be incinerated by a nuclear blast.

"There's something else about teaching to testing," says Felipe. "It drives kids out of school. Especially Latinx kids.

The more tests there are, the more dropouts there are. Kids who get low scores on the test feel like failures."

More kids come up to congratulate Felipe.

When they leave Treva asks, "When you boycotted last year, how did Ms. Delaney react?"

Felipe and I look at each other. "She was furious," I say. "Made all the boycotters attend a special after-school class for a week."

"What kind of class?"

"A class on the importance of state-wide testing," snorts Felipe. "And we know why she did that. The higher our school scores, the more money our school gets from the state. And that means Ms. Delaney gets a bigger bonus."

Treva sighs. "Her interest in the state testing is that she profits from it. So do the companies that design the tests. What is it about profit?"

Felipe straightens up and manages to look almost awake. "Lots of issues to bring up in the first meeting of class officers."

The bell rings. Treva leaves for her class, Felipe and I leave for ours.

When first period's over, I walk to my locker.

Jillian is standing there like she's waiting for me. Her eyes are red and puffy.

"I hate you, Cole Renner! Hate you!" she says. Loud. I can feel kids looking at us.

"Because you lost the election?" I ask. Okay, I can't help it. I don't mean to, but I know I sound amazed. Blown away.

Flabbergasted. F word: to be explored later. Man, people lose elections all the time. Big deal.

"This is all your fault. I know you're the one who came up with the photos idea. You did this to get even with me."

"No way, Jillian. I did it to help Felipe win."

"Same thing!" she shouts.

Kids are staring at us. This is going nowhere.

"Felipe won in a landslide, Jillian. Live with it."

I turn to walk into class.

But then I turn back to face Jillian. "You're the one who gave me the idea of how to fight back," I tell her. "You tried to appeal to everyone who thinks Latinos aren't real Americans. That's what gave me the idea to appeal to something better: a world where all colors and races and languages are equal."

Jillian smirks at this, and I can't figure out why.

Then I feel a thud on my shoulder. Strong fingers dig into my shoulder blade.

I turn.

As much as I can.

"Dead meat, Renner." Jared Anderson grips me harder. "You're dead meat."

I twist down and away from him, breaking his grip. "I don't think so, Jared." I walk into Nachman's classroom.

One of the things Dad always says goes something like, Past behavior is the best indicator of future behavior. So I know that somewhere in my future Jared Anderson is waiting to turn me into dead meat.

Waiting to *try* to turn me into dead meat.

Because Mom and Dad have taught me self-defense. Things like not having my back to a wall if somebody's coming at me. Crouching low. Twisting down and away. Falling backward, even. F word, *falling*.

FALLING

Sometimes it seems
the world is falling
all over us,

the world you
have broken and
have failed to fix

and I don't understand
why you don't understand
that when the world falls,
it will kill you, too

━━━

Dad never said anything about the future behavior coming instantly—which is what it does after eighth period as Treva, Felipe, and I walk toward the east wing. The boys' locker rooms are off the east wing, so I can change into my cross-country clothes and make it to practice with no problem. I'm thinking about cross-country. Treva is showing Felipe photos on her phone.

When we turn the corner, Jared Anderson is standing there. Arms crossed. Legs apart.

Like he's going to try to keep us from going where we want to.

"If it isn't the beaner," he says, "and his border-bunny-loving friends."

Jared has been calling Felipe a beaner or a jalapeño since third grade, so we've heard it before.

Treva hasn't.

"Why do you call people names?" she asks Jared. "Because you feel inferior?"

"Shut up, bitch."

"Great. More names. You really do feel inferior."

I can see Jared processing this. "C'mon," I say, nodding to Felipe and Treva that we should keep on going—around Jared and down the hall.

The three of us start moving and just then we hear a door opening.

All four of us look toward the sound.

Fatima walks out of a classroom, books in hand.

She takes in the scene and stops. For just a fraction of a second. Then she starts moving again.

Treva is holding her phone in the air. I notice it. I wonder if Jared does.

Jared moves, quick as a snake, and snatches Fatima's hijab off her head.

Which sends Felipe charging toward Jared, who holds the hijab high in the air.

Jared is going to stiff-arm Felipe, I can see it coming. I run forward, making Jared turn my way.

Then I swerve right, leap up, and grab the hijab.

Felipe rams into Jared, who staggers, but barely. Felipe's rush carries him past Jared, next to me.

We stop at the same time and turn around, facing Jared, who's also turned around.

He roars and runs at me.

I toss the hijab to Felipe and dodge left, keeping away from the wall.

Jared's going to crush me. I can feel it coming. I can't dodge forever.

And then I hear Treva shout. "You're on video, idiot! And I'm hitting send!"

We turn to stare at her. She still has her phone in the air and taps a button.

Jared makes a move toward Treva but stops.

Mr. Ortiz has just stepped out of the classroom. "What's going on here?" he demands.

"He ripped my hijab off my head," Fatima says. "Felipe and Cole tried to get it back for me."

Felipe hands her the hijab and she puts it on.

"Jared, is this true?" asks Mr. Ortiz.

"No," says Jared.

"Yes," says Treva. "I took a video and you can see that he ripped it off."

She shows the video to Mr. Ortiz.

"Jared," he says, "come with me. You and I are going to the principal's office. The rest of you, go home."

Which we don't.

We hang together a while, not saying anything. I feel the adrenaline draining away.

"Are you okay?" Felipe asks Fatima.

She nods.

"Quick thinking on the video," I say to Treva.

"Maybe we should move Muslim-hating to the top of the agenda," she says.

"What agenda?" Fatima asks.

Felipe smiles. "I'll tell you all about it."

CHAPTER 15

"**Y**OU GO, MAN, OR YOU'LL miss practice," Felipe says to me.

"Sure?" I ask, looking at him, Treva, and Fatima.

Treva and Fatima look at each other and nod.

"We're good," says Treva.

So I hurry to the gym, grab shorts and shirt and track shoes out of my locker, change as fast as I can, and then it's into the bus and the whole team is off to the suburbs. We take the school bus most days that we practice, but on Wednesdays we always go to The Hill.

Chicago doesn't have hills.

Some of the suburbs do.

Coach is into developing fast twitch muscles. And slow-twitch muscles. Coach is into developing muscles and stamina, period.

"You need both kinds of muscles," Coach shouts to all of us: sophomores, juniors, seniors. "You need both kinds of muscles," he repeats, "so you're ready for any situation." After he has our attention he speaks in his regular voice. Which isn't quite as much of a shout. "Fast-twitch for acceleration, slow-twitch for endurance. That's life, boys. A combination of acceleration and endurance."

I think about that a bit.

Ethan is sitting next to me. He looks upset.

"You okay, man?" I ask him.

He nods, then turns to me and whispers. "How's your father?"

I wonder why he's whispering. "Okay. He's doing okay. Thanks for asking, Ethan."

He looks straight ahead, at the bus driver. "I was going to. Ask. On my own. Mr. Nachman told me I should ask." He turns toward me. "But I was going to do it on my own."

"Wait. Let me get this straight. Mr. Nachman told you to ask me how Dad's doing?"

Ethan shakes his head. He's still speaking in a low voice. "Not exactly. We were talking about the last paper I handed in. The empathy assignment?"

"Yeah?"

"Well, we were talking about empathy and understanding, and empathy and reaching out to other people, and Mr. Nachman gave me some examples."

"Like?"

Ethan clears his throat. "You because your dad's in jail. Jillian because she lost something she really wanted to win. Felipe because he has, like, a big responsibility as class president. Emerald and Keeshan and Lawrence because they're seen as black people instead of just, you know... people. And Salma, because kids think wearing those head scarves is, like, I don't know, unAmerican?"

I nod at just about every person Ethan names. Sounds like he and Nachman discussed our whole English class. Maybe even Nachman's other English classes. But I feel good that Ethan asked me about Dad. And I hope that my saying Dad's doing okay means he really is doing okay. As okay as he can in jail. The largest jail in the country.

The bus finally stops. The Hill is waiting.

We all know what to do: lope the long flat prairie leading up to the hill, sprint the hill. Wait at the top until the whole team makes it. Then down the hill and up again.

Three times.

On the lope, things pour down on me. Jared calling Felipe a beaner and border bunny. Jared pulling Fatima's hijab off her head. Jared ready to pulverize Felipe and me.

The more I think, the angrier I get. Even before we reach The Hill, I'm *muy enojado*, as Felipe says. Furious. As furious as the night I painted the F word all over the school wall.

Maybe more.

F word: *furious*. I'm becoming good friends with F words—they express my feelings.

My feet barely touch the flat parts of the run. Going way too fast. Won't have anything left. For The Hill. I slow down… adjust my stride. I can feel Coach watching me.

Felipe is going to face more attacks. From Jared. From people like Jared.

So is Fatima.

And Treva, too.

Because she doesn't wear pink, the way Jillian does.

I laugh out loud.

Ricardo's behind me. "You won't be laughing long, Cole. The Hill."

"I can take it," I say over my shoulder.

I can't see Treva in pink. No way.

Treva says what she thinks. And she thinks about serious stuff.

Which is why she's in trouble, too.

Even with my reduced stride, I'm pounding out the footsteps. I notice there's nobody ahead of me. Which means— Duh!—I'm in the lead.

Which is sometimes good, sometimes bad. Depending on where the finish line is.

F word, *finish*.

We need to defend ourselves, so bullies like Jared can't beat up on us.

There must be self-defense classes all over the city. I see ads for them in little stores up and down Western Avenue.

After practice, I'm going to text Felipe and Treva, tell them about self-defense classes.

I reach The Hill and pump hard. And harder. I reach the top first.

Coach is there, stopwatch in hand. "I see you're back in form, Cole."

I don't say anything. I can't: I'm gasping for breath.

Coach pats me on the back. "I love having you on the team, Cole. You have great discipline, and you understand strategy."

I understand that in less than a minute I have to turn around and run down The Hill, across the flats, and then back up The Hill.

On the second round I think about Dad. I'm angry that he's in jail, angry that the visitation rules are such cruel punishment. I'm first on The Hill during the second round.

And the third.

Back in the bus, I'm still seeing red. The night I wrote the F words, my anger was like a fast-twitch muscle—drawing on all my energy at once. When Nachman caught me, he told me anger doesn't solve anything.

It didn't that night.

But maybe there are two kinds of anger: one fast-twitch, one slow-twitch.

What I feel now is the slow-twitch kind.

It's going to be with me for a long, long time.

Maybe forever.

FINISH

I won't be finished off
by some bully boy
who has no goals
except to crush
living things.

I won't be shellacked
and buffed
to a glossy finish
that covers
a hollow heart.

I will reach
the finish line—
where there are
no racial slurs
no fences
no jails.

CHAPTER 16

HEN WE GET BACK TO school I change into my clothes, hurry out the door, and am lucky enough to catch a city bus within three minutes. Usually I walk from school to Mrs. Green's—but not after The Hill.

I check my phone.

Whoa! More text messages than I have fast-twitch muscles.

Felipe: Demo Daley Plaz, Sun 6 pm. Going! U?
Me: What demo?

In a few seconds, he replies.

Felipe: 4 immigrant rights.
Me: How u know?

Felipe: Fatima

I think about this a sec. Felipe and Fatima?

Could be.

Me: 👍

The next text is from Treva. It's huge.

Treva: F & I went w Fatima 2 D's office, 2 report what hppnd. Had 2 wait til D finish w Jared. D told F & me 2 leave. F said he's class pres and reps all sophs. D repeated: Leave. Fatima said: No, I want Felipe to rep me. The 3 of them went into D's office. I 🖤 Felipe!

Me: I 🖤 him 2. What @ Jared & hijab?

She texts me back instantly.

Treva: Jared = 1 wk suspen. Jared = no ftball for 2 gms.

Me: J will b pissed. More than usual. We need 2 learn self-defense.

Treva: Let's do it! U, me, F, Fatima, Hasna, Salma.

Me: 👍 On way 2 work. TTYL.

The next stop is mine. There's a text from somebody who's not on my phone. I open it.

Fatima: Cole, Immigrant Rights rally at Daley Plaza Sunday, six p.m. Pls come if u can, to show ur support.

I don't know how Fatima got my number. Felipe must have given it to her. I add her to my book.

Me: I'll B there. Thx 4 let me know.
Fatima: Ask everybody you know.

This makes me think a minute.

I text Emerald and ask her to text others. Then I text Ethan and Ricardo and ask them to text others. On Ethan's text I type, PS: EMPATHY.

The bus stops, I hop off.

Starving.

I say hi to Mrs. Green and head straight back to the supply room, open the mini-refrigerator, and pull out the bag with my name on it. Mom packed me two sandwiches. One's meatloaf, one's turkey and avocado. I sit at the folding table and dig into the turkey one first. The supply room doesn't hold supplies, at least not anymore. It has a folding table and three chairs, the mini-refrigerator, a sink, a shower, and a cot. Sometimes Mrs. Green goes into the supply room and doesn't come out for an hour. Mom runs the cash register. I think Mrs. Green takes a nap.

Which is what I feel like doing right now. Too much of The Hill.

I finish the second sandwich, wipe any ketchup off my mouth, and head out to battle the bags.

I like working at the nursery, and I like Mrs. Green. She's always giving me information as I work, things like explaining that loam is a fertile soil composed of sand, clay, and humus. And that humus is decayed plants, like leaves and twigs. I love the smell of the loam, and I like lifting the fifty-pound bags on my shoulders and carrying them to the customer's cars. Or just moving them around.

Tonight it's mostly loam and fertilizer bags. F word, *fertilizer*.

Mom is helping a customer decide whether he wants asters, mums, or salvia.

When she's free and my path goes by where she's working, I tell Mom that Felipe and I are going to an immigrants' rights rally on Sunday. I don't tell her about Jared.

"That's great," says Mom. "So am I."

And then, before I can say anything, she adds, "Don't worry, I'll sit in a separate el car."

I grin. "That's extreme, Mom. Sitting at the opposite end of the same car is fine."

She laughs.

I like to make Mom laugh. Especially since Dad went to jail. We don't laugh as much with him gone.

I wonder if Dad gets to laugh at all.

A little before 7:30 Mom catches Mrs. Green's eye, points one finger toward the supply room, and flashes five fingers. Three times. She's telling Mrs. Green we're going to live chat with Dad and that we'll be back to work in fifteen minutes.

Once we're in the room Mom reminds me about talking in code. "They can probably figure out everything we're saying," she says. "But let's make them work for it, the filthy spies."

Fifteen minutes it's not, because even though Mom logs into the computer and is ready before 7:30, Cook County Jail takes its time in getting Dad's end set up.

The first thing we see on the monitor isn't Dad. It's a message in red letters. *Warning: this call is being recorded and monitored.*

My fast twitch muscles go crazy when I see that. I want to punch my fist through the monitor.

Mom puts her hand on my knee. "Calm down, Cole."

I take deep breaths. After about three minutes Dad's there.

"Hey," he says, "am I ever glad to see you."

Mom's sitting in front of the computer and I'm in another chair, pulled up close to her.

"Cole, I can't see all of you. Move closer to Mom."

I scrape my chair across the cement.

"Now I see you, Short Stuff. How's everything?"

If Dad were home, I'd tell him about Jared. I'd show him how Jared stood and where Felipe and I were, and Dad would give me some pointers on what to do. But I'm not going to worry him now. "Cool," I say. "Had a great practice today. The Hill."

"Good. Rain still expected for Saturday's race?"

"Yeah. I'll have my longer spikes ready."

"Cole and I went to a party last night," Mom tells him.

Dad raises an eyebrow. "Celebrating my jail sentence?"

"We're petitioning the court to make it longer," says Mom. "But the party was for a friend of Cole's."

"This friend won…" I stop, not sure if I should say "election for class president."

But Dad's already there. "That's great. Wish I could have been there to give my congratulations."

"I met a new friend of Cole's," says Mom. "She's striking."

"Mom!" I say, embarrassed. But I'm thinking, That's a great word for Treva. She's striking.

Dad laughs. "Is she intelligent?" he asks.

"Super intelligent," I say. Mom nods at that. "She dresses in black." I'm trying to figure out how to tell Dad Treva's an anarchist. "But she wears some red, too."

Dad looks at me. "She's finding her way."

"Yeah," I say.

"And you are, too," he says.

I think about that. "Yeah."

Mom clears her throat. "Cole and I have taken up walking together," she tells him. "It's good exercise. And you meet hundreds of people. We're starting this Sunday."

This code stuff is actually kind of cool.

Even though anybody can figure it out. Finks included.

Fink. I got that word from listening to Mom and Dad. *Fink.* A contemptible person who informs on others.

"Dad. Is there a guard in the room with you?" I ask.

"He's standing right behind me. Out of camera range."

And then somebody cuts off the computer connection.

I think it's because of what I said, but when I look at my watch, it reads 7:45. Our fifteen minutes—make that twelve—are up.

"I wish we could get Dad out of jail," I say.

Mom pats my shoulder. "I do, too. And so does he. But he won't get out until January."

We close the computer and move our chairs back into place.

Mom stuffs the computer into her tote bag and we go back into the greenhouse.

FINKS

snoop on links
even in clinks

make me think
before I blink

my mind kinks
my thoughts sink

finks stink

CHAPTER 17

ATURDAY MORNING ALL THE CROSS-COUNTRY teams,
boys and girls, sophomores through seniors, board
the school bus that takes us west to—duh!—West
Dundee. All of us are wearing our running shorts
and singlets in the August Mersy High School colors: crimson
and gray. Most of us are also wearing windbreakers because it's
October and the temperature is 50 degrees and pouring rain.

We arrive at the meet, which is in a huge park of some
kind, pile out of the van, grab our backpacks, and follow
Coach. "Five days of rain," he says, "and still coming down.
Most of the ground will be mud. Use your rain spikes." As if
anybody wouldn't.

I already have my half-inch spikes screwed into my track
shoes, which are in my backpack.

Coach discusses strategy, like he always does. He likes us
to run as a pack until the very end. Sticking together makes it

harder for other runners to pass. Sticking together allows us to encourage and support each other. That's always important. But it's especially important under bad conditions. Like the stinging rain.

In a perfect world all seven of us would cross the finish line ahead of anybody else. We'd score 1, 2, 3, 4, and 5 points. Only the first five finishers on each team score. In cross-country, lowest score wins the meet, and if five of us crossed first, nobody could come in lower than our combined total of 15. *Five. Finishers. Fifteen.* F words. But not every F word is going to be a poem. I'd, like, never graduate if I had to write a poem for every F word.

As I put on my track shoes I think about my strategy. Stay loose. Pace myself. Stick with the pack. Help the pack. Except I always try to be ahead of Ricardo Aguilar, who blows more snot than the whole rest of the meet combined. I hate being behind him when he does that. I sometimes think the Freshman All City statue I won last year was due to Ricardo: I ran fast to stay ahead of him. We're always telling him to wear a long-sleeved shirt and wipe the snot on his sleeve. I stick my hand out to feel the rain. It's one of those stinging rains that feels like it wants to slice you open. Coming down hard enough to wash away any snot.

We walk part way down the trail, studying as much of the layout as we can see. Dirt path. Correct that: mud path. Lots of trees lining the path.

"Follow the markers," Coach says, like he does every time. As if we'd forget. But sometimes following the markers isn't so easy. I remember my first race in sixth grade, where we thought we were following the orange markers. Three of us ended up somewhere in the woods and had to turn back. Because we got lost, our team placed last.

Tenth graders run first. The seven of us loosen up, talking to each other. "Stay loose. Stay together. Watch out for Kankakee, they're fast," and stuff like that.

It's pretty miserable weather. My legs are nothing but goosebumps. If I had to choose between having dirt, manure, worm casings, and perlite drip down my back as I carried sacks for Mrs. Green, and having rain run down my collar, I'd choose the dirt.

At last it's time to line up. We strip off our windbreakers and toss them aside. We line up together, shoulder to shoulder. Looks like there are two hundred of us altogether, grouped together in clumps of school colors.

The gun goes off and we sprint forward, trying not to trip, elbowing for position.

By the quarter mile most teams are running in clumps behind one another. I can see four different clumps ahead of us, so Mersy is in fifth position. I glance around to see how we're running. Ricardo's ahead of me, and so is Xavier. Deshaun, Ethan, Ibrahim, and Peer are behind me.

The rain's coming down, the mud's coating my legs. I hope my shoes are tied tight enough they don't come off in the mud. "When your shoe comes off, keep going," says Coach.

Yeah. Sure.

At the half-mile mark Ricardo shouts back at us: "Take green, next half mile."

He means pass the green-bibbed team in front of us. He picks up the pace and we move forward. Ricardo starts blowing snot. I stay to his left, which is usually safer. My spikes sink deep into the wet grass and mud, but with each long stride I take, my shoes stay with me.

By the half-mile mark six of us have passed the green team, and Peer looks like he'll do it soon. "Purple, next half mile," Ricardo pants. Some of the purple bibs hear him and stick out their elbows. We're in the woods now, where it's harder to run around anybody.

So we run through them, pushing hard, knocking their elbows aside. Ricardo blows some snot on them.

On purpose, I think.

Mersy's in third now, halfway through the course. Hill coming up, I can see it through the trees.

"Left, left!" I shout, using up valuable air—because Ricardo's confused about the orange markers. He's trying to move us to the right. But I'm taller than he is and I can see more markers in the distance. The markers go left.

"Orange markers," I pant. "Left."

Ricardo tilts left toward me and starts to take us through the white team in front of us. Or what's left of the white team, because by this time the runners in front of us aren't all one color. Runners from other teams have moved ahead, into the white pack and into the yellow pack.

Words are a waste of breath at this point. We know what we have to do. Two bunches to pass, a mile to do it.

I don't know where Peer is, but I can't be spending energy

looking backwards. None of us can.

By the time we gain second place, I'm even with Ricardo. He doesn't like that, he likes to come in first. Which is good.

Four runners. Two yellow bibs, one red, one white. I don't know who they are.

I don't care. I'm gonna pass 'em.

As we come down the hill Ricardo and I pass one of the runners. I hear somebody behind me. Footsteps and heavy breathing. It might be Ibrahim. Can't waste effort looking.

We're out in the open now, nothing but the muddy trail and rain. Everything's slippery.

I pass another runner at the same time Ricardo does. Only two runners ahead of us. Ricardo and I are running stride for stride in third place. And that's definitely Ibrahim I hear behind me.

I hear other things, too. I hear Ibrahim's family shouting for him. I hear Ricardo's Mom shouting for him. I hear people shouting for the other runners.

Mom's not here, like she always used to be. She has to work Saturdays.

Dad's not here because he's in jail.

Ricardo pulls ahead of me, passing the second runner. I force myself to follow, but the running feels harder. Like the mud wants to suck me in.

Ricardo takes the lead, yellow singlet is second, I'm third.

"Go, Coooooooooole! You can do it!"

I'd recognize that voice anywhere.

Felipe.

I glance over where the supporters line the path. I see him. He's jumping up and down. Rain is pouring off of him, but you wouldn't know it from how he's cheering.

"*¡Dele! ¡Dele!*" It's Tío Carlos. He's waving his fist in the air.

"*¡Coleto!*" shouts Tía Veronica.

I see Benito and Juliana and Isabella, and they're waving colored handkerchiefs and jumping up and down just like Felipe.

I give a little flap of my hand, which I hope they understand means I'm waving to them, and I find breath from somewhere deep inside and pass the second runner.

And then, just before the chute, I pass Ricardo.

My shoe comes off.

I keep going.

Stick to the center of the chute.

Ricardo's gaining. I see his feet alongside mine.

You don't pass me in the chute, dude!

I throw myself forward, breaking the finish tape and landing in the mud.

In cross-country it's the torso that counts.

I come in first, Ricardo second. We fall to our hands and knees, gulping air.

"G'run," Ricardo pants. Which I take to mean "good run."

"You, too," I gasp.

Yellow bib comes in third. Ibrahim comes in fourth. We high-five. A red bib is fifth. Deshaun is sixth and Xavier is seventh.

Our score is 20—the best we've done this season.

And in the rain and mud, too.

Coach is thrilled.

When there's a long gap in the field, I ask one of the judges if I can go retrieve my shoe. She nods, and I run out to where I lost my shoe and bend down, thinking to pull it out.

But my shoe isn't there.

Then I realize it is, it's just been pounded on by about fifty runners. I dig around the shoe with my fingers, yank it free, and trot back out of the chute.

"Gross," says Ricardo, looking at my shoe, which looks like a mound of mud.

I scoop the mud out as much as I can, squish the shoe on, and tell Coach I want to say hi to Felipe. He nods and I limp over to where they're all waiting for me. I'm limping because of my wet, smashed-in shoe, not because I'm hurt or anything.

Well, not more than I usually hurt after a race.

"*¡Gracias!*" I shout when I'm within earshot. "Thank you for coming!"

Now that they aren't clapping and shouting, they're all holding up umbrellas. Except Felipe, who places his hand over his heart. "Just one of the many duties of a class president."

I throw a fake punch at him and he throws one back. *Fake*. Fake punch. But not fake friends.

"You run a good race, Coleto," says Tía Veronica. She smiles and then gives me a big hug. Even though I'm covered in mud. Tía likes to hug.

"*Gracias.* The whole team ran really well. Your cheering helped me catch Ricardo."

"You came in *first*!" Benito's pulling at my elbow. "Are you going to win a track scholarship to college?"

"I hope so. Coach says I should be posting videos of my races on YouTube. I meant to start doing that."

Before Dad went to jail.

We're all quiet for a second, then Tía asks about Dad.

I tell them he looks good, which he did when we saw him, and that Mom and I can't wait for him to be back home. I'm thinking how different Thanksgiving and Christmas will be without Dad, but I don't say that.

I can't talk long, and Felipe explains to Tía that I can't ride home with them because the team sticks together. We say our goodbyes and I go back to Coach and the rest of the team.

He drives us to the nearby high school. We shower and then we dress in our street clothes. And shoes.

Coach takes us out to a pizza lunch, ordering four extra-large pizzas for each team: seniors, juniors, sophomores. There are twelve slices in each pizza, which is 48 slices per team.

The slices are gone in record time.

The pizza place is crowded with runners, parents, brothers, sisters, and friends. Mom and Dad always come to the post-meet lunches. Now they can't come: Dad's in jail, Mom's working two jobs.

Ricardo's mom comes over and says she'll treat everyone who wants ice cream to a sundae.

We all raise our hands. Even Coach.

She tells us we all ran really well. Then she tells me I ran especially well, but that Ricardo will win the next race.

I grin at that.
Maybe he will.
Maybe he won't.

FIRST

First is a place
ahead of the rest

but it can't be won
without the pack

First is knowing
you'll pass the test

because your friends
have your back

CHAPTER 18

UNDAY MORNING MOM AND I take the bus to Cook County Jail and stand in line to visit Dad. I look around for Emerald but don't see her. We wait an hour before we're allowed in.

We take off our shoes and deposit our wallets. I left my phone behind, but Mom brought hers. We walk down the hall and step up to the window to check in.

The guard behind the glass tells us that our visit has been cancelled.

"What?" asks Mom. "We didn't cancel our visit. This is our only chance to see him."

"Cancelled. No visit today."

"Who cancelled it?" Mom demands.

"Cancelled," the guard says again. "Check your email for information on your next scheduled visit."

"I want to see my husband," says Mom. "I need to know he's okay."

"We're scheduled to visit," I protest. "This visit was set up by you—by Cook County Jail."

"Department of Corrections," he corrects me. "Next!" he calls out to the people behind us.

"Who do I talk to about this?" Mom says. "Who's in charge here?"

"The supervisor won't be in until tomorrow morning. Come back then."

The next thing I know, a guard from behind grabs one of my arms and one of Mom's and starts walking us back to our shoes.

"Let go!" I shout, trying to pull my arm free. Which makes him increase his grip.

He practically pushes us into our shoes, then stands watch as we put them on and collect our stuff.

I glare at the guard. He puts a hand on his holstered gun. Mom puts her hand on my arm. "Let's go, Cole." She's warning me.

"This isn't right," I tell the guard. "We have a right to visit, and we have a right to know why the visit was cancelled." I'm scared—really afraid that something's happened to Dad.

"C'mon, Cole. We'll call Dad's attorney."

I go with Mom. When we reach the exit, I turn back to look. The steel door is closed.

As soon as we get away from the lines of people, Mom pulls out her phone and calls the defense attorney, Della Kazarian. She represents everybody who was arrested at the sit-in.

Mom leaves a message, asking Della to return her call today.

"Why doesn't she answer her phone?" I ask. "Don't lawyers always answer their phones?"

"It's Sunday. She might be taking the day off. Let's walk to the el."

"Which el? Where is it?"

"Pink line. There's a stop at California and 18th Street."

That's more than a mile away. No wonder we took the bus here.

We walk up California through working class neighborhoods. A lot of the stores have signs in Spanish. *Lavandería*, which is laundromat. *Tienda de segunda mano*, which is a second-hand store. I feel at home here, just like in Logan Square, where so many stores have signs in Spanish.

Mom walks faster than she usually does, which is how I can tell how worried she is.

"What could have happened?" I ask.

"He might have mouthed off to one of the guards and so they're punishing him by taking away his visiting privileges."

I think about that. The guard behind the glass did say something about a next scheduled visit.

"Have you checked your email? Just in case they've already scheduled the next visit."

Mom checks her email. She shakes her head.

I think about Dad mouthing off to one of the guards. I decide he wouldn't do that. Dad's pretty cool about keeping his temper. "Focus on the goal, Cole," he'd say to me even before I went to grade school.

Ahead of us I can see the round CTA sign.

Before we get to the el stop, Mom's phone rings.

From what Mom's saying on her end, I know she's talking to Ms. Kazarian.

She ends the conversation when we reach the el station.

"What'd she say?"

"She said she'd call the jail today, but it's a Sunday and she didn't expect any answer. She said she'd call Monday morning and if she didn't get a satisfactory answer, she'd go down to the jail before noon."

We catch the el toward the Loop. I look at the el map and see that we'll switch lines there, taking the blue line to Logan Square.

"Do other people get visits cancelled?" I ask. "Did she say?"

"She said it's happened before. She thinks it might be because the Euclid Defense Committee has been in the news a lot. The city doesn't like that, so the city wants to punish Dad even more."

Mom and I ride home in silence.

Halfway home, I think of something.

Emerald Jackson.

Maybe her brother has had visits cancelled, so she would know why.

Maybe her brother knows if Dad's okay.

I text Emerald.

Me: Hey, E. R visit to Dad cancelled. No explanation. Evr happen to U?

I wait for an answer.

Which comes when we're underground, switching to the blue line.

Emerald: No. Will ask bro later 2day.

Which makes me worry more.

CHAPTER 19

 OM PULLS OUT A BUNCH of baking pans. "Cole, please put out some napkins and glasses. Felipe and Treva will be here in"—she pauses to look up at the kitchen clock—"eighty minutes."

The "eighty minutes" makes me smile. Mom likes to be exact. But not seventy-nine minutes exact. She'll round up or down.

Felipe, Treva, and I are going to the immigrant rights demonstration, and they're meeting me here.

"I think Fatima might be coming with them," I tell Mom. "And maybe even Salma and Hasna. You don't have to bake anything, Mom. We're just meeting here, then catching a bus to the el."

"Baking is my therapy," she reminds me. "Halloween's almost here, I think I'll go with pumpkin chocolate chip cookies. And some dried cranberries for color."

My mouth is watering already.

By the time Felipe and Treva show up, I've already eaten four cookies.

It turns out Fatima is helping set things up for the demonstration, and Salma and Hasna are helping.

"We'll meet up with them somewhere," Felipe says.

"The cookies are delicious," says Treva.

"Thanks," Mom says. "I always wish that a demonstration is so large that I *can't* find my friends."

"*Podemos soñar,*" says Felipe.

Mom doesn't speak Spanish. Neither does Treva. So I translate. "*We can dream.*"

"I was about to translate," Felipe tells me, selecting another cookie. "Pumpkin is good, Tía. Origin: Mexico."

Mom laughs. "Yes, Felipe. According to you, the world originated in Mexico."

"Maybe not the *whole* world," he admits. "But definitely the pumpkin part."

Mom hands us plastic baggies and urges us to stuff our pockets with cookies before we leave. She takes a handful for herself and stuffs the baggie into her backpack, which is standing by the door, ready to go. The backpack's bulging, like we're going camping for a week.

The four of us catch a bus down Fullerton, then transfer to the el, taking the blue line south. Mom waits until we're seated, then goes to the other end of the car. "I have some calls to make," she says.

"My mom wasn't sure she wanted to let me come to this

demonstration," Treva tells us.

"Why not?" I ask.

"Because I always went with my father."

We don't say anything.

"I told her she could come," says Treva. "But she says she's not ready yet."

Felipe and I nod.

"Mamá didn't want me to go, either," Felipe tells us. "She's afraid the police will photograph me and keep a secret file on me, and that will have *repercusiones.*"

"Repercussions?" Treva asks

Felipe nods. "*Sí.* But at the same time, Mamá did want me to go." He thinks about this a bit. "She worries about all the people who get deported. More Mexicans are deported than any other nationality." He grips the edge of the plastic subway seat as if it's responsible.

He looks at me. "Bianca is one of the organizers of the demonstration."

I think that if Felipe's cousin is helping to organize, Tía should be fine with his going.

We wait for Mom when we get off the el, then the four of us walk toward the rally. The march starts in Union Park, which is a baseball-diamond shaped park at Randolph, Ashland, and Ogden Avenues. Ogden is one of the diagonal streets in Chicago, a kind of hypotenuse through the grid of north-south and east-west streets.

"Wow!" says Treva as we approach the park. "There are *thousands* here!"

"Fantastic!" shouts Felipe. "Tía, how many do you think are here?"

Mom and Dad are pros at estimating crowd size. "More than fifteen thousand," she says. "And more will probably join as we march."

People of all ages are here. Our age. Younger. Older. Much, much older. People wearing hoodies. Blackhawk jackets. Sox jackets, Cubs jackets. Brown people, black people, white people. Mexican flags. Irish flags. Palestinian flags. U.S. flags.

"There's a Japanese flag." Treva points it out as we walk around three women pushing wide strollers. Each stroller holds two small kids. "I saw a lot of those in Portland."

Almost everyone's carrying a poster—posters a lot bigger than the ones I made for Felipe. Lots of banners, too. One cries out, SMASH ALL BORDERS. A kid about ten years old is carrying a sign that says DON'T DEPORT MY DAD. I stumble into somebody and say I'm sorry. He's carrying a sign that says EDUCATION, NOT DEPORTATION.

Lots of signs in Spanish. NO A LA DETENCIÓN, DEPORTACIÓN Y SEPARACIÓN.

Felipe sees somebody handing out lots of those posters. He takes one, holds it up, and joins the chants.

I see groups that identify themselves as Chinese. Japanese. Korean.

Mom sees some friends and waves goodbye to us.

Somebody's giving out signs that say RESIST! I grab one. Treva does, too.

Felipe, Treva, and I shoulder our way through the crowd, looking for Fatima.

More signs.

NO MUSLIM BAN. NO BORDERS. NO WALLS.

IMMIGRANTS! WE ARE THE WORLD!

STOP THE DEPORTATIONS!

DESCENDENT OF JEWISH REFUGEES

DOWN WITH CAPITALISM!

NO HUMAN IS ILLEGAL

NO BAN, NO WALL. BLACK LIVES MATTER

NO JUSTICE, NO PEACE

I like that one, so I look around to find somebody giving them out and I take one, holding RESIST in one hand and NO JUSTICE, NO PEACE in the other. There are so many good signs, I'd have to be an octopus to hold all the ones I like.

Part of my brain is looking for F words. But I don't see any. Maybe the F words are supposed to come to me, rather than me going out to find them.

I look around for Emerald, but don't see her. I look for Ethan, but don't see him either. In a crowd this size, it would probably be sheer accident to run into them. I text them both to tell them we're at the northwest corner of Washington and Ogden.

Neither one texts back.

Maybe Ethan didn't come. Maybe Emerald isn't here. Maybe she's visiting her brother.

And asking him about Dad.

We walk around, wondering how we'll find Fatima.

LGBTQ AGAINST DEPORTATIONS!

END OPPRESSION—BUILD A WORKERS PARTY!

CAPITALISM IS THE DISEASE, SOCIALISM IS THE ANSWER

Treva grabs one of those. Now she's carrying a sign in each hand, too.

HATRED COMES NOT FROM THE MOUTH OF GOD, BUT FROM THE MINDS OF IDIOTS!

FREEDOM FOR ALL!

I've never seen so many protest signs in my life.

I've never been in such a large crowd in my life.

"There!" shouts Treva. We have to shout to each other to be heard above the crowd. Felipe and I look to where she's pointing, and we see **FREEDOM AND JUSTICE FOR ALL**, with Arabic writing underneath.

"I see Salma." I point, and we shoulder our way in that direction.

By the time we reach the Arab-American signs, the march has begun, heading east on Washington Avenue, so we're moving forward with thousands of others, but we're also marching sideways to reach Salma.

Ahead of us are hundreds of women wearing hijabs.

I don't know what color hijab Fatima's wearing. How are we going to find her?

Just like that, she's there next to us. Salma, too.

"Where's Hasna?" Treva asks.

Fatima smiles and points.

Hasna's standing two black hijabs away. Hers is black, too. But she has it wrapped around her head, over her mouth and nose, and down her forehead. All we can see are her eyes. She sees us and flashes the peace sign.

"You came!" Fatima says. And smiles at Felipe. "Thank you." Her sign says WE THE PEOPLE.

We amble along at a slow pace, because of all the people. Definitely not a cross-country meet. The air is filled with good food smells: barbecue… curry… tortillas. Food trucks are lined up on both sides of Washington along the route of the march.

Mom was right about thousands of others joining the march. I see them ahead of us, standing on the sidewalks, holding posters. They're standing on apartment balconies. Some are cheering, some are just staring. People from the sidewalks step into the moving mass.

Dad would love this.

He might even be invited to be one of the speakers, as head of the Committee to Save Public Education.

Treva starts shouting. *You Have Made This World a Mess! Capitalism No, Socialism Yes!*

I like her shout, so I join in.

Felipe's talking to Fatima.

Treva stops shouting and elbows me. "Cop. Guy with the camera."

I see a guy taking pictures. I watch him for a while, and it looks to me like he's zooming in on individual faces. He turns his camera our way. I turn around and march backwards, blocking his view of Felipe and Treva. Hoping to, anyway. Fatima sees what I'm doing. She turns to give an angry stare right into the camera. Hasna doesn't: she turns her face down and away.

When we reach Daley Plaza we keep up the chanting. Daley Plaza is where the famous Picasso statue sits, the one that doesn't have a title but looks sort of like a baboon, even though I don't think that's what Picasso intended.

Most of us are shouting *No Bans, No Wall, No Deportations!*

Somehow the huge crowd divides itself in half, and in the narrow space between halves, protestors step in and shout, then step back into the crowd. It's like they're strutting down a walkway. Or inventing a new line dance.

But about serious stuff.

A guy with a megaphone steps into the walkway. He looks Arabic.

We Are Young!, he shouts through the megaphone. *We Are Strong! We Can Rally All Day Long!*

This makes us laugh out loud. We join him. So do thousands of others.

The guy with the megaphone runs up and down the aisle, chanting his chant.

When he comes back to the middle, he jumps up and down, still chanting.

Big jumps, way into the air, legs tucked under.

The crowd responds louder than ever.

Felipe and I look at each other.

We ask Treva to hold our signs.

The next time the guy reaches the center of the walkway, we're ready.

He shouts and jump, we shout and jump.

And shout and jump.

And shout and jump.

And we aren't the only ones. All over Daley Plaza I can see people bobbing up and down over the top of the crowd.

The megaphone guy keeps it up for quite a while.

But even he needs a rest.

He disappears back into the crowd and somebody else steps in.

Mom.

I can't believe it.

She has Dad's new megaphone strapped on. That must be what she had in her backpack.

Freedom's Right, she shouts, *Walls Are Wrong! When United We Are Strong!*

We all join her.

I mean all: like twenty thousand people!

Mom does what the megaphone guy did: she starts at one end of the walkway and marches down it, chanting and aiming her megaphone first to one side, then the other.

"Your mom is fan-*tas*-tic!" shouts Treva, pounding me on the back. She hands me back my signs: RESIST and NO JUSTICE, NO PEACE.

"*¡Bravo Tía!*" shouts Felipe.

Megaphone guy steps back in and waits for Mom to finish. She sees him and stops at one end of the walkway.

We Are Right! They Are Wrong! But United We Are Strong! he shouts, running down the walkway with his megaphone.

He reaches the end opposite Mom, then motions for her to go.

She walks backward down the walkway shouting, *Freedom's Right, Walls Are Wrong! When United We Are Strong!*

Then it's his turn.

Then hers.

The crowd goes wild on the *We Are Strong* parts.

I see men with cameras taking pictures.

I wonder if they'll try to put Mom in jail.

And then I realize that they want me to feel fear—to feel that they have the power and there's nothing we can do about it.

But I'm holding the answer in my hands.

RESIST!

The rally goes on a long time, but finally people start to leave.

Felipe, Treva, and I meet Fatima's mom and dad, who thank us for coming. Felipe thanks them for coming, too.

They grin at each other.

"We are in the same boat," they say to him.

"But United We Are Strong," he says to them.

We shake hands all around, then Felipe, Treva and I head toward Jackson and State to wait for Mom.

"Tía Stacey may be a while," says Felipe. "She's probably signing autographs."

Treva smiles at this. "Your mom is cool, Cole. And she bakes a mean chocolate chip pumpkin cookie."

It's like we remember all at once that we have cookies on us. And that we haven't eaten for hours. We reach into our pockets, pull out our cookies, and chow down.

By the time Mom shows up we've eaten all the cookies and are looking around for a pizza joint.

"There," says Mom, pointing to a place a block up. As if she can read our minds.

Which maybe moms can.

We walk in and who's standing there but Ethan. Turns out he was at the demo but is just now reading his texts.

"That was awesome!" he tells us. "Thanks for telling me about it, Cole." He looks at Mom, who he knows from all the cross-country meets. He just stares at her. "That was, like, awesome, Mrs. Renner,"

"Just saying what needs to be said, Ethan," she replies.

We all order slices of pizza and talk about the demonstration. When the pizza slices come we gobble them down, then find the nearest el stop.

All five of us get off the el at Logan Square, and walk south on Kedzie Boulevard to Fullerton. Felipe, Treva, and Ethan wait for a bus to go west, and Mom and I walk home, down Kedzie Boulevard and through Palmer Square Park.

As we're walking in the door, I get a text.

Emerald: Fight. Ur Dad ok. Other 2 guys not.

Holy shit. Dad was in a fight?
I show Mom what Emerald texted.

Me: U know what fight abt?

Mom reads over my shoulder.

Emerald: Turf war. Hppn all time. He OK.
Me: THX, E. Very much.

Mom and I look at each other.

"She says he's okay," Mom says. "But I still want Della to see him tomorrow morning. Just to make sure."

CHAPTER 20

FEAR

punches me in the throat,
knocks my breath away

fear of losing
who I love.

This is not
an accident.

Someone wants to drill
fear deep into my heart

and mind.

Into our hearts
and our minds.

I hate the system
that grows rich and cruel
from prisons
and ghettos
and starvation wages

and allows beatings

and uses fear

as a weapon

to contain us.

CHAPTER 21

ONDAY FELIPE AND I ARE standing around after school. He won't be over to my house until later because he's helping coach Benito's soccer team at Euclid Grade School.

"When's student council meet?" I ask.

"Tomorrow."

"Wish I could be there," I say.

"After cross-country ends, you will be my enforcer."

"Is that an elected position?" I kid.

"Let me table that discussion for now."

I can tell he's joking, but I punch him in the arm anyway.

"Stop talking like an official," I say. "I can't be friends with a bureaucrat."

"It is my sworn duty to sound official," he says. "To know rules, regulations, procedures, and *Roberts Rules of Order*."

"I gotta go," I say, "before I fall asleep listening to you."

"What's for dinner tonight? *Presidentes* need to be fed."

"I'm going to grill some burgers and Mom's making oven french fries."

Felipe steps back, raising his hands in horror. "*You* are going to cook?"

"*Sí.*"

He considers this. "Tío Hank grills monster burgers. Did he show you how?"

"Yeah. Before he went to jail. Besides," I add, "I've watched how he does it."

"And Tía Stacey is fine with this? The fire insurance policy is fully paid?"

"Each guest is required to bring a fire extinguisher."

Felipe jumps on this. "*Each* guest? There's another guest? Treva?"

"No. Just you."

"But you would like it if Treva were there, *sí?*"

"Yeah."

"Let's discuss this," he says. "You and Treva."

"Let's table it," I say.

"Hmmmm." Felipe rubs his chin. "*El Presidente* will honor the motion to table. But this topic will be re-introduced for future discussion."

We slap palms and head in opposite directions. Me to get the backyard grill ready, Felipe to coach soccer.

At home I text Treva to see what she's doing.

Visiting Morton Arboretum with her mom and uncle.

Me: Like it?

Treva: Can't see a thing. 2 many trees.

Me: 😊

When Mom gets home she mixes some stuff into the ground beef. I watch. Salt, pepper, mustard powder, barbecue sauce. She shapes the meat into five patties. I go out to get the grill ready, following the instructions Dad gave me.

Felipe arrives just as the fire kicks to life. I ask him how soccer coaching went.

"*¡Excelente!* Thanks to *el Presidente!*"

"That rhymes," I say. "Maybe you should be writing my poems."

"Man, are you still writing those poems?"

"Every week until the end of the school year." I think about the poem I wrote last night, "Fear." I gotta admit that, as F words go, *fear* is pretty powerful. But it's not something I want to live with.

Felipe shakes his head, probably grateful he doesn't have to write poems from now until June. We shoot hoops while we wait for the fire to get hot

When the briquets are glowing I spread them across the grate with a long fork, the way Dad does. I snap a few photos, so I can show him how I did. But not until January: we can't take photos into Cook County Jail.

When I go inside to get the patties, Mom tells me the fries will be ready in ten minutes.

"So will the burgers," I say.

"Don't get too good at this. Dad and I may turn the job over to you permanently. While you were playing basketball Della Kazarian called."

I stop at the door, plate of uncooked meat in my hand. "What did she say?"

"She saw Dad today. She's stopping by here on her way home."

"Is he okay?"

"She says he is. We'll ask her more when she gets here."

I step outside and start laying the patties on the fire.

"You have a look on your face," says Felipe. "Something wrong?"

"Della Kazarian saw Dad today. She's coming by later on."

"Is he okay?"

"She says he is. I don't know."

Felipe pats me on the back. "*Tenga coraje.*"

Being brave isn't easy.

After a minute I turn the burgers to sear them on the other side.

Felipe points at the biggest one. "That one has my name on it."

———

Mom's plucking a french fry out of the bowl and Felipe and I are finishing our second burgers when the doorbell rings.

Mom jumps up to answer it and comes back with Della Kazarian.

I stand up and shake her hand, the way Dad does. Felipe stands, too, and I introduce him to Ms. Kazarian.

Mom tells her she can speak freely in front of Felipe.

"You were at the Euclid sit-in," she says to him.

"Yes. Tío Hank helped me get out the window and away from the cops."

"Hank has good instincts," she says.

Mom invites her to sit at the table, which she does. Mom clears off most of the dishes. Felipe and I kind of hurry with our burgers. It's really awkward eating food when somebody else isn't.

Like magic, Mom puts a plate of pumpkin chocolate-chip cookies on the table and puts a plate in front of Ms. Kazarian. They're the cookies she baked before the protest rally yesterday. She puts on a pot of coffee.

Ms. Kazarian, meanwhile, is unstrapping her watch. She places it on the table and taps it.

We hear her voice. "So what would you say to your wife and son if they were here?"

Then we hear Dad's voice. "I'd tell them I'm fine. Bloody but unbowed. No, I take that back, I'm not bloody. Black and blue but unbowed. I didn't expect this attack—the guys who jumped me. But I fought back and I'm fine. I'd tell them not to worry and that I'm looking forward to seeing them."

Mom, me, and Felipe are all leaning way forward, as if we could find Dad inside the watch.

"Why did they jump him? How many of them?" Mom demands.

She turns to Mom. "Two of them. Nobody knows why. Could have been a turf war, could have been the guards told them to, could have been they were just spoiling for a fight. Could be they hate socialists."

Nobody says anything.

"These things happen in jails and prisons," says Ms. Kazarian. "Hank is basically okay. Beaten up, but okay."

"Is it going to happen again?" Mom asks.

Ms. Kazarian starts to say something, then stops. "There are no guarantees, but Hank doesn't think it will happen again. Chances are it won't."

"Can't he get out somehow?" I ask.

Everyone looks at me.

"I mean, you're appealing his conviction, right? How long will that take?"

"He'll be out of jail before the next court even gets around to considering the appeal."

More silence.

Ms. Kazarian eats a cookie and drinks a whole cup of coffee in almost one gulp.

"There are two things," she says.

From the look on her face, they aren't good news.

"What are they?" asks Mom.

Ms. Kazarian looks uncomfortable. She reaches into one of the pockets of her suit and pulls out a cell phone. "Would you like to see a picture of Hank?" she asks. "So you know that he's basically okay?"

"Yes." Mom reaches for the phone.

Ms. Kazarian pulls it back. "You have to look past the… damage," she says.

Mom nods.

Ms. Kazarian passes her the phone.

Mom's eyes widen. She bites her lips together and then presses the phone to her chest.

After a bit she looks at the picture again, studying it. "Yes," she says. "I can see that Hank is… basically okay." Mom looks at me. "Do you want to see this?"

No.

Yes.

I need to know.

I take the phone and look.

Except that my eyes are closed.

I open them.

Two different feelings run through me at the same time. One is that Dad looks horrible. The other is that Dad looks great. Horrible: one eye is swollen shut; black and purple all around; black and blue marks cover his face; his lip is cut and swollen almost as big as his eye. Great: he's smiling—as much as he can with a swollen lip. And the eye that's open looks at me with confidence. No fear.

I pass the phone to Felipe, who grips it hard.

"How'd you do that?" I ask the lawyer. "Are you allowed to take your phone in?"

"Of course not," she answers as she takes another cookie. "A smart attorney might be wearing a couple of small cameras on her person."

Mom and Felipe and I look at her.

"Large ring, right hand?" guesses Felipe.

"Medallion hanging from your neck?" I guess.

"Frame of your thick tortoise shell glasses?" Mom guesses.

If it's one of those, or even two of those, Ms. Kazarian isn't telling. She proceeds straight to the second thing she wants to say. "Hank's visitation rights are cancelled for the next two weeks."

"What?!" we shout.

"He didn't start it!" I argue.

"Why?" Mom demands. "The other guys started it! You said so."

"Yes, the cameras show they jumped Hank. That's not the problem. The problem is that they're in the hospital."

Silence.

"Tío Hank beat them up?" Felipe ventures.

"Yes. And then the guards beat them up, too."

"What Tío Hank did is self-defense," Felipe says. "Self-defense is a human right!"

"Yes, it is," says Ms. Kazarian, looking at Felipe. "But in jail you're punished no matter which end of the fight you're on."

"They don't want you to fight back," I say. "They want you to lie down and take the beating."

"Hank would never do that," says Mom.

"Neither would I," I say.

CHAPTER 22

FEAR 2

There's a lesson
in fear.

Fear doesn't leave,
but it does lessen

when
you
fight
back.

CHAPTER 23

MOM'S STANDING ALONGSIDE MRS. GREEN'S cash register, trying to find a space for the shiny poster boards and her stencils. Every year Mrs. Green asks Mom to stencil new signs for the fall and winter holidays. PUMPKINS. WREATHS. CORNUCOPIAS. CHRISTMAS CACTUS. Mom loves doing this, even though Mrs. Green always jokes about not being able to pay her union wages for such professional work.

Mrs. Green's Greenhouse is a super-busy place from late October through the end of December. Sometimes it seems like half of Logan Square shops here.

"Sorry that I can't give you a fun job, too, Cole," Mrs. Green tells me. "But it's time to wash out all the galvanized trays. I want everything spiffy for the big buying season."

Spiffy. Nobody else in the world uses the word *spiffy*. Mrs. Green's great-grandmother must have used it.

There are so many galvanized trays I just know I'll be working on this all week long. I walk down to the end of the furthest aisle, hook up a hose, find the cleaning powder, and start moving plants off the first tray I'll wash.

That's when I hear Felipe's voice.

"Hello, Mrs. Green. Hi, Tía Stacey." I look up toward the front counter and see Felipe giving Mom a hug.

"I am here to buy a plant for Mamá," he tells Mrs. Green. "And to say hello to Tía Stacey and Cole."

From where I'm scrubbing the first tray, I see Mrs. Green duck her head and smile. She's used to this. Whenever Felipe wants to talk to me and I'm at work, he comes to Mrs. Green's and buys a plant for Tía Veronica. Mrs. Green once told him he could come talk to me now and then without buying a plant. Which embarrassed Felipe, 'cause he thinks that would be rude.

"What do you have in mind," Mom asks him.

"Something small. Something that blooms."

"Kalanchoes are good winter-light plants," Mom tells him. Mrs. Green nods her agreement.

Mom and Felipe disappear down another aisle, and after a while they're back at the counter, with Felipe holding a kalanchoe with bright red flowers. I think the plant will make Tía Veronica very happy. And that makes me think of Dad, and how a bright green plant bursting with red flowers might cheer him up. Him and the other prisoners. But I know that if visitors aren't allowed to bring food or pictures or cell phones, they sure aren't allowed to bring flowering plants. I hope Dad's okay, that he doesn't need a doctor, 'cause even though Ms. Kazarian said he's okay, that doesn't mean he is.

Felipe pays for the plant, Mrs. Green wraps it in orange paper (that's her October wrapping-paper color), and Felipe walks back to where I'm working.

"'S up?" I ask.

"Jillian came to the officers-only meeting today."

I tilt a tray away from Felipe and spray it, making sure no water hits him. "Why? Does she expect you to say it was all a mistake and she should be president?"

"Close. She offered her 'experience and knowledge' to the rest of us, suggesting she could work as a special advisor."

I can just see Special Advisor, in caps, on Jillian's resume. "What'd you say?"

"Your class president responded immediately. Before any of the other officers might think that Jillian had a good idea. 'Thank you, Jillian,' I said, 'but I think we need to go through the experience on our own. Like you did.'"

I laugh. "Great response!"

"But then," Felipe continues, "she did not go. No, she did not leave. Instead, she sat down, pulled out her phone, and put it on her lap. I think she was probably going to record what we said."

"Man!"

"Your president then asked Jillian to leave the room, so the class officers could have their first meeting."

"Let me guess," I say, replacing the now-clean tray onto a cart. I start loading plants into the tray. "She wouldn't leave."

"*¡Exactamente!* But that is where Mr. Ortiz comes in. He's the tenth grade student council advisor."

"He was there?"

"*Sí.* And he told Jillian she had to leave. The rest of us waited until she finally closed the door behind her. Probably standing out in the hallway, her ear pressed to the keyhole."

Felipe moves his kalanchoe from hand to hand. "Wanna know how the meeting went?"

"Yeah. Sure. You know I do." I start working on another tray.

"It was divided into two parts. The first part was Mr. Ortiz going over our responsibilities. *¡Aaayyy!* Who knew we had so much to do with organizing dances and all kinds of other class events. Each of us is required to spend two hours a week on club activities."

"Like what?"

"Like joining the chess club or the debate team or the chorus or any one of the clubs that meet after school. We don't have to join them, exactly, but we need to attend some of their meetings and make sure everything's running well, that they have space to meet, help them recruit new members, take their suggestions or requests to the principal, that kind of stuff."

"Sounds like a lot of work," I say.

Felipe waves it away: all part of *el Presidente's* duties. "Then," he says, "we got to the second half of the meeting: the things we think our tenth grade class needs. To function as good students and—quoting Mr. Ortiz here—good citizens of the world."

He points at the tray I'm working on. "You missed a spot."

I aim the hose in his direction. He pretends he's terrified.

"How did that go?" I ask.

Felipe ponders this. "Okay, I think. We decided two things, the first with the help of Mr. Ortiz."

I wait for him to continue.

He does. "First, everyone wants love, respect, and harmony. Well, not everyone. Not people like Jared. But everyone on the student council. Mr. Ortiz thinks we should teach racial, ethnic, and cultural respect. So we came up with the idea—and he says we can do it—to use the display case in the main hallway to teach about different cultures. Each month, a different one. One represented in our school."

That sounds good to me.

"We'll ask for volunteers and the first display should go up in November. Indian."

"You can ask Sanjana and Raj," I suggest. "They'd love doing something like that. And maybe they'd bring in some naan or samosas we could all eat."

I'm leaning down, pulling out another tray. Felipe pats me on the back. "Indian. Illini, Fox, Sauk, Menominee, Ho-Chunk."

Wow, I was way off, heading in the wrong direction. Embarrassing, but not fatal. F word. Strong one, too. "Got it. You gonna talk to Henry Thunder?"

"Yeah, I'm hoping he'll be interested. I think he will be." Felipe looks back toward the counter. "I should get going. Mrs. Green might not want me talking to you so long. The other thing we decided, which Mr. Ortiz wasn't so keen on, but didn't veto, is to start a study club on Alternative Social Systems."

"Felipe," I say, pointing a finger at him and using my Ms. Delaney voice, "Don't be a troublemaker."

He raises a fist. *"¡Viva Zapata!"*

CHAPTER 24

"**O," SAYS FELIPE, SCRAPING HIS** hand back and forth across the links on the fence. He's studying me out of the corner of his eye, but I don't know why.

I wait, but nothing follows.

"Where's Treva?" he asks.

"Dentist appointment."

Felipe runs a hand over his jaw. Maybe checking that his teeth are all there. "How do you know that?"

"She texted me."

He keeps studying me.

"Why are you looking at me like that?" I ask.

"You and Treva."

"What?"

"You and Treva," he repeats.

"What about us?"

"Aha!" Felipe grins and points a finger at me. "Got you to say it, dude."

"Say what?" I'm not sure where this conversation is going.

"Us. You said 'us'!"

Now I see where the conversation is going. I try to think of a way out. "I'd use the same word if Treva asked about you and me."

Felipe shakes his head. "You and Treva. Are you, like, a thing?" He makes the last word sound like one of those meme headlines: here today, gone today.

I hesitate. He waits. Finally, I answer. "I don't know."

This stops him. I guess it stops me, too. Because I know what I'd like. I'd like—no, love—for Treva and me to be more than just friends.

Neither of us says anything for a while. Then Felipe tries again. "Are you afraid?" he asks. "Because you can't be afraid, man. Treva will sense it. I could give you some pointers."

I laugh. "As class president?"

He puts a hand to his heart. "The burden," he says. "Heavy." He keeps looking at me. "Seriously, Cole."

"Yeah. I'm afraid. But not in the way you think."

"How, then?"

I stall. Think about how I feel. Then I plunge in. "I met Treva right after Dad went to jail. In the hallway outside Nachman's class. Jillian was there, and, I don't know, I kind of thought if I talked to Jillian she might, like, change her mind about dumping me. But she just wanted my vote."

Felipe waits.

"Treva was standing there, in a corner, seeing it all. That's when she said she knew who she was going to vote for."

"Smart," says Felipe. "Just like you."

I don't say anything.

"So what's the problem?" he prods.

"Treva knows that Jillian dumped me. I don't want Treva to think that I'm bouncing from Jillian to her, just because she's there."

"Hmmm."

"Yeah."

"The class president will think on this," he says.

"What about you?" I ask.

He doesn't answer. "You and Fatima," I push.

"Our families are negotiating the prenuptial agreements."

"Yeah. Right. Just be sure—"

I'm interrupted by Nikki Zurlo. She's tapping me on the back.

"Hi, Nikki," I say.

"Hi, Cole. Hi, Felipe. Ms. Delaney wants to see you in her office. Now."

"Me?"

"And Felipe."

"Us?" I ask.

Nikki nods. "Yes. Both of you. Come with me."

Felipe and I look at each other. Neither of us knows what this is about.

We follow Nikki through the doors and down the hallway and into Ms. Delaney's office.

Nikki leaves, closing the door behind herself. Ms. Delaney motions to two chairs and tells Felipe and me to sit down. But before she can say anything, Felipe speaks. "You still haven't signed off on our Alternative Social Systems Club, Ms. Delaney. I've turned in the statement of purpose. We need your signature and a time and room assignment."

"That discussion is for another day, Felipe." She motions to the chairs, which are pulled up close to her desk. "Sit down, the two of you."

After we sit, Ms. Delaney turns her computer around, so that we can see the screen.

YouTube?

Ms. Delaney surfs YouTube?

She hits a button, and the next thing I know, Felipe and I are watching ourselves at the pro-immigrant demonstration. We're both jumping as high as we can, shouting, "We are young! We are strong! We can rally all day long!" You can see the huge crowd, with the Picasso in the background.

This was almost two weeks ago. Why are we being called in now?

She lets the whole video play out, maybe two minutes long. Both Felipe and I are leaning forward in our chairs, watching closely. I don't know what he's thinking, but I'm thinking we look good. All 20,000 of us.

The clip ends. Ms. Delaney looks first at Felipe, then at me. Neither of us says a word.

She starts with him. "What have you got to say for yourself, Felipe?"

He rubs his chin. "I can't jump anywhere near as high as Cole."

I grin at this but cover it with a cough when Ms. Delaney glares at me. "This is not a laughing matter," she says.

"I agree," says Felipe. "Immigrant rights are a serious matter. All human rights are a serious matter."

This time I grin inside, where Ms. Delaney can't see it.

"This reflects poorly on the school," she says.

"No, it doesn't," I say. "We weren't wearing school jackets or school colors. There's no way anybody can identify us with August Mersy High School. And even if they could," I continue, "it's our right to demonstrate. It's everyone's right to fight against their own oppression."

"Not when you're in school," she shoots back.

"We weren't in school. We were in Federal Plaza."

She ignores me. Concentrates on Felipe. "Who told you about this demonstration?" she demands.

Felipe shrugs. "Information is everywhere. Who told you about the video?"

"Videos are everywhere," she smirks.

I butt in. "You don't seem like someone who watches YouTube," I argue. "So if you didn't find this video on your own, that means somebody told you about it. Maybe somebody who's hoping you'd call Felipe and me into your office."

"I want nothing but silence from you, Cole Renner. I'm talking to Felipe. Are you related to Bianca Sanchez?"

What?

What kind of question is that?

Felipe must think the same thing. He frowns. Finally he says, "Yes. She is my cousin."

I wish he hadn't offered that extra information. Never offer information to the interrogator, Mom and Dad say.

"Why do you want to know?" he asks.

"Do your parents know you were at this demonstration?" she asks, ignoring his question.

Two things run through my head at the same time, each fighting for the only space on the running path. First I think her question makes it sound as if we're in grade school. Second, I see something in Felipe's face… something I can't quite read. But I can tell he's not comfortable.

"Why does it matter about my family?" he asks, angry. "I don't need their permission to attend a demonstration."

Yeah, I think. And we don't need your permission either, Delaney.

"I asked if your parents knew."

Felipe kind of shifts in his seat. I can't figure out what's bothering him about the question. Tío Carlos and Tía Veronica both knew he was going to the demo. Wait. Felipe said his mother sort of didn't want him to go. And what's Bianca have to do with this? I hope Ms. Delaney doesn't pick up on Felipe's posture.

I decide to help out by butting in. "My mother knew," I say. And when Delaney turns to frown at me, I give her the zinger. "So did my father. He wished he could be there—protesting injustice. Leading the way to a better world." Against people like you, I think. The word *foe* bangs on the door of my mind and lets itself in. *Foe.*

Felipe gives a small nod. I can sense him relaxing a little.

But then she turns to look at Felipe again.

So I speak again. "My mom helped lead the chants."

"Really?" says Ms. Delaney, turning toward me. She says it in a way that means she doesn't care. "Who else was there?"

"It would be hard to name them all," says Felipe. "Over twenty thousand people."

"Name a few," she says. She actually takes a pen out of its holder as she asks this.

Neither Felipe nor I say anything.

"What other students were there?"

"Thousands," answers Felipe. "Thousands of people our age." He glares at her.

"Who else was there from August Mersy?" she asks.

Felipe looks at me. "I don't remember. Do you, Cole?"

"No."

Ms. Delaney puts her pen down. "I'm not surprised at Cole's unwillingness to cooperate," she says, not even looking at me. "But you, Felipe. You're different. You're the class president. You have a responsibility to present August Mersy in its best light."

Felipe nods. "I agree."

I think it takes Ms. Delaney at least ten seconds to figure out that Felipe's saying he *was* presenting August Mersy in its *best light*. Whatever the words *best light* mean.

She sits back in her chair and studies Felipe, then me. "If at any time in the future you remember details you want to share with me, I'm willing to listen. And I'm willing to extend certain privileges to students who cooperate for the good of the school. Hallway passes, for example. You could go anywhere at any time. Handy for a class president to have."

My mouth falls open.

I've never been offered a bribe before.

Is this how it's done?

Felipe looks angrier than before.

Which is how I feel, too. Angrier. "What would you do with the names of students who attended the demonstration?" I ask. "Hand a list to the cops?"

Delaney looks at her watch, then stands up. "I may choose to continue this discussion at a future time."

I notice she didn't answer my question.

Felipe and I stand up and walk out the door.

Neither of us says goodbye to Ms. Delaney.

Nikki gives us passes to get into our first-period class.

"You looked worried back there," I say to Felipe as we walk down the hall. We walk as slow as we can because it's almost time for second period to begin.

"When?"

I'm pretty sure he knows when. "When she asked about Bianca and if Tía and Tío knew you were going to the demonstration."

He shrugs. "My family is none of her business. I don't like her asking about them. Especially when she's keeping a list."

I believe him.

But not totally. I try to figure out why Delaney asked about Bianca. "Wasn't Bianca expelled from August Mersy?" I ask. "Back when you and I were in second or third grade?"

"She punched a teacher in the mouth when the teacher told her to speak English or go back to Mexico."

Right. How could I have forgotten that?

"Bianca was born here," Felipe adds. "Not in Mexico. If she had been speaking French or German, the teacher would have thought she was cultured. But when you speak Spanish and have brown skin, teachers think you're ignorant."

By the time we get to history, students are pouring out the door. Felipe heads to his next class. "See you at lunch," he says.

My path takes me through the entrance foyer, where a crowd of students are surrounding the display case.

I stop and look. It's full of Ho-Chunk Nation stuff. Baskets, beads, fishing spears, corn, squash. And a map of North America with INDIAN TERRITORY written across it. A map of the Midwest and the Great Lakes, with the territory of Ho-Chunk and other tribes labeled.

Henry Thunder is standing alongside the display case, answering questions.

"Awesome, Henry!" I bump fists with him and hurry to Nachman's class.

Nachman's waiting outside the door, rounding up students, and when I walk by him he says. "I want to talk to you, Cole. See me today after the last period ends."

CHAPTER 25

FTER THE FINAL BELL I walk to Nachman's room, wondering why he wants to see me.

He's there alone, standing behind his desk, sorting papers.

"Cole," he says when I walk in. "Have a seat."

Part of me wants to walk to the back row, where I always sit, but the smarter part of me knows that's not what Nachman wants. So I sit in the front row.

"How are you doing, Cole?" he asks, still sorting papers. He looks away from the papers and right at me.

"Okay."

He pulls his chair away from his desk, moves it to the side, and sits down.

"Is there anything bothering you?" he asks.

Bothering me? Well, yeah. Ms. Delaney keeps calling me into her office. And now she's calling Felipe in, too. I took first place in cross-country in a muddy race, but I've come in third every race since. Dad's in jail, he got beat up, the city won't let us visit him. Mom's working two jobs. Felipe's worried about something but he won't tell me what. Treva might like me the way I like her… or she might not.

I drop my backpack on the floor and stretch my legs out. "I don't think so," I answer.

"How's your father doing?" Nachman asks. "How are the visits going?"

I don't say anything.

"Cole? Are you visiting your father?"

"I was. But…"

He waits.

"The jail took away his visiting privileges. For two weeks. But it's more like three weeks, because they didn't start to count until after the fight."

I can feel Nachman tighten, then I can see him make himself loose again. Maybe he was an athlete in college. "Is your father okay? Was he in a fight?"

I pull my legs back and tuck my feet under the chair. Not consciously, it just happens. "Two guys jumped him." I tell my legs to get out from their tuck. I straighten them in front of me again. "We get to see him again this Sunday. I think… I think he's okay. He shouldn't be in jail." I have a hot feeling behind my eyes. I rub them with both hands.

"Governments that want to quell dissent press false charges, Cole. They want to intimidate people, keep them from making demands." He studies me.

I'm quiet, thinking about Dad.

"What are you and your mother doing for Thanksgiving?"

What?

"Uh, we're eating at Tía's. I mean, Mrs. Ramirez. Felipe's family."

"That's good. I'm happy to hear that."

"We're having Christmas dinner there, too. They don't want Mom and me to be alone. Without Dad, I mean."

"Holidays can be tough," says Nachman. "Very tough."

I look at him, wondering if the holidays will be tough for him. If I could, I'd invite him to our house for Thanksgiving.

"Are you familiar with the Crow's Nest?" he asks me.

Huh?

I guess I stare at him too long because he laughs. "It's a coffee shop not far from here."

"Uh, yeah. I know where it is. Mom and Dad go there sometimes. On the weekend. For brunch."

"Well, I eat breakfast there six days a week," he says, "Monday through Saturday, from six a.m. until school starts. Later on Saturday." He pauses. "If you ever need to talk, Cole, or need help with anything, you can find me here at school, or you can find me at the Crow's Nest."

"Why were you here that night?" I ask him. "The night I…" I look around, to make sure the door is closed and nobody's sneaked into the classroom, "tagged the wall."

"I was walking home and took a shortcut through the schoolyard." He leans back in his chair. "That led, indirectly, to your writing F-word poems."

Uh-oh. Is this about my poems? They aren't good? I thought Nachman was liking them.

"I enjoy reading your poems, Cole. I think they're good."

Maybe Nachman's a mind reader.

"How do you feel about writing them?" he asks.

"Uh. I don't know. I promised you I would."

He smiles at this. "So you feel they're an obligation? Nothing more?"

"More," I say before I can even think about not saying it.

He looks at me, expecting something… more.

"They're more than an obligation," I admit.

"In what way?" he wants to know.

That's the thing about Nachman. He always pushes. Beyond. Beyond where you think you are.

"They let me say how I'm feeling. And they make me think. I mean, writing them makes me think." I don't say anything for a second or two, then I add. "And even when I'm not writing, I'm thinking."

He nods. "That's good. What about the words you've chosen. Have you noticed anything about them?"

Yeah. They all begin with F.

But that isn't what he wants, so I dig deeper. "The words are short," I say. "Except for *fusillade*."

"You're right. And that's a good observation, that the words are short."

I ask why it's a good observation. I really want to know.

"When something is really, really important—urgent, even—it's usually expressed in a short word. *Now! Yes! No!*

Don't! Flee! Fire! Friend. Foe."

"So most F words are short words? Why?" I reach down and pull my tablet out of my backpack. "Can I take notes?"

"Of course. Did you look up the origins of any of the words you used? I'm not avoiding your question, Cole, just taking a less direct route."

I open my tablet and open my Poems file. Just in case I need them.

"I looked up *fartlek*, which comes from Swedish."

He reaches an arm sideways to his desk and grabs the file folder that's on the end. He opens it. "*Far*," he says. "What's the origin?"

That was my first poem.

I look down at my notes. "The dictionary said Old English and Old Saxon."

"*Force*," he says.

I look at my notes. "The dictionary said Old Norse."

"*Falling*."

"The dictionary said Old English, Old Norse."

"*First*."

Okay, I'm getting it. My notes will say the word comes from Old English.

They do say that.

I tell Nachman. He nods.

"What does this mean to you, Cole?"

"I have Viking blood in me?"

He laughs at this. "Well, you might. I wouldn't be surprised. But let's talk about words of Anglo-Saxon origin."

He stands and opens his desk drawer, pulling out a laptop. He sits back down and opens it.

"I'm going to a website you might want to visit. It lists all English words of Anglo-Saxon origin. Here, let me read you a few of the f words."

He clears his throat and starts reading. "*Fair, fall, fang, far, fast, father, faze, fear, feed, feel, fetch, few, fickle, field, fiend.*"

Wow! I'll bet I could write a poem about each word he reads. I have written poems about some of them—*far, faze, fear.*

"Do you feel anything when you hear those words?" Nachman asks me.

"Yeah. I feel… I don't know, I feel something inside me. I don't know what it is. But it's there. Inside."

"*Visceral.* Relating to deep inward feelings rather than to the intellect." He watches me.

I think about this. "So you're saying I was feeling. I wasn't thinking, I was *feeling.*"

He nods.

"The words made me do that?"

"Words of Anglo-Saxon origin go back—way, way back. They've been in our language the longest. They're about our most basic needs. Fears. Desires."

"What about other words? The ones that don't come from Anglo-Saxon. Like *fusillade*?"

He chuckles at this. "Well, Cole, if you recall, that word didn't come to you immediately, did it?"

"You're right. I had to ask you for the word."

"Do you feel anything when you hear *fusillade*?" he asks.

"It's interesting," I say. "It makes me think. I wonder what it means and why it means it." I sit there and think. "But no, I don't really *feel* anything."

"Thinking is good, though," he says. "Words of French and Latin origin help us express our thoughts, and I guess you can say they help us think."

I look down at my Poems file, then back at Nachman. "This is awesome. It's sort of like a poem begins with a feeling, but then I have to think about the feeling."

He nods. "You're doing a great job, Cole. Every Friday I look forward to reading your poems."

I don't know what to say.

Nachman stands again, closes his computer, and slides it back into the center drawer of his desk. "Are you interested in trying some poetic forms? Or some syllable count poems? You don't have to if you don't want to. But writing poems that fit a certain form challenges poets in ways that free verse doesn't."

"*Forms?* Is that an Anglo-Saxon word?"

"No. Old French and Latin."

Which explains why my gut instincts felt nothing.

But my mind sat up and paid attention.

I ask him what kind of forms.

He bends down and writes something on a sheet of paper.

"Here are two web sites that explain poetic forms and give good examples of each. If any of these interest you, try them. You might even take one of the poems you've already written and try rewriting it in syllable-count or as a form poem."

He hands me the paper. I take it.

CHAPTER 26

WHAT NACHMAN SAID ABOUT WORDS is fascinating. F word, *fascinating*. Doesn't sound Anglo-Saxon, so maybe French or Latin? I think about words and feelings, and I think about thinking. I think so much I trip on a tree root and fall, cutting my knee and my palm.

"Careful, Cole," Ricardo warns as he runs around me. He's wearing a long-sleeved tee, but that's because the weather's colder. Not because he wants to wipe his snot on his sleeve.

Ricardo's been pretty happy lately. Probably because I haven't been there to challenge him. I've been there physically, but I haven't really been there, on the course. Not since Dad went to jail. Not since he got beat up.

I wasn't there a second ago, when I tripped.

I push myself up by instinct and keep on running, almost without breaking stride.

"Good recovery!" shouts Coach. "Pump it up a bit!"

So I do.

But on the bus ride back to school, and the whole time I'm working at Mrs. Green's, I'm thinking about Dad and when we see him next. And I'm thinking about F words. And syllable counts. And forms.

At home I finally have time to visit the two web sites Nachman gave me.

Lots of information. Like, more information than I can grasp all at once.

I read about sonnets, sestinas, and ghazals. Way, way hard.

The triolet. Only eight lines long. But tight rhymes. Not sure I could do that. Maybe later.

Okay, here's one I really like, the tanka. Japanese origin, sort of like the haiku, only older. Five lines, syllable count 5/7/5/7/7. I can do that.

Cinquain. I remember that one from last year's English class. Five lines, syllable count 2/4/6/8/2. Cinquains have a noticeable shape because of the growing line length and then the sudden drop off. There's something I really like about the cinquain shape.

I'm going with syllable-count poems. Syl-la-bles. Treva would love it.

If she knew I was writing poetry.

I kinda want to tell her, but I kinda don't want her to know how lame my tagging the building was. Treva's serious about political action.

I decide to do what Nachman suggested—rewrite one of my poems.

To choose one, I scroll through them.

"Force" kind of jumps out at me. Because it's okay. But not great.

"Force" is going to be forced into shape.

I stare at my poem.

FORCE

Don't force your police
force on people,
people who ask for
better jobs
and homes
and schools

Don't force your
red-white-and-blue
thinking
on others

because

they will join forces
to force
you
out.

At first I try taking what I have and putting it into syllable-count lines.

That turns out to be awful, with

Don't force
your police force
on people, people who

Problems. Lots of problems.

I insert a page break and start again. This time, before I write a single word I think about force and what I said about it. Do I still think the same way, that the ruling class is forcing people rather than listening to them?

No-brainer. Look at the para-military police forces in every large city. Look at the world's largest standing army. Look at ICE, uniformed and armed.

I start to write.

Force us
into corners
where we can barely breathe

I count the syllables. I think about where the poem is taking me, and what its last two lines should be.

FORCE

Force us
into corners
where we can barely breathe,
force us back so far we explode
on you.

Wow.

I didn't know what I was going to say until I said it.

For a while I just look at the new poem, admiring its shape.

I open the old poem and read it again.

I like the new one better. The limited syllable count made me think in a different way. The syllable count and the subject work together: I have to force—ha!—a lot of information into a tiny space, and the two-syllable line at the end kind of explodes.

Now I'll have to stop myself from writing nothing but cinquains.

CHAPTER 27

EDNESDAY MORNING I RUN MY usual short run to Felipe's. This Saturday is the last meet of the season. Coach will tell us to keep running all winter long. "Winter runs are pleasure runs," he'll say. "No pressure."

Dad's been in jail for two months. Which means he gets out in two months. Early January.

I wonder what his Thanksgiving will be like, without us. At least we get to be with Tía and Tío. Tía says she'll be feeding twenty people. Mom's baking five pumpkin pies. She says I'm supposed to make cranberry sauce. Which I've never made in my life. But which I've downloaded a recipe for.

After breakfast Felipe and I watch until Benito, Juliana, and Isabella turn the corner toward Euclid Grade School.

"Felipe," I ask, "what's bothering you?"

"Nothing."

"Is it something I did?"

He shakes his head. "No."

We walk in silence.

Felipe turns around and gives one last look at the corner his brother and sisters turned down. "I wish I could talk to somebody," he says. "Somebody like Tío Hank."

He wants to talk to Dad?

"You want to talk to Dad about what's bothering you?"

"*Sí.*"

"Have you talked to your father?" I'm still clueless about what's bothering him.

"*Sí.* Many times."

Let me figure this out. Felipe's already talked to his own father. Now he wants to talk to Dad. Which he can't until Dad gets out of jail in January.

And he's not going to tell me what's bothering him.

But then I remember what Nachman said. "If you need to talk to somebody, what about Nachman? He told me he eats breakfast at the Crow's Nest six mornings a week. And that he encourages kids to talk to him if they need to. I think Ethan's been there to talk to him."

Felipe looks at me. "Have you talked to him?"

"No."

"But he said this to you because he thought you might want to talk to him. *¿Por qué?*"

Our bus stop is just ahead.

"The poems, I think."

"*¿Los poemas?*"

"Yeah. Well, not them exactly, but what's in them."

He waits.

"Nachman can tell I'm worried about Dad. From the poems. So he said I could talk to him if I need to."

Felipe pats me on the back. "Tío Hank is strong. He'll be out in two more months."

"Yeah."

___

When we get off the bus I'm hoping Treva is already at the fence.

But she isn't.

Jillian is.

"*Hola,*" says Felipe. Without much enthusiasm. I'm pretty sure he's speaking Spanish just to irritate Jillian.

"I want you to know that I'll be attending each open student council meeting," Jillian tells him. "And I'll be taking notes."

"*Bueno ¿y qué?*"

I can tell she has no idea what he just said. And I'm sure not going to translate for her.

"You really should speak English, Felipe. As class president, you need to speak English."

"You really should learn Spanish, Jillian," he shoots back. Angry. "Spanish and English are the languages of the Americas."

Jillian readjusts the books she's holding. I think she's the only student in all of August Mersy High who doesn't wear a backpack.

"The things you're working on are all wrong," she continues, still talking only to Felipe. "Like the display case idea."

"What's wrong with that?" I demand. "It looks great, and it's a great idea."

Jillian turns to look at me. "Henry Thunder is the only Indian in all of tenth grade."

"Whose fault is that?" I ask.

She's about to say something, but she looks past me and stops.

I turn and see Treva walking toward us. Her coat is unbuttoned. I can see she's wearing all red today. Except for the black coat, of course.

I turn around to hear Jillian's next bright idea. But she isn't there. She's already halfway to the school door.

"Hey," says Treva.

"Hey," Felipe and I say.

"Usually people wait until I say something before they leave the battlefield," she says.

"Jillian's probably reporting to Ms. Delaney," Felipe mutters. Then he studies Treva more closely. *"Rojo,"* he says, pointing to her clothes. He's trying to teach Treva one Spanish word a day.

"Rojo," she repeats. "Red."

We nod.

"I saw ICE," Treva says.

Felipe stiffens. "Where?" he asks.

She points behind herself, back to the corner where we saw the ICE patrol car last month. When they marched into the school and took Gi Pak away. Nobody's heard from him since.

"I yelled at them," Treva adds.

We stare at her. "Yelled what?" I ask.

"No Deportations! Disband ICE!"

"Intenso," Felipe tells her.

"Intense?" she asks. "What I shouted?"

"Strong, hard, powerful."

She smiles at that.

"Treva. Cole's last race is this Saturday. He would like you to go."

Treva and Felipe both look at me. Treva with a smile, Felipe with a grin.

"Rojo," says Felipe, pointing to my face.

"I'd love to see you race," Treva says. "But only if you want me to."

"Yeah. Yes. Yeah. I do want you to," I manage, my words bumping into themselves on their way out of my mouth.

"I'm there!" she says. And does that little dancing-in-place with her feet. She's wearing red shoes and short white socks with lacy edges.

The bell rings. Which saves Treva from a grammar lesson of *más rojo* and *el más rojo*. And me from whatever the Spanish is for *further embarrassment*. What a great F word, *further*. Probably Old English.

All that day, whenever I get a chance, I work on a poem.

The same poem. Over and over.

Trying to get it right.

It's not *further*. I might save that for another time.

I'm working on a form poem. That's one of the things that makes it hard. It's a rondelet. Seven lines long, with lines one, three and seven being identical.

This is hard. Like hopping a three-mile cross-country race in a potato sack.

I work on the poem in study hall. On the bus ride to cross-country practice. On the bus ride to Mrs. Green's. And then up in my room.

FLYING

I'll be flying
When I pass the place where you stand
I'll be flying
Even though my strength is dying
Aid this runner across the land
Add shouting voice and waving hand
I'll be flying

When I finish, I feel like I've run twenty miles. Make that thirty. I read the poem again and feel *rojo* all over.

I'm not going to show this poem to Nachman. No way.

I move it into the Poems: Private file, where I have "Face Time" and "Faze."

I want to give the poem to Treva.

Should I? What will she think?

If I do give it to her, how? Text? PDF via text, so the lines stay true?

Print it on paper?

I can't decide which. Or whether.

CHAPTER 28

ACE DAY IS CLEAR BUT cold. We're out in the southwest suburbs. A fifty-mile bus ride. Most of us are wearing long-sleeved shirts to run in. All of us are wearing warmup suits.

Coach is going around to each runner. When he gets to Ricardo and me, he places a hand on each of our shoulders. "Last race of the season. Give it your all. Finish strong."

We nod.

"Both of you can make varsity next year. Keep up the training, rain or shine."

I'm moving my knees up and down, keeping warm. I nod at everything Coach says. So does Ricardo. Coach pats our backs and moves on.

Then he's there again.

"Watch Palatine," he warns. "And Tinley Park. Pace yourself. Take the team with you. The last half mile, the two of you pull ahead."

Ricardo and I glance at each other. Last *half mile?*

Sophomores run first, so before the race starts all seven of us do an easy lope around the course, checking it out.

No forests here. Not many hills. The track's a mile long, so three times around. I prefer the long, winding courses with no turning back. Most schools don't have the space to do that, so we're used to the loop courses.

The crowd is large and noisy. Moms, dads, sisters and brothers, friends. The last meet of the season is a big one. If Mom and Dad were here, they'd be standing near the finish line.

Felipe couldn't come to the meet. His whole family is in Wisconsin, visiting relatives.

I hear loud cheers and look to see who they're for. A bunch of Palatine fans are whooping for their team. Palatine's favored. But Ricardo and I are going to be troublemakers.

I look for Treva but don't see her.

The butterflies never leave my stomach until the gun goes off, so I'm always walking around, trying to ignore the flutter.

Time to line up. My mouth goes dry.

The gun goes off.

August Mersy springs forward, into the fray. Seven of us running together.

The first half mile is all about keeping from falling into, over, or on somebody else. There's nearly two hundred of us, and we don't get sorted out until we're halfway around the loop.

We keep close, like Coach wants us to for most of the race. Ricardo's a step ahead of me. I'm to his left. Out of snot range. "Breathe easy," I say to Peer, who always starts too fast and then falls back. He nods and loosens up a bit. Ibrahim's right behind me. "With you," he says. "With you," Ethan grunts. "With you," says Deshaun.

There are maybe thirty runners in front of us. I glance over my shoulder. Xavier's running seventh in our pack and I can tell he won't be with us by the mile, not unless something helps him pick up the pace.

Cheering and shouting comes from all directions. We round the final curve, coming up on the first mile. Coach is standing on a chair, halfway between the last quarter mile and the chute. He'll shout something to each of us as we pass.

Then I hear *"Way to go, Cole!"* Treva.

Inside, I grin. Outside, I grimace as Ricardo picks up the pace. "Take ten, next mile," he says.

Which is not easy.

But we do it, with me pulling alongside Ricardo as we round the curve for the second time.

"Cole Cool! Cole Rule!"

What?

I take a quick glance. It's Emerald Jackson, standing next to Treva. And there's Michael... Patricia... Beth... Collins...

All from English class.

"Right flank, Cole, right flank!"

It's Mr. Nachman.

I can't believe it. He came to the track meet?

To shout F words?

Oh. Wait.

He's warning me.

I glance toward my right just as a Palatine runner tries to overtake me, hoping to slip into the breach between me and Ricardo.

No way, dude. I pick up my pace and veer a bit to my right. Ricardo sticks his elbows out. Palatine has to go around if he wants to pass us.

We pass two more runners.

"Eight... more," I pant to Ricardo as we enter the last mile.

We pass six of them by the two-and-a-half-mile mark.

Only. Two. More.

"Crush 'em, Cole! Crush 'em!!" It's Treva. I can see her jumping up and down.

"Go, Mersy, go! Mersy, Mersy, Mersy!" Emerald.

With my friends watching and cheering me on, I want to place in the top three for sure. Somewhere inside me there's room for more. I find it. Lengthen my stride. Increase my pace.

I glance at Ricardo, to see if we're together. He shakes his head and motions me to go.

I pull ahead. Pass one.

"Flashy finish, Cole! Flashy finish!"

Nachman.

Somewhere inside I'm laughing.

I'm running so hard I think I'm going to faint. Everything is blurry, like colors swirled together.

I'm flying. I pass Palatine just before the chute.

In the chute I sway, hitting the ropes to my left. Then right.

But I throw myself across the finish line.

And collapse.

A judge helps me up. "You okay?" she asks.

I nod, breathing hard.

Ricardo comes through third, falling down alongside me.

"G'race," I gasp.

"G'race," he gasps back.

We help each other off the ground. Behind us, we see Xavier cross the finish line. He found something to help him pick up the pace. "Good race," we tell him.

"Ninth," he pants, telling us where he placed.

We find our warmup suits and stumble into them, then wait at the end of the chute until all of August Mersy is in. Even though only the first five runners' places count toward the score, you don't desert your teammates.

Coach tells us we ran really well and that August Mersy might win the meet. We won't know until the numbers go up.

When they do go up, Mersy has a score of 36. That's good, but not great. Great is in the low to mid twenties.

Palatine comes in at 39. We breathe a sigh of relief. And then Tinley Park comes in with a total of 44.

Yes! Our 36 is the lowest number on the board—we win our last meet of the season!

Ethan nudges me. "Did you see everyone from our class?"

"Yeah. Let's go thank them." And so we walk over to where part of our English class is standing around, waiting for us.

I thank each and every kid who came out and shake each of their hands. So does Ethan. Treva holds on to my hand long enough that I think she might be doing it on purpose. Her hand is warm.

I brought the poem. It's in my hoodie pocket. Should I give it to her?

"How'd you all get here?" I ask.

Everyone points first at Treva, then at Nachman. Both of them look ready to accept praise.

"She organized it," Emerald says. "He was merely the chauffeur."

We laugh at that.

"Treva's a great organizer," Nachman says.

"Hey," I say, "you all wanna come to whatever pizza place Coach is taking us to? Lots of family and friends come. I have to sit with the team, but I can, like, sneak over to the English-class table for a while."

"I'm up for it," says Nachman. "Does anybody have to be home by a certain time?"

"Pizza! Pizza!" everyone shouts.

So we all eat pizza and then ice cream, and I eat with the team, but Treva's table is right next to ours and I scoot my chair that way whenever I can. Coach gives a speech that ends with what he always says: "Believe in yourself and believe in the team."

We all cheer.

"And train," he reminds us. "All winter long. Short runs, long runs, bike rides, weights, stretches. Fun. Fun runs."

Everyone on the team promises he'll do that. I know I will.

And, because it's our last meet, Coach lets us ride back with whoever we want to ride back with.

I manage to squeeze into Nachman's SUV.

Next to Treva.

When nobody's looking, I slip the poem out of my pocket and into Treva's. She feels me doing it and gives me a questioning look.

"For you," I say.

She smiles.

———

When I get to Mrs. Green's, she and Mom greet me with a cake. A big "1" candle is burning in the center. Mom has her camera on a tripod. She's been doing that the last few weeks, so that when Dad comes home he can see some of the things we did. The camera's on as I blow out the candle. It's on as Mom, Mrs. Green, and I all take a piece of cake and move toward the phone as we bite into the pieces. Dad will laugh when he sees this. He'll want chocolate cake, too.

My phone pings.

Treva: I 🖤 the poem. You are a poet.

I open the attachment.

At first I can't figure out what it is. Something hanging on a wall. I enlarge it.

It's my poem. In big, bold, blue ink. Framed.

Wait. The poem's superimposed over a photo.

Of me. Winning the race.

I compress the photo to normal size and stare at it.

I think Treva likes the poem.

Really likes the poem.

Like, she typed it out.

Took a photo of me.

Printed the poem over the photo.

Framed it.

And it's hanging on her bedroom wall.

Work is a blur. I get through it somehow without knocking anything over.

———

That night in my room, I think about writing another poem to Treva.

Somehow, though, nothing comes to me.

I find myself thinking about the race, about Treva coming to watch me run.

About Nachman bringing so many kids to the meet.

I think about the F words Nachman was shouting. Like when he warned me to watch my right flank.

I look up *flank* and learn—no surprise—it's an Old English word that comes from the German. *Flank* can be a verb or it can be a noun.

Noun: *The section of flesh on the body of a person or an animal between the last rib and the hip; the side.* Also: "The right or left side of a military formation."

Verb: *To protect or guard the flank of.* And also the opposite: *To menace or attack the flank of.* So I could flank or be flanked.

When Ricardo and I stopped the Palatine runner from coming through, we were protecting our flank. When I passed the lead runner, I flanked him.

This definitely calls for a poem.

Maybe Nachman was even telling me to write a poem about flank.

I log onto one of the poetic forms web sites he gave me.

It's hard to choose a form when I don't know what the poem's going to be.

Maybe that's the point: maybe I'm supposed to let the form guide me to what I want to say?

I choose a form called the fib, short for fibonacci. This is a syllable count poem based on the Fibonacci sequence. So the syllables and lines will go 1 /1 /2 /3 /5/ 8. And so on. I get it.

FLANKS

Flanks
guard
the sides,
protecting
the main body from
sneaky maneuvers or attacks

Friends
flank
their team
by instinct,
committing themselves—
doing right to help each other

CHAPTER 29

AD COVERS THE DISTANCE FROM the door in three strides, pushing both hands against the plastic, fingers spread wide. Mom presses her hand against Dad's left one. I press mine against his right one.

We're really pressing against the dirty, scratched plastic window. But it feels like we're touching Dad.

Almost.

"Hank, are you okay?" Mom bends toward the speak-through grill as she sits down. I kneel on one leg in front of the grill. There's a guard standing in the corner on Dad's side. Another standing in the corner on our side.

"Yeah, I'm okay," he says in the general direction of the speak-through grill. "I doubt there will be more attacks."

I study Dad. I can see the cut alongside his eye. It required stitches. But it's mostly healed. There's an almost-gone black-

and-blue mark on his jaw, and four—no, five—fading yellow-green ones on his arms. There's probably more that I can't see.

"That's good," says Mom. "Why do you feel that way?"

"First tell me about the outside world," he says. "Then I'll answer your question." He turns to me. "How'd you do in your last meet?"

I'm happy to tell him the good news. "Mersy won the meet. I came in first, Ricardo third. And Xavier had a personal best—he came in ninth. A bunch of kids from my English class came to cheer. That really helped."

"Nothing like support. Great way to end the season, Cole," Dad says as he bends into the speaker grill. "And speaking of support, the reason I don't expect more trouble, Stacey, is that I'm now a respected teacher."

"What?" she asks, staring first at the speak-through grill, then back at Dad.

He grins. "I volunteered to teach reading to anybody who wants to learn. It started out small, with just three prisoners, an hour a day. Now each class is up to five students."

"Each class?" Mom asks. "How many classes are you teaching?"

"Four. Each meets five days a week. And I think I'm going to add another one. If you can't read, the past is lost to you. Which means the future is, too." He straightens to look at us.

Wow.

"You must be a good teacher, Dad," I say into the grill.

"Hey, don't you remember who taught you the alphabet?" he asks, bending down.

"It was Mom," I kid. "You might have helped a little."

"Ha! Who hand-carved you twenty-six alphabet blocks when you were two years old?"

"I can't remember that far back," I say. It's good to see Dad laugh. It's good to be laughing with him. "And the D was a bit too round. To this day I get my capital D's and capital O's mixed up."

"He doesn't know whether to say DOH or OOH," Mom says.

Dad laughs again. "And another thing," he says. "The prison library stinks. Nothing political. I've been putting in five book requests a day. *The Autobiography of Malcom X; Malcolm X Speaks; The Communist Manifesto;* Lenin's *State and Revolution;* Trotsky's *History of the Russian Revolution; Imperialism in the 21st Century; October; Fighting Fascisim.* Books on racism, colonialism, imperialism, war."

Double wow. Treva would love hearing this. I love hearing it. "Are they going to get any of the titles?" I ask.

Dad straightens and looks at me through the plastic window. It's his are-you-seriously-asking-me-that-question look. He bends back down. "Unlikely. But not impossible. Especially if other inmates also request them. Over and over."

"Which means somebody tells them about the books," Mom adds.

"I'm going to see if I can start teaching a history class," says Dad.

He straightens, points at me, then flexes a bicep. "I'm back to lifting weights, Short Stuff. Can't let you gain on me."

"Track is over for the season," I say. "Which means I can spend a lot more time in the weight room."

"The weight room is mine!" Mom says. She's definitely worked out more since Dad went to jail.

Just as Dad is about to say something, the guard on his end steps forward and taps him on the shoulder. Our guard does the same. They must practice synchronized repression.

I press my hand against the glass and Dad does the same. His other hand has been pressed against Mom's the whole time. She blows him a kiss and I give him a wave. Then he disappears through the metal door.

———

"I feel a lot better than before we came," I tell Mom as we walk north to catch the el.

"Me, too. Resilience is heartening to see."

I think about this. *"Resilience* means bouncing back?"

Mom looks at me. "I wouldn't say bouncing. That sounds too... too something. Too cheerful? Resilience means something like flexibility, the ability to come back, to rally." She looks at me to see whether I understand.

"To rally. I like that," I say. "Like, it could mean to gain strength."

"And I like that, Cole. To gain strength." She gives me a grin. "But not from weight lifting."

We wait at a corner until the Walk sign flashes, then we cross. "From something that's inside you," I say.

"Yes. From an inner strength. Dad has a lot of inner strength."

I look at Mom. "You do, too," I say. "And I think I do, too."

"I know you do, Cole."

Once we're on the el I pull out my phone and start working on a poem. Mom asks what I'm doing and I tell her I'm working on another assignment.

By now I know the poems are for me every bit as much as they are for Nachman.

And I realize, just then, that Nachman wants to teach me flexibility. Poetic flexibility. Which is why he wants me to try some syllable-count poems and some form-poems. So far I've done two syllable-count poems, the cinquain and the fib. And one form poem, the rondelet. Except the rondelet not only uses rhyme, it counts syllables, too. That poem was really hard. The more discipline a poem requires, the harder it is to create.

I go to the poetry forms site.

Tanka.

Pure syllable count: 5 / 7/ 5/ 7/ 7.

I type the title: Flexibility.

Man, no way! That one word is five syllables long!

But hey—there's the first of five lines.

I work on the poem.

Mom shakes my arm. "This is where we transfer, Cole."

After we catch a blue line train, I work on the poem again.

Our visit with Dad was early morning, ten o'clock, so there's still a lot of Sunday left. Felipe's still in Wisconsin. Treva's going to a play with her Mom. Ethan doesn't answer his texts. Ricardo asks if I want to meet him, Peer, and Ibrahim at the Regal Webster movie complex. I say sure, grab my jacket, tell Mom where I'm going and when I'll be back, and head out the door.

Later that night, I work on the tanka again. Sometimes it's hard to know if a poem is finished or not. Needs more work or not.

FLEXIBILITY

Flexibility
in the claws of injustice
doesn't mean we slide
free, escaping their pain, but
that we mend to rise again

CHAPTER 30

HEN WE GET OFF THE bus Felipe and I see that Treva's already waiting in our spot by the fence.

"Hey," she says. "How was Wisconsin, Felipe? And how was your visit with your father, Cole?"

"Nice," Felipe answers. "I'm training my younger cousins to run for class president."

Treva gives him a thumbs up, then looks at me.

"Good," I say. "He's doing okay." I tell her and Felipe about the reading classes Dad is teaching.

Treva smiles and nods as I talk. "Hank Renner is a hero," she says when I finish.

Which she said when I first met her.

"Yeah," I say. "He is. To me for sure."

"To me, too," says Felipe. "I wish he could be home for Thanksgiving."

Which makes me wonder—again—what Felipe wants to talk to Dad about.

The bell rings. When we walk inside, we stop. Up on the huge electronic message board there's a photo of me, the Palatine runner, and Ricardo at the finish line. MERSY WINS LAST CROSS-COUNTRY MEET OF SEASON is captioned beneath it.

"Wow!" says Treva. "Cool! Almost as good as the photo I took."

I feel myself turning red. Hope Felipe doesn't see it.

"Way cool," he says, studying the photo. "I'll bet Hannah Iwata took that picture. Hey, Cole—maybe she's gonna run it on the front page of *The Fire*!"

"As if," I say. "Not when she can run a football photo instead."

We stand and stare at the photo a while. I do look cool, actually. I pull out my phone and take a photo to show Mom. A lot of kids stop, stare, then congratulate me. Another bell rings.

Felipe and I go to history class, and when that's over we head our separate ways through the halls. A couple of turns through August Mersy and I'm almost at my locker.

The next thing I know, somebody grabs me and slams me against the wall.

The force snaps my head back and forward. My backpack slips off my shoulder and to the floor. "Hey!" I shout, pushing back at somebody solid.

Then I see who it is.

Jared Anderson.

I haven't seen him since he got back from being suspended, and that was maybe two weeks ago.

I can't say I've missed him.

He lets go of me but forces me against the wall. "Leave Jillian alone, Renner."

Jillian?

Except for seeing Jillian in English class every day, and that one time at the fence, I haven't thought about her. At all.

"I'm not bothering Jillian."

"It's your fault," he shouts. "All of it!"

Yeah, right. It's my fault he's a bully who snatches hijabs off the heads of other students. "I didn't make you steal that hijab, Jared. You did it on your own."

He backs away a bit. Not enough for me to slip to my left or right, though.

He frowns. "I'm not talking about that. I'm talking about Jillian."

"Jillian?" Man, I am confused.

He moves closer, pressing me against the wall again. "She dumped me. All because of you."

Oh.

Okay. Jillian dumped him. Now I get why he's angry. At least five of my F words were for Jillian.

"Uh, that's not my fault, Jared. I had nothing to do with it."

I can feel his breath on my face. Almost as bad as being hit with somebody's snot in a race.

"She wants to get back together with you."

"No," I argue. "She doesn't. No way."

He backs away a bit. But not enough.

"Then why'd she do it?"

I can think of lots of reasons why. Mainly that Jillian doesn't want to be associated with somebody who steals hijabs and gets suspended. Not good for her resume. But I'm not going to say that to Jared Anderson.

"Maybe it's a pattern," I suggest.

"Pattern?"

"Of dumping guys. First me, then you. And there was Zachary before me, I think."

He's still breathing hard. But he steps back, and I think fine, we've got that settled. I pick up by backpack.

He knocks it out of my hand.

"You're saying Jillian's a slut! You saying there's something wrong with her!"

There's a crowd around us. All I see is other kids fanning out to my left and right and behind Jared.

Around, but not too close. Nobody wants to get too close to Jared.

I try again. "Calm down, Jared. This isn't between you and me. It's Jillian's choice, and she chooses neither of us."

He's quiet, and I think I'm out of it. I look down at my backpack, wondering if I should risk picking it up again.

"You want Jillian!" he shouts, his face in mine. "Say it! Say you want her and can't have her 'cause she's mine! Say it, Renner! Say it!"

"No!" I shout back. My *No* means No to everything in his wacko mind. So it's a pretty loud *No*.

Teachers must be running out of their rooms by now to check out the trouble.

Which escalates like a rocket when Jared punches me in the face, knocking me against the wall. I stumble and fall to the floor.

Blood's spurting out of my mouth and on my shirt and all over the floor.

I look up to see Jared standing there. Thinking he's right. Thinking he's won.

I pull my legs back and kick them out straight, at his shins, hard as I can.

He comes down almost on top of me, but I'm expecting it and he isn't. I roll out of his way, climb onto his back, pull one of his arms behind his back, and slam his face into the floor.

Just like Dad taught me.

No time to enjoy the victory, though—somebody grabs me from behind and hauls me off Jared.

At first I try twisting away, but then I see it's Turner Blevins, so I stop. Turner's captain of the football team, and he plays centerfield on the baseball team. Turner's a good guy.

Turner lets me go, then turns to Jared, who's back on his feet, blood gushing out of his nose.

"This stops here," Turner says to Jared.

I can see Jared disagrees. But he listens to the captain of the team.

For now.

Holding his hand to his nose, Jared brushes by me, trying to knock me to the ground. I stay on my feet.

"What's going on here?!" a voice demands. Students back up out of the way, and suddenly Turner and I are left standing there, far from anyone.

"Jared Anderson, come back here this instant!" Mrs. Teklova commands. Her class is somewhere near here. I'm kind of mixed up on exactly where I'm standing. Or even where my next class is.

Not that it matters. Mrs. Teklova marches both me and Jared straight to the nurse's station. Jared glares at me, but I give him a tougher-than-you look and he turns his head away.

The nurse takes care of Jared first. He's in worse shape. I'm pretty sure I broke his nose. It's mashed off-center and gushing blood.

I hear Mrs. Teklova call somebody, asking them to lead her class for the period. She teaches typing. Which is, like, a prerequisite to taking computer classes.

"I'm staying right here until you're both taken care of, and then we're all going to see Ms. Delaney," she says. "I saw everything that happened."

I almost ask her why she didn't stop Jared before he punched me. But that's probably not the smartest thing to do, so I don't say anything.

I take out my cell and start typing.

"What are you doing, Cole?" she demands. "I won't have you spreading word of this before we see Ms. Delaney."

"I'm writing a poem."

She sticks her hand out and wiggles it.

I hand her my phone.

She sees:

FIST

I wish
his fist

"This isn't finished," she says, handing the phone back.

Well, Duh!

How can I finish my poems if people keep interrupting me?

I continue typing, then hand her my phone again.

FIST

I wish
his fist
had missed.

She reads it and hands the phone back.

Hmm.

I think the poem's kind of cool. For an on-the-spot creation.

By somebody whose lip is bleeding down his chin and onto his shirt.

"It's got off-rhyme," I tell her. "And assonance. Which is the repeating of vowel sounds."

"I didn't know you were a poet, Cole."

But I am.

I am a poet.

"By the way," she says, "congratulations on the cross-country win. Nice photo of you and Ricardo."

"Thanks," I say.

And then Jared comes out of the nurse's room, his nose splinted and taped. Mrs. Teklova points to a chair and Jared sits. He doesn't look at me.

The nurse takes me into her room. There's not much she can do for me she says as she wipes my cut with the sharpest stinging liquid on earth. They must keep it on hand just for students. I try not to wince, but sometimes you can't always do what you try.

"Ice on the jaw tonight and tomorrow. You know how to make a cold compress, don't you, Cole?"

"Yeah, Coach taught us how."

"What kind of pain reliever does your mother give you?"

"Aspirin, I think."

She writes something on a slip of paper and hands it to me. "Give this to your mother tonight."

She looks into my eyes again. "Do you want a pain killer now?"

I shake my head. "I'm okay."

When I come out, Mrs. Teklova motions to Jared and me to follow her.

My backpack feels ten pounds heavier. I make the mistake of slinging it over my left shoulder, which makes my jaw hurt. I quickly switch the backpack to my right shoulder and step into line as we march toward Ms. Delaney's office.

CHAPTER 31

RS. TEKLOVA GOES INTO THE principal's office with Jared, which leaves me sitting in the outer office. "What happened to you, Cole?" Nikki Zurlo asks. "Jared punched me."

"You've seen the school nurse?" she asks.

"Yeah. Thanks."

She asks me how Dad is and I tell her how he's doing. She asks if I think he'll be willing to lead another protest in front of Euclid Grade School. "If that becomes necessary," she adds. I have to think about that, but only for a bit. "Dad won't stop fighting for what's right," I say. Nikki nods and goes back to work.

I pull out my phone. When she's not looking, I take a selfie and send it to Felipe and Treva.

Me: Jared. In D's office now.

Felipe's in study hall. He texts back right away.

Felipe: Por qué?

Me: Cause he's Jared.

Treva: 😠 U OK?

Me: Will be. CU @ fence?

The door opens and Jared marches out, not looking at Nikki or me.

I hope his nose hurts like hell.

"Cole." Mrs. Teklova is standing there, motioning me into Ms. Delaney's office.

She holds the door open for me and I walk in. She comes in, too, closing the door behind herself.

"Sit down, Cole," says Ms. Delaney.

I take my favorite worn-out wooden chair. There are two of them, so she could have had Jared and me in at the same time if she wanted to. Like she did with me and Felipe.

"Emma, you can go now," Ms. Delaney says to Mrs. Teklova. Who looks confused at that.

I must look confused, too. If Mrs. Teklova stayed for Jared, shouldn't she stay for me? She said she saw the whole thing.

"You sure you don't need me?" Mrs. Teklova asks Ms. Delaney. "My class is covered."

"I took notes," says Ms. Delaney. "And I'm unlikely to forget in this short space of time."

Which is, like, a dismissal. So Mrs. Teklova leaves.

My gut tells me this is not a good thing.

After the door closes, Ms. Delaney is silent for a while, staring at me. I stare straight back at her.

Finally she says something. "This is a very serious offense, Cole. Fighting in school."

"It's Jared's offense, not mine. He attacked me, I defended myself."

"Jared has been suspended for one week. Again."

So?

That makes sense to me.

Ms. Delaney is watching me. She wants something.

I have no idea what.

She moves her chair back from her desk. She crosses her legs and leans back. She plays with a pen. "Let's relax a minute, Cole, and reflect on other matters."

What other matters? Where's she going with this?

"I've been watching you on YouTube," she says.

That again?

"Somebody took videos of your last race and posted them. Good job, Cole. Very good."

Oh. Not the demonstration for immigrant rights.

She waits.

I think I'm supposed to say thank you. "Uh, thanks," I manage. "Our whole team ran really well: first, third, and ninth. Then tenth and thirteenth. That's what helped us win the meet."

Ms. Delaney smiles.

It's not a real smile.

"Your win is very good for August Mersy," she says. "And potentially good for you, too. If you compile enough of these wins in your junior and senior years, you could win a college scholarship."

I'm about to say something like, "Yeah, I'm hoping for that." But I don't.

Because I still think she's up to something.

"A scholarship would not only benefit you, it would reflect well on our coach and, most importantly, our whole school."

"Yeah," I say, because it's kind of hard to say nothing when somebody is waiting for you.

"Unlike your participation in last year's test boycott."

For a second I don't get what she means or where we are in this conversation. Which is pretty much one-sided.

And shouldn't be happening at all. Except maybe she should compliment me for fighting back against a bully.

But then it hits me, what she means. Running is what she thinks I should be doing. Protesting is what she thinks I shouldn't be doing.

Man, this was a setup, the way she led me there. Ms. Delaney is good at this.

I don't say anything, just stare at her.

She uncrosses her legs and moves her chair forward. "Will you be participating in a testing boycott again, Cole? At the end of this school year?"

"I don't know," I say, shrugging. "That's a long way away."

She taps her pen on her desktop. "Answer my question. Do you intend to boycott student testing this coming spring?"

"I did answer your question. I said I don't know. That's my answer."

"That's not good enough. I want your word that you won't boycott student testing this spring."

I shake my head. "I won't give you my word."

Delaney pushes her chair back. "Very well, Cole. For your participation in today's brawl, I'm giving you a three-day suspension."

"What?!" I shout. "Brawl? No way! That's unfair! It wasn't a brawl! Jared attacked me! All I did was defend myself. It's a human right to defend yourself!"

"Do not shout at me," she says, already writing something out. My suspension, probably.

I'm on my feet, worried about cross-country because Coach doesn't allow kids who get suspensions to be on the team, and even though this year's season is over, I'm worried about next year. Worried about what Mom and Dad are going to say. I've never, ever received a suspension.

"I was attacked!" I shout. "You're treating the attacker and the person he attacks as the same." I'm filled with enough rage to pick up the heavy wooden chairs and throw them at her. To kick over her desk. To spray paint the walls of her office at the very least. Her, too.

But I don't do those things. Even though doing them would feel good. Really good.

Throwing and kicking and spray painting aren't the way to fight back. I realize now that's what Nachman meant when he caught me tagging the wall.

They're basically ineffective. Pointless. *Futile*. F word.

"I've buzzed a security guard to escort you off the school property, Cole. You will leave as soon as he arrives."

Which he does even as she's speaking.

Man, she must have security guards stashed five steps away.

Which she probably needs, considering the injustice she's dealing out.

He grabs me by an arm and starts hauling me out the door, but I manage to shout back at Delaney. "No justice, no peace! No justice, no peace!"

The guard marches me out the door and down the hallway and out the closest door. He even walks me to the edge of the school property and doesn't let go until I'm on the public sidewalk. Behind me I hear traffic zipping by on Pulaski.

I stand there. The guard stands there, too.

I don't know what he's doing, but I know what I'm doing. Thinking.

Thinking first of something Dad always says, "The carrot or the stick. The ruling class controls us through the carrot or the stick."

Ms. Delaney offered me the carrot first: praise about my running. The suggestion of a scholarship. Then, when I didn't do what she wanted, that's when she used the stick—the three-day suspension.

Man, she's wicked good at this.

But I'm going to be good, too.

Good at fighting back.

And I don't mean tagging the walls of buildings.

CHAPTER 32

WISH DAD WAS HERE. HE'D understand. I don't know how to break the news to Mom, or even when's the best time to tell her. So I stand there on the sidewalk and text her.

Me: Jared punched me, I broke his nose. Principal suspnd him 5 days, me 3.

Mom: Where are you?

Me: Sidewalk in front of school.

Mom: There in half hour. Stay put.

It's cold outside, that thin November cold with no wind, no rain, no snow—just bleak cold. Winter's coming. My jacket is better for riding the bus than it is for standing outdoors, so I jog back and forth from one end of the block to the other, then back again. The guard finally gives up and goes back into the school to do whatever other injustice Delaney has in mind.

August Mersy High School and its grounds occupy one full city block, side to side and front to back. Fullerton and Pulaski is a major intersection, so a lot of traffic creeps by as I'm jogging. I know there's a lot of traffic in the mornings, but I never realized how much there is in the middle of the morning. Maybe it's like this all day long.

I stop.

If I did something here, in front of the school, lots of people would see it. Everyone traveling on Fullerton. Everyone traveling on Pulaski.

Students. Teachers. People going to and from work.

I could make picket signs protesting what Delaney did.

As I'm standing there thinking of what the signs should say, Mom gets off the #53 bus.

"Tell me what happened," she says.

When I'm done telling, Mom asks me to wait while she goes in to talk to Ms. Delaney.

"Mom, wait. There's a big smudge of blue paint on your forehead."

She reaches up and touches the smudge. "Good. That will let Ms. Delaney know she seriously interrupted me."

———

While I wait I decide to write a poem. I sit at the bus stop, pull out my phone and look up *ballad*, something I remember from Nachman's class last year. I don't know why I'm thinking ballad. Good guys and bad guys, maybe?

I remember that ballads are written in quatrains, but I don't remember the rhyme scheme.

Okay, it's abab. Iambic tetrameter.

FAIR

She throws me out into the cold
Without a thought to what is fair
But I am strong and will be bold
And she'll be caught by her own snare

At least I hope she will be, because I have some ideas on how to fight back. I'm just not sure how well they'll work.

After I'm pretty much frozen, Mom finally comes out of the school.

"You're freezing," she says, "so let's be quick about this. Did you spray paint the school wall earlier this year?"

Oh, man.

Is that why Delaney gave me a suspension?

Mom's looking at me.

I nod. "Yeah. I did. I'm sorry, Mom, it was the day Dad went to jail. I wouldn't do it again."

"Did you tell Ms. Delaney you spray painted the wall?"

"No. She called me into her office. I told her I had the right to remain silent."

"Good. That you used your right to remain silent. Bad that you spray painted the wall. You know better than that. What makes her think it was you?"

So I tell Mom exactly what happened, with Nachman catching me in the act and promising he wouldn't tell.

"You ended up cleaning the graffiti off the wall?" Mom asks.

"Yeah. Felipe helped me. It's all gone."

She looks at me. "You realize that Mr. Nachman jeopardized his job by not reporting you, don't you? If it ever came out that he knew and didn't tell, he would be in trouble."

I look down at the sidewalk. "Sort of. I mean, I know now. But I didn't think about it then."

"What kind of poems is he making you write?"

"Uh. Poems about words that start with F."

Mom gives a smile over this. "Mr. Nachman has a sense of humor."

"He's a really good teacher."

"I'd like to read some of your poems, if you want to show them to me."

"Okay," I say. "I'll pick a couple to show you."

Mom sighs. "Well, I couldn't get Ms. Delaney to rescind your suspension, no matter how hard I argued. She kept bringing up that you spray painted the wall. Which I told her she apparently had no proof of, and which was irrelevant to the issue of Jared attacking you and you defending yourself."

Mom looks at me. "Let's walk to the Crow's Nest. You'll be warmer inside."

"Cole," she continues as we walk, "if you had told me you spray-painted the wall, I'd have gone into Ms. Delaney's office with you, and we would have worked something out.

Maybe she would have given you a suspension, but at least it would have been for something you did. You should not be suspended for defending yourself against an attacker."

"I don't want to tell her now, Mom."

"I agree. That would be a mistake."

Whew!

I don't have to confess to Delaney.

"For one thing," says Mom, "it would get Mr. Nachman in trouble. You can't give up somebody who's stuck out his neck to help you."

I nod.

The sign for the Crow's Nest is just ahead. Warmth.

"Also," Mom continues, "you've cleaned the wall." She looks at me. "And you've promised you won't do anything like that again. It's misdirected. And it defaces the building."

"I won't, Mom. I'm going to fight back in a different way."

We reach the Crow's Nest and slide into a booth.

"How?"

"I'm going to picket the school tomorrow, with signs about my suspension. But I want to talk to Felipe and Treva about what the signs should say. Is it okay if Treva comes over for dinner tonight?"

'Sure," says Mom. "I made enough lasagna to feed you, me, and Felipe twice over. Heat it up. There's broccoli salad in the fridge, and a chocolate pudding cake. You know how to make garlic bread."

"Thanks, Mom."

"Clear your strategy with me before you implement it," she says.

"Okay. But Mom…"

She raises her eyebrows, to let me know she's waiting.

"Why is Ms. Delaney picking on me? Is it because I protested all the stupid state testing?"

Mom nods. "That's part of the reason, I'm sure. She wants to toe the line and get her bonus if all students take the test. But the main reason she's picking on you, Cole, is because you're intelligent, articulate, and you want to see a different world than the one Ms. Delaney defends." The server drops two menus on the table and holds a glass carafe of coffee in the air, like a question mark. I nod yes to the hot coffee and so does Mom.

"That's why sports franchises get rid of quarterbacks who speak out for racial justice," she says, "and basketball players who do the same. I'm sure Ms. Delaney has it in for Felipe, too. He's Latino, he's bright, he's articulate, he wants social and political justice."

"That's why Dad was framed. Because he fights for justice." I watch Mom sip her coffee. "He's not going to get out early, is he? He'll be in jail until January."

She nods. "The masses are not ready to storm Cook County Jail and release the prisoners."

I think about how wonderful it would be to storm Cook County Jail. Tear it down, from the barbed wire outside to the demeaning visiting booths inside.

"So," Mom says, "I want to see how you propose to fight back. What your strategy will be. Lead, but don't get so far in the vanguard that you're cut off. Do you understand?"

"Uh-huh. Like not getting so far in front of the other runners that they see me and can concentrate on running me down."

She stands up, opens her purse, and hands me a ten dollar bill. "I can't stay, Cole, I have to get back to work. I won't be home until maybe eight. Save me some dinner."

I order a burger and fries. I'd like a shake, too, but between Mom's ten and my four dollars and the ten percent city tax and the tip, I don't have enough.

As I eat, I look around the Crow's Nest. I'm thinking about Dad, wondering what he's doing at this very minute. Man, he's not going to be happy to hear I was suspended.

But I think he'll like the way I handled Jared Anderson.

I'm thinking about Nachman, too, realizing how much I appreciate what he did. Not telling.

Making me write poems.

I wonder which table Nachman sits at each morning when he has breakfast at the Crow's Nest.

CHAPTER 33

"**T**HAT'S NOT HOW MAMÁ MAKES garlic bread." Felipe's looking over my shoulder, crowding me into the counter.

"What do you mean? I haven't even started making it. She doesn't take the bread out of the bag?"

"Your technique," he says. "It's all wrong. The knife is too big."

"Is not," says Treva, coming to stand on my other side. "You need a big knife to slice the loaf down the middle, lengthwise."

"Lengthwise?!" he shouts. "Never! You're supposed to make little cuts halfway through it. Crosswise."

"Nope," she says. "Give it one good whack down the middle lengthwise, slather both sides with butter, olive oil, garlic, put them back together, wrap them in tinfoil, heat them in the oven. Garlic Bread 101, *compadre*."

"Back off, both of you." I lift the knife into the air and wave it around a bit.

"Grump." Treva sits at the kitchen table, which I've set with plates and silverware, napkins and glasses.

"Touchy." Felipe sits across from her.

"Getting suspended does that to you," I say as I start to slice the bread.

"*¡Ayyyyy!*" he wails. "Treva, he is slicing it *diagonalmente!*"

"Frou-frou," she says. "Not the way a serious fighter against injustice would slice garlic bread."

Frou-frou. Interesting word.

"Neither of you is obligated to eat it," I say, brushing melted butter into the partially-cut loaf. "I can eat it all."

Felipe touches his hand to his heart. "You are wrong. I am obligated to eat it because you, my friend, made it. They are never ending, the obligations of a class president."

"And I'm obligated to eat it just to fortify myself for our meeting," says Treva.

Fortify. Good word. We're going to fortify ourselves with food, and then we're going to fortify our position against Delaney.

I take the lasagna out of the oven, put the pan on the counter, and slice the lasagna into rectangles. Then I put a serving spoon into the broccoli salad Mom made.

"How much longer for the garlic bread?" Felipe asks.

"About five minutes," I say.

"Tía Stacey makes delicious lasagna," he tells Treva.

"I can smell it," she says. "How much longer for the garlic bread?"

They keep that up for the next five minutes or so, until the timer goes off and I take out the garlic bread, open the foil, and put the bread alongside the lasagna. "Help yourselves," I say.

And they do. And then I do.

And then Felipe smacks a hand to his forehead. "I completely forgot! Ms. Delaney called me into her office after lunch."

Treva and I look at him.

"You got suspended, too?" I ask.

He shakes his head and swallows his food. "You'll never guess. She called me in to tell me she's approved the Alternative Social Systems discussion club."

"That's great," I say. Treva nods.

"But," says Felipe, examining a piece of garlic bread, "it won't start meeting until after Christmas break."

"What? Why? That's two months away," I say.

He shrugs. "I argued and argued. She wouldn't budge."

Treva frowns. "This is suspicious. That she suspends Cole in the morning and approves our extracurricular club in the afternoon."

"How's that suspicious?" he asks.

"It's like, I don't know, she wants to play you off against one another? Cole bad, Felipe good?"

"Everyone knows Cole bad, Felipe good. Except maybe Cole."

For a while we talk about whether this is a coincidence or a plan on Ms. Delaney's part.

Felipe hesitates about something. Then says, "Mamá is a bit worried."

"About?" I ask.

He leans forward, into the table. Then back. "About everything that is happening. At school. In the world."

Then he shakes his head. "But for the Alternative Social Systems discussion club, we will have to wait 'til January." Suddenly he smiles. "Tío Hank will be home!"

That makes me smile, too.

"Back when I was an anarchist, this long waiting period would have called for severe action," Treva tells us.

"Back when you were an *anarquista*?" Felipe ponders this. "Like, yesterday?"

Treva dismisses his sarcasm with a wave of her hand. "Like weeks ago."

"She's been talking to people," I say. "But she won't say who."

Treva smiles. "Best not to name names."

We kid around for a while longer. "No talking about our strategy until after we've had the chocolate pudding cake," I tell them.

"Any chance of coffee with that pudding cake?" asks Treva.

"Big chance."

We all have second helpings of the lasagna, and then I clear the table and cut the cake into squares.

Felipe and Treva crowd me into the counter again.

"The squares aren't equal," Felipe complains. "Tía Stacey cuts equal pieces."

"How can we discuss equality if the squares aren't equal?" asks Treva. "I think Ms. Delaney suspended Cole for the wrong reason. We need to tell her about his unequal pieces."

"*Sí*. We need to tell her everything Cole does wrong, starting with the garlic bread. She will suspend him for months. I will have to graduate without him."

Treva pats Felipe on the back in commiseration.

"Coffee's ready," I tell her. "Mugs are in the cabinet next to the refrigerator."

I'm the only one who has a second helping of cake.

When we're done we clear the table, move to the front of the house and plop into easy chairs. I take Dad's.

"Okay," I say. "I'm going to fight this suspension. Really fight it. It's unfair to suspend somebody who defended himself against an attack."

"It's like saying we should all let Jared Anderson beat us up," says Treva.

"What is your plan, *hermano*?"

"I want to make posters and hold them up as I march back and forth in front of the school. It's a public sidewalk, so it's my right to do that."

"Great idea!" Treva pumps a fist in the air. "What will the signs say?"

"No Suspension for Cole Renner," Felipe answers.

"Expunge the Suspension!" Treva looks at us for approval.

"Expunge." Felipe tries the word out a couple of times.

"Who's going to understand that?"

"Okay, Erase Cole's Suspension."

"That sounds like we're in grade school," he says.

"I don't want to be fighting for just myself," I say. "This isn't just about my suspension, it's about all suspensions."

Felipe and Treva wait.

"Why does she have the right to suspend a student?" I ask. "Because that's the way the school board sets things up— that somebody else rules us. Why can't we rule ourselves?"

"This is good." Treva twirls a lock of hair in her fingers. "We should have student government. Not token student government, but one with power. Students should determine if a suspension is right or wrong. You can bet that if we rule ourselves, we aren't going to suspend somebody who fights back against a bully."

"But we would uphold expelling Jared Anderson," Felipe volunteers.

"Not necessarily," I argue. "We might make him go to anti-bullying classes for a couple of months."

"Which means we need such classes," Treva points out.

"We need self-defense classes, too," I say. "If the school is going to allow bullies inside its walls, then it has to give us self-defense classes. Look at what Fatima faces every day she's in school."

"Where is Fatima?" asks Treva. "I haven't seen her in, like, three days." She looks at Felipe.

"I don't know," he says. "I've texted her every day, but she doesn't answer. She's not in class."

"Want me to text her?" Treva asks.

"*Sí. Por favor*. I'm worried about her."

Treva takes out her phone and starts texting.

"Self-Defense Classes for Students," says Felipe, spreading his hands outward. "That's a good demand, Cole. Underneath, it should say something like Rescind Cole Renner's Suspension."

"Oh, *rescind*. Nice easy word," Treva says, still typing.

Felipe shrugs. "*Rescindir*."

"Maybe revoke?" I ask. "And that's two posters so far. First one: Student Control Over Suspensions—Revoke Cole Renner's Suspension. Second one: Self-Defense Class for Students—Revoke Cole Renner's Suspension."

"Give Cole Renner a Medal for Busting Jared Anderson's Nose!" That's Treva.

"I like these," says Felipe.

"I want other kids to see them," I say. "So I'm going to be out there walking the sidewalk all day long. I'm going to get there at 7:00 a.m."

Treva sits up and points a finger at me. "Let's make more signs. I can carry one until class starts."

"Me, too," says Felipe.

"And I can bring lots of extra poster board," I say. "Mom and Dad have a stash in the basement. And I'll bring markers. Kids can make their own protest signs."

"¡*Brillante*!"

"In Portland we always sent out a press release before we held an anti-testing demonstration," Treva says, looking at me.

"Good! I wouldn't have thought of that. Mom and Dad have a press release template somewhere on the computer. Mom can give me the newspaper list and I'll send them out tonight."

"I can meet you at the school at seven," Felipe tells me.

"Thanks," I say. "That sounds great."

"I can get there early, too," says Treva, "and start talking to everybody about your suspension. Maybe kind of shoo them in your direction, so they can see the signs." She checks her phone, but I guess there's no text from Fatima. "Oh, another thing! I can write a leaflet, telling everybody what happened. I'll do that when I get home and send it to you tonight. You can make changes and then I'll run it off on my printer. How many should I make?"

"Five hundred?" I ask.

"Okay. What else? What else can we do? Is what Delaney did even legal?"

I shrug. "She says it is. She says she can suspend anybody she wants. She says she has a lot of power, and that Illinois law is on her side."

"On her side and against the students," Treva answers. "We need to organize against the state, too."

"A state that rounds up poor people and ships them away," mutters Felipe. "A state that hates you if you're black or brown or Mexican or Arab or Asian."

"Or female," adds Treva.

"Or poor, or working class," I say.

Mom gets home not long after Felipe and Treva leave. As she eats, I tell her my plans.

"Excellent demands, Cole. Things like student control and self-defense classes not only address today's problems— they help point the way to what the future should be like."

"Yeah," I say. "I learned a bit from you and Dad."

She smiles. "Bring me the computer and I'll show you the press release form and the database of TV stations and local newspapers."

After Mom shows me what to do, I go to my desk and write a press release and send it out. Basically I say that I, Cole Renner, was unjustly suspended from August Mersy High School because I defended myself against a bully and that I'll be protesting this injustice tomorrow morning and afternoon, picketing in front of the school.

"Mom!" I shout down the stairwell. "Can I take Dad's new megaphone with me?"

"Bring it back in good shape," she shouts.

CHAPTER 34

HEN I HOP OFF THE bus Felipe and Treva are already waiting for me, on the public sidewalk in front of August Mersy. Felipe has a stack of posters under one arm and Treva's holding two clipboards.

"Check this out," she says. "I made a petition for kids to sign."

REVOKE COLE RENNER'S SUSPENSION is written across the top, with room for twenty signatures per page. She has more pages underneath the first one.

"Look at the right-hand side of the petition," Felipe urges. I do.

Treva has a little square box after each signature. Above the box she has, **CHECK HERE IF YOU WANT STUDENT CONTROL OVER SUSPENSIONS.**

"Cool," I tell her. "Really great."

She laughs. "You sound funny with a swollen lip."

"He is talking out of one side of his mouth," says Felipe. "We cannot trust him!"

I shrug off my backpack and stash it under the nearest tree on the lawn. The backpack's bulky—Dad's megaphone is inside.

Felipe hands me a sign and takes another for himself. Mine's the SELF-DEFENSE CLASSES poster, his is the STUDENT CONTROL OVER SUSPENSIONS. I notice he used all red and black lettering on the posters—the same colors we scrubbed off the school wall. We walk in opposite directions, me east on Fullerton, Felipe north on Pulaski. Treva stands at the intersection, ready to show kids the petition.

Felipe and I cross paths as he walks east and I walk north. We aren't at it very long before a security guard comes out and asks us what we're doing.

"Protesting my suspension," I tell him.

He tells me I can't do that. I tell him I can, it's a public sidewalk and I'm not setting foot on school property. Treva has her phone aimed at us. The guard notices. He glares at us a while, then goes back into the school.

"I'm moving to the back entrances," Treva calls to us. "To get signatures and send students in this direction."

As she hurries across the school lawn a TV truck pulls up to the curb. Three people climb out. They approach Felipe, who points to me. By this time I'm walking in their direction. They're filming. I'm holding my sign square in front of me, so their cameras pick it up.

A woman comes up to me with a mike in her hand. She sticks it in front of me, almost into my split lip. I rear back. "Are you Cole Renner?" she asks.

"Yes," I say, and before she can ask another question, I continue. "Yesterday I was attacked by a fellow student." I point to my swollen lip as I say this. It's black and blue in a good way—it should show up on camera. "I fought back and broke his nose. Because I fought back, the principal of the school, Ms. Delaney, suspended me for three days."

"Doesn't she have the right to do this, Cole?" asks the reporter.

I think about this, because only part of this is about Delaney and me.

"School principals shouldn't have total authority over what happens in school. Students are citizens. We're thinking, feeling people. We need a voice in what happens to us. We need control over our school lives."

She's about to ask something else, but I rush on. "The attacker and the person he attacks should never be treated the same way. That's what the principal did. She suspended both of us. But only one of us did something wrong."

Now she does stick the mike in my face. "Do you think you'll win?" she asks.

Just as she asks this I look up. Treva is leading students—like maybe *two hundred* students—down the sidewalk toward us.

I try to say something but can't. I'm choked up. I just point.

The two camera guys and the reporter all turn. Then they leave me standing there and head toward the other students.

Which makes me laugh. In a happy way.

Felipe is handing out posters left and right. He's even handing out blank ones, and extra magic markers.

"Let's fight for what's right," I hear him say. "Any one of us could be the next one suspended. Or expelled."

"Let's stand united," I shout over to the group. "We all have the same fight—control over our lives."

Emerald Jackson grabs a blank poster and some markers and begins to write. In no time at all she's chanting the words on her poster: WHOSE SCHOOL? OUR SCHOOL! WE RULE! COLE COOL! Emerald's loud and soon other students are shouting along with her.

And then I see Mr. Nachman walking out the front door, toward us.

The reporter and cameramen run up to him while he's still on school grounds. Probably because he's the only adult around. I see her talking to him and I see him talking into the mike, but I can't hear what they're saying.

Kids are talking to me, pounding me on the back. The size of the crowd keeps growing. Somebody shows me a Tweet. Me, holding a sign. I look around and see just about everyone on their cells.

Eventually the bell rings and kids hand their signs back to Felipe and Treva, who stash them under the tree. They all file into school and I'm left there. Alone.

Back and forth I walk, back and forth. South to north, east to west. When a bus goes by on either Fullerton or Pulaski, I hold up my sign. Some people from the bus shelters come out to talk to me, asking me what happened. Most want to know why I'm doing this. I say that I want to fight back against injustice. Some of them tell me I'm an idealist. Most of them wish me luck.

I keep walking back and forth.

My text signal keeps pinging, but if I stopped to read every text I'd be standing there reading all day long.

But the signal is, like, constant, so I tell myself I'll read five messages every time I complete a circuit.

I'm about to do that when a truck from another TV station pulls up.

I wish I wasn't alone. But everybody else is in school.

The camera people are filming from the minute they step out of the truck. I can see the cameras sweep across the school... across me... my sign... the pile of posters leaning against the tree... my backpack... the bus stop.

"Cole Renner?" asks the reporter.

"Yeah. That's me."

"Got your press release," he says. "Turning on the mike." He holds it toward himself first. "Are you Hank Renner's son?" he asks.

I nod. "I'm Hank and Stacey Renner's son. I wish my father could be here with me, to protest yet another school injustice. But he's in jail for helping neighbors defend their right to a public school."

Man, I don't know how I'm able to say these things so clearly. This is like running a race, seeing the openings in front of me.

The reporter asks me a few more questions, then the three of them pile into the truck and pull away.

I take a break to read my texts.

OMG.

189 texts.

Most from students.

One from mom.

Mom: You're on Channel 2 news! Great answers! Love You!

I send her back a 🖤.

There's a text from Nikki Zurlo, in Ms. Delaney's office. What? I open it.

Nikki: Keep it up, Cole! Don't stop!

Is Nikki telling me that Ms. Delaney is weakening? That I could maybe win?

There's somebody talking to me. I look to see who it is. Somebody I don't know. She says she's a reporter from the *Tribune*. She wants to know if she can interview me and if she can record the interview. I say sure.

That goes on for a while. Newspaper reporters take a lot more time than TV reporters do.

She leaves.

I go back to scrolling the texts. Which are now up to 244.

I'm going to spend the rest of my life just answering texts.

Felipe: Most of hist class on ur side. CU @ noon. Venceremos!

Treva: Lflts gone. 240 signatures!

I hear something and turn.

Kids are coming out the front door.

I look at my watch. Second period.

They're walking toward me. It's my whole English class. Mr. Nachman is with them. When they reach the public sidewalk, he tells me their assignment is to interview me.

So they form a group around me and ask questions.

Jillian's first. She's holding a pen and notebook. The paper kind. "Is this street behavior the public image we tenth graders will have with you and Felipe representing us?"

Whoa.

Street behavior? Public image? Me and Felipe?

Her question is so convoluted I have to think a bit before answering.

"I don't know what you mean by *street behavior*, Jillian, but when injustice is done to people they want to appeal to others, whether it's through writing, speaking, or marching. The streets and sidewalks belong to us: the people."

"Amen," Emerald chants.

"Also," I continue, "Felipe is the elected class president. You're implying I somehow control him, or that I'm the real president and Felipe's just a puppet. You're wrong. Felipe is a strong person and a good class president. I'm not part of student government at all." I feel myself getting more and more angry at all the implications of Jillian's question. I take a deep breath and step back a bit.

"Do you think your actions will inspire others?" asks Emerald.

"I hope so. We should have control over how we're treated. I think we can be fair judges of what's right and what's wrong."

Treva speaks up. "How do you think your actions today compare to Thoreau's actions of civil disobedience?"

I can see Nachman smiling. Probably because I wasn't expecting any questions about Thoreau.

"Um, well, Thoreau did what he did alone. As an individual. I'm not acting alone. I have the help of friends. And I hope the number of friends helping me grows and grows. This is a fight for all of us." I think about Thoreau for a bit. "Unlike Thoreau, I don't particularly want to go to jail." This gets some laughs. "I want to change the power structure in our school. In all schools. So that *we* make the decisions on what we need. If we were in charge, there wouldn't be teaching to the test, for instance." Everyone cheers at this. Except Jillian.

"Boycott state testing!" shouts Emerald, raising a fist.

There are more questions. Including ones on where I bought my poster board, have any neighborhood residents come out to talk to me, and whether Ms. Delaney will let me into school to use the bathroom.

Which, I realize, I need to do.

Just before the bell goes off, they all file back into school and I'm alone again.

Except that Della Kazarian, Dad's defense lawyer, is walking toward me.

CHAPTER 35

"**HI, COLE. HOW ARE YOU** doing?"

"Uh, pretty good. Did my mom ask you to come?"

Ms. Kazarian laughs. "Nope. I came because on the morning news I saw a young man—a tall young man—who comes into my office once a week and gives my secretary fifty dollars for the Euclid Grade School Defense Fund." She gives me a serious look. "I came for him."

I don't know what to say.

"I'm here to represent you, Cole. If you want me to, that is."

Represent me? Like, defend me against Ms. Delaney? That's kind of cool.

But I know we're paying a lot of money for Dad's defense, and giving money to everyone else's defense, too. And I want Dad to come first. He's in jail. I'm only in school.

"Thank you," I say. "I really appreciate that. I wish I could say yes, but… uh, we can't pay for two defenses at once."

She smiles and pats me on the arm. "It's *pro bono*."

"What's that?"

"*Pro bono* comes from the Latin phrase, *pro bono publico*, which means *for the public good*. Today it means work done for free. Donated work. In other words, I wouldn't charge you for this, Cole."

"Oh." I think about this. "What would you do, exactly?"

She looks at her watch. "Tell you what, you could probably use a break. Why don't you take fifteen minutes. I'll stand here and watch the posters and your backpack." She walks over and looks through the posters, then pulls one out. "I'll even march around with this one. We're set, right? I am representing you?"

"Yeah. Thank you!" I look at my watch. "I'll be back in fifteen."

I take off toward the Crow's Nest, running fast. I kind of rush in, order a sandwich to go at the cash register, and head toward the bathroom.

While I wait for my order, I ask if I could have a glass of water. The server pours me one and I gulp it down. She looks at me and pours another. I drink that more slowly.

In fourteen minutes I'm back in front of the school. Ms. Kazarian's the only one there, walking up and down with a sign that says REVOKE COLE RENNER'S SUSPENSION. It doesn't say anything else. I don't know who made it. At least they spelled everything correctly.

"So here's what I want to do, Cole. I want to walk into the school and see the principal. You mentioned her name in the newscast. Ms. Delaney?"

"Yeah, that's right."

"I will demand that she set things right by revoking your suspension and removing all references to it from your student file."

"That sounds great."

She says, "This will take a while."

I nod.

"Keep doing what you're doing. In fact, do more... though I don't know what that could be."

"I have Dad's megaphone," I say, looking at my backpack.

"And you intend to use it how?"

I smile at the way she talks.

"I'm not sure. I haven't used it yet because I don't want anybody to say I'm disturbing the public or other students with the sound. But at lunch time nobody's in class, so I figure that's the time to use it."

She nods. "Good thinking. Do you know what you'll say?"

"Not sure. Do you have any ideas?"

"What would your father do?" she asks.

Just like that, her asking the question tells me what I should do.

"He would make what people want even more visible. So I'm going to call on students to come out and join me. And then to march around the school with me."

She grins. "Great plan. Keep the times around the school finite. Say two times around the school for sure, maybe three. Enough to make an impact, but they need time to get back to class. And Cole?"

I look at her.

"Keep your demands in the foreground."

Foreground. An F word. She must mean keep my demands up front. Prominent. I know Dad would give me the same advice. Mom, too.

"Got it," I tell her. "And we should all be chanting."

"Excellent," she says, looking at her watch. "When it's done, come back here, keep carrying the signs, and wait for me."

I tell her I will, and she walks away, going into August Mersy through the front door.

The sun is starting to shine. I take off my cap and stuff it into my backpack. I unzip my jacket. Then I strap the megaphone over my shoulder and around my waist, pulling the straps until the belts are snug. I hold the megaphone in my right hand, turn it on, and give it a *Testing-one-two-three* try.

Pretty loud. Kids in front of the school will definitely hear it. The cafeteria's on the north side, so I walk to that end of the sidewalk. I want the sound waves to go straight into the cafeteria.

When I hear the lunch bells go off, I switch on the power. Then I start talking.

"This is Cole Renner. Fight for our rights. Join me on the public sidewalk during lunch break. Show your support. March with me, twice around August Mersy. Twice around August Mersy. Join with me. Protest unfair suspensions. Protest injustice. This is Cole Renner."

I keep it up, nonstop, aiming the megaphone at the cafeteria.

Treva and Felipe are the first ones out the door. But they were coming to help anyway. Will there be anybody behind them? I keep talking. "Join with me. March twice around our school. March against unfair suspensions. March for student control over suspensions. March for self-defense classes. March for student power."

Out of the corner of my eye I keep watching the front door.

Students aren't just coming out. They're *pouring* out.

I see Felipe and Treva look behind themselves. Then they run to the tree and pick up the posters, handing them to anybody who wants one.

A couple hundred students are coming toward me, carrying signs. More are coming out the door. "Felipe!" I shout, covering the megaphone with my hand. "Can you lead the march?"

He runs to the front of the crowd and points in the direction they should go. Eastward around the school. I keep talking into the megaphone, toward the cafeteria. More students come out.

"Cole, let's go," says Treva, grabbing my arm. "You should be near the front of the march. With the megaphone."

She's right.

The two of us race past everybody, find the front of the crowd, and step in behind Felipe.

"Look!" he says, pointing.

Another TV crew.

I start chanting into the megaphone. *"One, two, three, four—We are students, hear us roar!"*

Everybody picks it up. There must be three or four hundred of us now. With more students coming out of the side doors.

Treva motions I should give her the megaphone. I do, and she chants: *"Five, six, seven, eight—We will command our fate!"*

I love her chant.

Hundreds of voices pick up on that, too. Treva and I keep passing the megaphone back and forth, chanting.

We go around the school once.

People from the neighborhood come out on their porches to see what's happening.

The TV crew is racing up and down the sidewalk, filming.

Security guards come rushing out of the school. Then they just stand there, on school property. Arms crossed.

As if anybody wants to go back to school.

We march around twice, and then I stop and face everybody.

"Thank you all for coming out," I say into the megaphone. "We're standing up for the rights we should have, but don't. Whether my suspension gets revoked or not, we're letting Ms. Delaney and the Chicago Board of Education know that we know what's right and what's wrong—and we're going to fight for what's right."

Kids cheer at this.

The first warning bell goes off, letting everyone know the lunch period is over. They file past me, telling me they're glad I'm doing this. I recognize a little more than half of everybody who's there. Felipe recognizes them all. And I swear he manages to say something to just about everyone.

The whole day so far has felt like a roller coaster ride. The slow climb up: that's when I'm out there by myself. Then the downward rush, the excitement of so many other people working together to change things.

I lean against the tree and eat my sandwich. When it's gone, I straighten up, change the sign I'm carrying, and begin walking the sidewalk. Back and forth, back and forth.

When I see Ms. Kazarian walking out the front door, that's when I remember that she was inside, talking to Ms. Delaney.

She comes up to me and smiles. "I could hear the chanting inside Ms. Delaney's office." She chuckles to herself.

She reaches into her briefcase and, pulling out a sheet of paper, hands it to me.

I have to read it three times, the words just won't register.

"You've won, Cole. Your suspension has been revoked. As you can see, that letter of agreement from Ms. Delaney promises that any and all mention of a suspension will be removed from your record."

I can't believe it.

I won.

"Wow." That's all I manage to say at first.

"Thank you," I say next. "Wow. How did you do this?"

"First, let me say that I'll be back next week to inspect your student records, Cole. To make sure that all reference to a suspension has, in fact, been removed."

I nod. I don't trust Delaney, either.

"Then, let me say that you did it yourself. You and your friends and everybody who came out in your support. You organized well, you spoke well, you fought well."

I nod, still fazed by the whole thing.

Ms. Kazarian smiles at me. "I did happen to mention to Ms. Delany that I intended to contact national news programs this evening, and that they would be out in the morning. And I implied you would get talk-show interviews. You're a good speaker, Cole."

Wow.

"That's… that's great. I don't know what to say."

She pats me on the arm. "It's my pleasure, Cole. I'm seeing Hank tomorrow morning and I can't wait to tell him all about this."

"And now," she says, glancing at her watch, "you should probably get yourself back into school."

Crap!

Why couldn't this have been settled at 3:30 instead of 1:30?

I say goodbye to Ms. Kazarian, pick up my backpack, and walk onto school property.

CHAPTER 36

E: WANNA GO 2 MOVIE SAT NGT?

After writing and rewriting the text a dozen times, I hit Send.

Treva: 🖤 Where?

Her reply is, like, instant.

Me: Regal City, Western. Off wrk @ 4. CU there @ 6?

Treva: Will B there. Lv protest sgns at home. 😊

Felipe studies me as we lean against the fence, waiting for Treva. Now it's me that other students high-five and pat on the back.

"You look *muy contento*," he says during a lull. "Because you're back in school?"

I shake my head. "Treva said she'd go to a movie with me. This Saturday."

Felipe grins. "She asked you?"

I shake my head. "I asked her."

We talk back and forth until Treva arrives. Then Felipe gets serious. "I went to Ms. Delaney's office three times yesterday."

"What? Why?" I ask.

"The signed petitions. All those X marks on whether we should have student control over suspensions and expulsions."

"What'd she say?" Treva asks.

"She didn't. She wouldn't see me."

I look at him. "She can refuse to see a student who wants to see her?"

He shrugs. "Maybe it's never come up before."

All three of us laugh at this.

"But your class president is fearless. I made copies of the sheets and put them in an envelope and asked Nikki Zurlo to give them to Ms. Delaney."

Treva points a finger at him. "Making copies of the sheets was a good idea."

"Your class president is clever. And careful."

Felipe starts to tell us that he's going to meet with the other class presidents to see if they agree about student control over suspensions and expulsions—but all of a sudden Fatima and Salma walk up to us.

"Fatima!" all three of us say at once. "Salma! Where have you been?"

Then I notice they're holding poster boards. But I can't see if anything's written on them because they're holding them downward.

"Are you okay?" Treva asks them.

Fatima shakes her head. So does Salma.

"Hasna has been deported," says Fatima.

"What?" I manage.

"ICE came for her brother last Monday, very early in the morning. He and his wife are college students. Hasna lived with them." Fatima is speaking so softly it's hard to hear her.

"I thought Hasna was a citizen," Treva says.

Salma and Fatima both shake their heads. "We were born here," says Fatima, indicating herself and Salma, "but Hasna came here five years ago."

"Terror," Felipe growls. "This is terror. Terrorizing people who aren't citizens."

Salma coughs. Clears her throat. "We were afraid," she says. "That's why we didn't come to school."

"Did somebody threaten you?" I ask, thinking of Jared Anderson.

Fatima shakes her head. "We are afraid that the government wants to deport all Muslims, whether we were born here or not."

Nobody says anything.

Fatima puts an arm around Salma's shoulder. "And we needed to give comfort to Hasna's aunt and uncle, who are afraid for Hasna and her brother. And for themselves."

"The ruling class exploits differences between us and them," says Treva, "trying to make us glad we aren't them—immigrants, Native Americans, African Americans, lesbians, gays, homeless, mentally ill, you name it. I hate capitalism!"

Fatima looks at me. "But then we saw Cole on television, marching in front of the school. And later we saw that he won."

Salma nods. "So now we are here. And we, too, are going to demonstrate." She holds up the sign she's carrying. On it is a large picture of Hasna. Her name is written at the top of the photo, in English and Arabic. At the bottom is written, YOUR FELLOW STUDENT WAS DEPORTED FOR BEING MUSLIM. AND BEING ARABIC.

Fatima holds up her sign. It has Hasna's photo, and the words, STOP THE DEPORTATIONS. STAND WITH IMMIGRANTS!

"We are going to march in front of the school before classes begin, and on our lunch hour, and for half an hour after the last period," Fatima says.

"Me, too," says Felipe.

"And me," Treva and I say in unison.

"Can I write something on your sign?" I ask Fatima.

She hands me her sign and, along with it, a marker she pulls out of her purse.

I draw an octagon shape, like the ones I watched Hasna draw in geometry class. Then I begin to fill it in with more lines, the way she did.

Fatima laughs. "That is a good way to remember Hasna," she says, "but maybe I should fill in the lines for you?"

I hand her the marker and in no time she creates a beautiful design. I can see that it's more complex than I could have done.

Then Felipe writes on Salma's sign. WHO IS NEXT? STOP DEPORTATIONS NOW!

Treva takes a turn, too. She writes on Fatima's sign: ICE DEPORTS OUR FRIENDS—DOWN WITH ICE!

So the five of us go to the same sidewalk I walked all over yesterday, and we begin walking back and forth.

Some kids come up to us, mainly Latino, Arabic, and Korean kids, and ask us about Hasna. Next thing I know, Hannah Iwata's there, kneeling on the sidewalk, taking photos. I hope they get into *The Fire*.

Across the street I spot the same ICE car that keeps coming back, parked on a corner, with two people standing outside it, looking right at us. They're wearing dark blue uniforms. Handguns and billy clubs holstered to their belts, and microphone clips attached to their shoulders.

They're standing with their legs wide, their arms crossed.

Everything about them, especially their hostility, shouts out Police State!

FOREGO

Fee fi fo fum
We smell the blood
Of rebeldom

Fee fi fo fum
Black, White, Brown
To us all are one

Fee fi fo fum
You'll not escape
Your shackledom

Fee fi fo fum
You must forego
Your rights or run

That evening Mom and I set up the computer in Mrs. Green's storage room so we can talk to Dad. Mrs. Green comes with us because each of her two granddaughters drew a card for Dad. They both go to Euclid Grade School. The first grader drew flowers and a heart. The third grader drew a picture of the school and wrote *Thank You for Saving Our School*.

When we connect with Dad, Mrs. Green asks him how he's doing, then places each card in front of the screen, one at a time. "From Casey and Colleen," she says.

Dad smiles and thanks her. "Be sure to give my thanks to both Casey and Colleen," he says. "And please save me the cards."

She says she will, then leaves us to talk to Dad alone.

"Tall Stuff," he says. "Saw you on television. Great work!"

"I learned from you and Mom," I say. Then I talk to him in code, trying to tell him about Hasna and how Fatima and Salma came to school with posters. I think he gets some of what I'm trying to say.

"Watch your back," he warns.

Dad tells us that he's now teaching six reading classes and two history classes. "But not a single book I requested for the library has been ordered."

He and Mom tell each other that the Cook County Department of Corrections is never going to order *The Communist Manifesto*. Or any other book on Dad's list.

The time is up way too soon, like it always is. We tell Dad we'll visit him Sunday.

On Saturday I run home after work, shower, and dress in clean clothes.

"Any particular movie you want to see?" I ask Treva as we head toward the popcorn stand and study the movie titles and times.

We buy some popcorn and stand there eating it, spilling some. We agree on a movie and buy our tickets. Then we sit in the back, where nobody else is sitting.

It's easy for us to see over the heads of people.

CHAPTER 37

THE WEEK OF THANKSGIVING MEANS we have three free days—no school. On Wednesday morning I sleep in, figuring I'll take a three-mile run later in the afternoon. Breakfast at Felipe's house is an hour later than usual. Everybody wants to sleep in. And Felipe has invited Treva, Fatima, and Salma to breakfast. During Thanksgiving week everyone seems more generous. People on the street and in stores are friendlier. I hope that's true in Cook County Jail, too.

The closer we've gotten to Thanksgiving, the more I've been thinking how Dad deserves to be home. Not in jail. At home he'd have good food. And freedom. Two F words. Thinking about Dad not having them chokes me up.

I swallow hard and work to put myself "in the moment," as Coach says. Here and now. This spot on the race course.

Felipe has a reason for inviting us. Well, not me, 'cause I'm there every Wednesday morning. He wants us to brainstorm ideas for both student council and for the Alternative Social Systems club.

The breakfast table is more crowded than usual. Benito, Juliana, and Isabella are very quiet. They keep looking at Fatima and Salma's hijabs. Tía tells them the hijab is like a rebozo, only smaller.

"Mamá," says Felipe, "please sit down and eat with us."

"No, no. I will eat later. I have much to do on the Thanksgiving meal." She looks at me. "Have you made the cranberry-orange *áspide* yet, Coleto?"

"Tomorrow morning," I promise.

Tía gives the whole table an inspection, I guess to make sure it can hold up under the amount of food. Then she walks back to the kitchen.

Felipe grins. "Have you ever made cranberry-orange aspic?"

"Not yet. How hard can it be? Couple bags of frozen cranberries, some oranges and other stuff."

"Cinnamon," says Fatima.

"Cloves," adds Salma.

"Simmered," says Treva. "Not boiled. Then refrigerated."

"What are you doing for Thanksgiving?" I ask her as I eat some black beans and scrambled eggs.

She smiles. "We're spending it with my uncle. He's a great cook. And I don't have to make the cranberry aspic. Relish. Sauce. Topping."

I love it when she talks in synonyms. I think she does it just for me.

Breakfast goes on a while because we're all having fun. Juliana and Isabella and Benito leave first, taking their dishes into the kitchen. Then the rest of us follow.

The dirty dishes are stacked higher than textbooks. "Can we help you?" I ask Tía.

"No, no," she admonishes, shooing us away. "Juliana and Isabella will help. You go with Felipe into the front room and have your meeting."

So we do.

Fatima and Salma sit on the couch next to the bay window, which is full of Christmas cacti, jade trees, kalanchoes and other plants that Felipe keeps buying at Mrs. Green's. Tía loves her collection of plants.

Felipe pulls a wooden chair up to face them, his tablet in hand.

"Where's your gavel?" I ask. "Don't all class presidents get one?"

"Ms. Delaney's afraid to give me one."

Treva and I grab wooden chairs and place them so they face the plants and the window. The five of us form three sides of a rectangle, with the plants and bay windows forming the fourth side.

Felipe begins. "Our world is full of wrongs," he says. "Injustices of all kinds. We need to speak up, to help change the world."

"It is up to us," says Fatima. "Our generation. I do not see how the world can survive all the invasions, the bombings, the civil wars."

We talk about these things, back and forth, each of us giving examples. Each of us bringing in other injustices.

"Deportations are cruel," Salma says. "They separate families."

"And they're arbitrary," adds Treva. "ICE just picks names, rounds people up and deports them. That randomness makes people even more afraid."

"It's meant to," I say.

"So," says Felipe, typing on his tablet, "do we want student council to ask for something like August Mersy High observing a pro-immigrant week?"

"Part of the pro has to include the anti," I argue. "We're pro immigrant, and we have to be anti-deportation. We want kids to go beyond just being pro—we want them to fight the roundups and deportations."

Back and forth we go, with lots of ideas. A demonstration every week? No, kids would get tired of that. A tenth-grade educational assembly once a month? Our own newsletter? What would we call ourselves? Should we all volunteer to write articles for *The Fire*? Build an August Mersy contingent for every major demonstration against injustice? What other kids are interested in social justice? Can we get them to come to meetings and talk about what they think is important and what we can do?

After about an hour I stand up. "Stretch time," I announce, doing a few backbends.

Fatima and Salma stand, too, stretching their arms wide.

Felipe sits, typing away.

Treva stands and looks out the window.

She freezes.

"ICE!" she shouts. "ICE! Immigration!" she points out the bay window.

An ICE car is in the street, its doors open, two uniformed men walking toward the house. Felipe's house

Fatima and Salma back away, into a corner.

Felipe jumps to his feet, dropping his tablet, staring out the window.

"Mamá!" he shouts at the top of his lungs. "¡*Inmigración! ¡Corre, corre!*" He runs to the front door, throws the deadbolt, and leans against the door.

In the kitchen I see Tía drop the wooden spoon and run out the back door.

"Stall them," I say to Treva as I run after Tía.

On the way out I grab Felipe's hoodie off the peg rack near the back door. I grab mine, too. And a couple of caps, I don't even look to see what, just something.

Tía Veronica. She must not be a citizen.

I didn't know that.

She's running up the alley, heading north.

"Tía!" I shout, but not too loud. "¡*Camine, no corra! ¡No corra, no corra!*"

She stops running and walks. I take really long steps and catch up to her.

"Put this on," I say, handing her Felipe's jacket. "Quick. Pull up the hood."

She's super quick about it. The alley's about to intersect the next east-west street. I don't want to look backward, in case ICE is coming toward the back door. I push Tía around the corner, east, then take her hand and pull her with me onto the sidewalk.

My body screams *run* like it's the last quarter mile! But my head screams *be smart, be calm!*

Cars are parked front to back, filling both sides of the street. I pull us in front of a van, stop, and put on my hoodie. I leave the hood down, just so ICE doesn't see two hoodie-ed people. I don't want us to get shot.

From in front of the van I peek to see if ICE is coming down this street. They must have broken into Felipe's house by now. That's what ICE does: it crashes through doors to grab people and deport them.

The coast is clear. I'm still holding Tía's hand. We cross quickly to the north side, slip between two more cars, and then I spot a house that isn't fenced. We walk from its front to its back, and now we're in another alley. I turn east again, and then north.

We zigzag back and forth like this, walking quickly but not conspicuously. At least I hope not. I've never been more grateful for Chicago's alleys than I am right now.

A siren shrieks. We both jump.

I can't tell which direction the sound is coming from.

We're in an alley, where people's fenced-in back yards have gates. Some locked, some not. Some wooden fences, some chain link. I'm tall enough to see over most of the wooden fences if I jump up for a second. Which I do.

Wooden fence. Jump. Clear. No BEWARE OF DOG signs. I reach an arm over and unlatch the gate. We slip into some stranger's back yard. I hope nobody's home. I latch the gate. Tía and I squat down alongside the garbage cans, our backs to the fence.

The siren screams louder.

And louder.

A car comes screeching down the alley. Blue lights flash. The blue glare bounces off the back windows of the houses.

I keep staring at the back windows of the house whose back yard we're in. I'm so afraid somebody is home. So afraid they'll look out their back window to see what the sirens are about. They'll see us, and they'll call the cops.

More screeching as a second car races down the alley. More sirens. More blue lights.

Tía and I huddle there.

I see that she's shaking.

I put my arms around her. *"Está bien,"* I whisper. *"Espereremos un tiempito."* We'll wait a while.

She nods, grabs me and holds me.

We wait there for ten minutes. There's no sound anywhere.

Finally we stand, unlock the gate, and leave.

"¡Los niños!" Tía cries. She reaches into the pockets of Felipe's hoodie. Then her dress pocket, looking for her phone.

"No llame," I beg her. "Maybe they can trace your position. Please don't call." But I'm worried about Felipe and Treva and Fatima and Salma, too. And Benito and Juliana and Isabella.

"Mi teléfono está en la cocina," she says after searching her pockets three times. "Please call, Coleto."

I don't know what to do. "Tía," I argue, "I'm not sure it's safe for me to call Felipe. They might be tracing all your phones." Even mine, I think.

"Debemos regresar,' she says, telling me we have to go back. "I must make certain they are safe."

Tía turns back.

I grab her arm.

"Wait," I say. "Just let me think a minute."

She watches while I think.

"I'll text Fatima," I say.

Me: We're OK U all OK?

Tía and I watch my text app, waiting. After a few seconds we see a reply.

Fatima: OK here. Where U?

All of a sudden, I'm on guard. Is this really Fatima? Is it Felipe using her phone?

Or is it ICE?

Me: Later.

I hit Send, then I shut down my phone. I don't really know if that works or not, as far as tracing signals goes. But it's the only thing I can think of.

"Tía," I say, "let's go to someplace else, find a Starbucks. Maybe they'll let me use their phone. I can call Mom and she can call Felipe to make sure everything's okay."

But everything isn't okay. What's Tía going to do—go back home?

She thinks about this a while.

"If we go back, they'll grab you and deport you," I plead, hoping she'll listen. Hoping Treva, Felipe, and everybody else really is okay.

"My purse is at home," she says. "No CTA pass, no money."

That's a yes, I think.

"We'll walk," I say. "Starbucks are everywhere."

"Starbucks will not let you use their phone. I know a *cantina* that will."

CHAPTER 38

"GO TO BARNEY," SAYS MOM. "Tell me you understand."

It takes me a second, then I get it. "Yeah. I do."

"Keep your phone off. Wait for me. It'll take a few hours. I'll call Mrs. Green and tell her we have a family emergency."

She hangs up and I look at the phone. Then I hand it back to the cantina owner.

"Gracias," I say.

He looks at Tía, and he looks at me, then he looks back at Tía.

"Sit, please," he says, pointing to a table. "And eat."

"No tenemos dinero," Tía tells him.

Which isn't exactly true, because I might have five or six dollars on me. But that's not enough to buy two meals, even at a Mexican *cantina*.

"*Págame luego,*" he says.

"*Sí.*" I promise I'll pay him later.

He doesn't even ask what we want, just brings us two plates of rice and beans and burritos.

I eat everything on my plate, but Tía barely touches hers.

The cantina owner boxes up her food and hands it to her. Tía is staring into space and doesn't see it. I take the box. "*Gracias.*"

And then I take Tía's arm and guide her out the door. "We have to walk another mile," I tell her. "To the garage Dad rents."

She nods.

We walk east and south. I keep to the alleys wherever I can. Tía walks alongside me, but she's not really there. I tell her where to cross, but she just comes to a stop. So I take her hand and she follows me from one alley to another.

"Tía, why did you run? You aren't a citizen?"

"*Sí.* No citizen. No Green Card." She starts explaining why. After Juliana and Isabella were born, she stopped working. She had no time to study for citizenship papers, it was more important that Tío get his. She forgot to renew her Green Card. Then she became afraid to reapply. "*Los fríos,*" she whispers. It's complicated, and I understand only some of it. I understand *Los fríos,* though: the cold ones. The ones who have no heart or soul.

I lead us north and east, sticking to the side streets. Mostly sticking to the alleys that run behind garages.

We're going to the garage where Dad keeps his Suzuki. Because it's a deep purple color, when I was in grade school I used to call the bike Barney, after the cartoon dinosaur.

When we get to the garage I look around. No cars driving by. Nobody peeking out their window that I can see. I unlock the side door and Tía and I step inside. I flip on the light switch, close the door behind me, lock it from the inside, and put Tía's food on Dad's workbench.

Barney is there, under an old nylon cover.

Tía touches the motorcycle. "*Tu papá* took me on a ride once," she says. "And he let Carlos ride it himself."

I look around for the electric heater Dad keeps in the garage. I find it, plug it in and turn it on. "Mom says we might have to wait a long time," I say. "You should eat something, Tía."

"I am worried," she says. "Are you sure *los niños* are okay?"

I think no, they are not okay — they've heard the police pounding on the door, seen their brother try to prevent ICE from entering, seen their mother run out the back door to escape. "Felipe said everybody is fine," I tell her. "He'll take care of them."

"Carlos," she says. "He will be angry."

"Angry? At ICE?"

She shakes her head. "At me. He has told me over and over to study for citizenship papers."

I find a folding chair in a corner and open it for her. She sits on it. I lean against the workbench. "I always thought you were a citizen, Tía."

She shakes her head. "We have told nobody. Nobody. Felipe wanted you to know, but Carlos forbid him from talking about it. Ever. And he kept telling me to study."

She stares at the wall, where Dad had hung pegboards that hold tools, gaskets, and cans of spray paint. "I was always so busy with the children. It is all my fault. We will all suffer because of me."

"It's not your fault, Tía. You should have the right to live here without being terrorized."

She shakes her head. "No. It is my fault. Whatever happens, it will be because of me."

I begin to pace back and forth in the narrow garage, but that seems to make Tía nervous, so I stop and push myself up onto Dad's workbench. I sit there with my legs dangling down.

Two or three hours go by. I try to not look at my watch.

Finally, we hear a key in the lock. I jump off the bench. Tía just sits and stares.

The door opens and Mom walks in, followed by Bianca. Bianca grabs Tía and the two of them hold each other. Hard. They talk in really rapid Spanish, their words interrupting each other. As far as I can tell, they're talking about citizenship, Green Cards, and ICE.

Mom's holding a big shopping bag. She puts it on the floor and we wait while Tía and Bianca talk. Mom asks me what happened, and I tell her.

She hugs me. "I'm so proud of you, Cole."

Tía pulls away from Bianca and hugs Mom. Tía's crying. Mom tells her she's strong and will get through this.

My stomach feels hollow, like there's a hole in it that can't be filled. All I can think of is Felipe, and what will happen to him if his mother is deported. Will the whole family move to Mexico to be with her?

Mom turns and starts to take clothes out of the shopping bag. "This is for you, Verónica. All the clothes in the bag are for you."

She pulls out a heavy sweater. Tía pulls the sweater on over Felipe's hoodie.

Bianca puts her hands on Tía's shoulders. "You must hide for a while. I will call a lawyer I know and we will go to Immigration and see what we can do." She waits until Tía nods. "Cole and Stacey will see Carlos and Felipe tonight. It is best if I am not seen at your house too much. That would encourage ICE to follow me. If they aren't already."

Mom hands Bianca the shopping bag. Bianca reaches into it and brings out three boxes. She opens one, pulls out a phone, and hands it to Tía. Then she pulls out two more boxes, each with a phone in it. I watch as she programs phone numbers into the phones.

"Carlos will call you tonight," she tells Tía. "After that, you can call him on this phone if it's an emergency. But you can't call *anybody* else." She nods toward Mom. "Except for Stacey. Her number is in the phone, too. Each call increases the risk of discovery. *¿Entiendes, mija?*"

"*Sí.* Yes. I understand. I won't call any number but the one for Carlos."

"Or the one for me," Mom reminds her.

Tía nods. She looks at her phone. Then she puts it in the pocket of her sweater. She keeps her hand inside the pocket.

"We're waiting for a knock on the door," says Mom.

We are?

I look at the door, as if somebody is already there.

"I have a friend who will be here soon," Bianca tells Tía. "You and I will go with her, and I will stay with you tonight. We will talk about what to do."

"Do I know this person?" Tía asks.

Bianca shakes her head. "No. But you will like her. She will take you into her home for a few days. Until you and Carlos decide what to do."

Tía frowns. "Tomorrow is Thanksgiving." She starts to cry.

Mom and Bianca put their arms around her.

Not too much later, there's a knock on the door. Mom unlocks it.

A short blonde woman steps into the garage. She has a head full of curly hair, like an Afro except that it's pale yellow.

Bianca introduces her as Gretchen. The next thing I know Gretchen's speaking Spanish, telling Tía that she is welcome to stay with her and her husband for as long as necessary.

Bianca, Gretchen, and Tía walk out of the garage. I'm surprised it's already dark out there. I look at my watch. 5:30 p.m.

Mom and I watch them get into Gretchen's car. A Volvo. They drive away.

I unplug the garage heater and grab the bag of food from the *cantina*. Mom and I look around to make sure everything's okay. Then Mom turns off the light and we leave.

Forty-five minutes later we knock on the door to Felipe's house.

Tío Carlos pulls the door open so hard I think he'll tear it off its hinges. Felipe's behind him.

"Where is Verónica?" he asks Mom.

"Let's take a walk," she says. "In case they've bugged the house."

"What?! How could they?"

"Papá," says Felipe, "Tía Stacey *tiene razón*. I'll get your jacket."

"Who will watch the kids?" Mom asks.

"Benito," he replies.

The four of us walk down the street. We pass a bus stop. "Next bus stop," Mom says.

We find it and the four of us sit down. There's nobody else around. I guess everybody is home from work and getting ready for Thanksgiving.

Tío and Felipe ask a lot of questions, first of me, then of Mom. They want to know everything that happened from the time Tía and I ran out the back door. I fill them in on the first part of the day, and Mom takes over from when she called Bianca. She pulls out one of the two burner phones and gives it to Tío Carlos, telling him that it's programmed with two numbers: hers, and Tía's. I'm not sure it's really a burner phone unless you use it once, then toss it. But that doesn't matter. It's a phone that can't be traced. We hope.

"You and Verónica will talk," says Mom, "and decide what to do."

"What can we do?" demands Felipe. "ICE wants to deport Mamá."

Tío sighs. "We will talk about it, Felipe. You and me."

Felipe nods.

A bus wheezes its way toward us. Stops. Spews exhaust everywhere.

The bus driver opens the doors and stares at us. Felipe shakes his head.

The bus moves on.

And then we move on, too, walking back to Felipe's house, where we say good night.

"You will come tomorrow ¿*no?*" asks Carlos. "For the Thanksgiving we had planned?"

"Yes," Mom and I say together.

They go up the stairs to their house, and Mom and I decide we'd rather walk home than wait for a bus.

We walk straight east on Fullerton, in plain sight of whoever's looking. We aren't running or hiding.

"Mom. Have you ever done this before? Helped somebody escape ICE?"

"No, Cole, I haven't."

"Has Dad?"

"No."

I think about this a while. "What about Bianca?"

Mom looks at me. "I've never asked her."

I think. "But you knew to call her."

Mom smiles a small smile. "I suspected she would be a good person to call. And I was right."

We walk slowly. I'm thinking about Bianca, wondering how long she's been helping people hide from ICE. Wondering if she was doing this when she was sixteen years old and punched the teacher who told her to speak English or go back to Mexico. Mostly, though, I'm trying not to think about Felipe and what's going to happen to him if Tía is deported.

We're halfway home when Mom stops in the middle of the sidewalk, shouting "Oh, no! Cole!"

I look all around, to see if somebody's about to jump us. But there's nobody there.

"No, no, NO!" she shouts.

"Mom! What?!"

"It's Wednesday night! We missed our phone call with Dad!"

CHAPTER 39

 OM SITS AT THE KITCHEN table, head in hands. "I don't know what to do," she groans. "Dad will be worried about us. There's no way to reach him."

"Can you call Ms. Kazarian? Can she get a message to him?"

Mom shakes her head. "Tomorrow is Thanksgiving. I don't want to bother her. I'll call the jail tomorrow and see what they say."

"I can go there tomorrow and ask them in person to give him a message," I say.

She reminds me that the jail won't let "unaccompanied minors" through the door.

We see Dad again on Sunday morning. I hope we can get a message to him between now and then.

But I'm betting we can't.

Mom and I run through more possibilities, but we can't come up with anything.

"Go to bed, Cole," she says. "It's late and you look beat."

"So do you."

"I have four more pies to bake for tomorrow."

"Can't you just forget about them?" I ask. "I mean, everyone would understand."

She stands up, goes to a cupboard, and begins pulling out bowls. "No. If it were me hiding out, Verónica would bake the pies she promised."

I watch Mom a while, thinking I should offer to help. Thinking I would mess up the pies. So I go upstairs to my room and sit on my bed, my head in my hands.

That's just what Mom was doing—sitting at the table with her head in her hands. Maybe that's what Dad's doing, sitting on his cot in jail. And Tía.

I straighten up.

What's going to happen to Tía? She can't hide out forever.

What's going to happen to Felipe? If his mother's deported, his father might move the whole family to Mexico.

Not *might*.

Would.

My legs and arms twitch. I run my hands down my jeans, rubbing them up and down like I'm trying to start a friction fire.

Felipe and I have been friends forever.

For some reason I think of Treva's father, who's gone forever.

Treva!

Felipe said she was okay, but I haven't talked to her. I grab my phone to see if she's been texting.

Shit.

My phone is still *off*.

I turn it back on. It takes forever.

No. Two minutes is not forever.

Only forever is forever.

Finally it comes on.

Three texts from Treva.

First Text: U OK?

Second Text: Cole?

Third Text: Let me know UR OK

I type.

Am OK. U?

I hit Send and wait.

And keep waiting.

Then I look at my watch.

It's midnight.

I kick off my shoes and flop onto my bed, telling myself that Treva's probably asleep.

How did this happen? The ICE raid on Felipe's house. How did it happen?

Why, I mean. Why did it happen?

Did somebody call ICE and tell them about Tía Verónica not being a citizen?

I didn't know. How would anybody know?

Maybe they didn't, maybe they just reported the Ramirez household in general.

Jared Anderson?

Yeah, he could have. He hates Latinos.

Jillian?

Yeah, she could have, just so she could be class president.

Muffled sounds from downstairs seep through the floor and walls. It used to make me happy, hearing them, because that meant Mom and Dad were downstairs, doing something that made them happy. Or something that had to be done. Now the sounds of pots and pans are strange clankings. Like somebody trying to break out of prison.

Ms. Delaney.

She asked Felipe about his mother. And about Bianca. It made him nervous.

Ms. Delaney doesn't want Felipe to be class president because she thinks he's a troublemaker. Ms. Delaney especially doesn't want Felipe and me taking part in another test-boycott this coming spring. If not enough students take the test, Ms. Delaney doesn't get her big bonus.

And the test companies will make less profit.

Is it our fault? Mine and Felipe's?

I cross and recross my ankles about a thousand times. I flop onto my stomach and then onto my back. And then do the same thing again and again. My mind spins round in circles.

Tía and Tío. Was it because they were part of the thousand people surrounding Euclid Grade School, demanding it stay open?

Bianca. If she helps people escape from ICE, is this ICE's retaliation?

Dad. Was it because he fought to save Euclid Grade School from people who want to sell schools to private companies for profit?

Profit.

Profit.

It's all about private profit.

Capitalist profit. Not public profit, like free schools and free health care.

Private profit. For mansions, yachts, and to buy and control armies that invade other countries.

Profit.

Fuck profit!

What about our *lives?* What about our so-called right to life, liberty, and the pursuit of happiness?

Profit stomps all over life, all over liberty, and way, way all over the pursuit of happiness.

Me, to Treva and Felipe: Meet 9 am @ fence?

I wait, but nobody texts back. So I open my tablet and write.

There's only one F word in the whole world for what has happened.

FUCK

Fuck you,
you capitalist fucks,

you've fucked up my best friend's life,
which means you've fucked up my life,

THE F WORDS

you've fucked over billions of lives,

fucked over the whole world.

And I will fight you
the rest of my life,

I will fight you forever,

you contemptible
fuckheart
fuckers.

CHAPTER 40

'M THE FIRST ONE AT the fence, but I see Treva a block away, so I walk to meet her.

"Are you okay?" she asks. "Is Mrs. Ramirez okay?"

"I was so worried about you," I say. "I didn't want to leave you there. But I had to help Tía."

She reaches out a hand toward my face, then draws it back, almost before I can register what she's doing.

I grab her hand and hold it.

I grab her other hand and hold it.

Our faces move close. Our foreheads touch.

"Cole."

"What?"

"If you let go of my hands, I can hold you."

That sounds even better. I let go and as Treva holds me I hold her, too. She smells so good. And she feels warm.

After a bit, I pull back. "Treva. Can I kiss you?"

She pulls her head back to look at me. "I don't know. Can you?"

I grin at that.

Then I press my lips to hers.

Hers are warm and cushiony. She tastes even better than she smells.

I could stand like this forever… but somewhere nearby I hear a bus lurch to a stop. We pull apart and watch Felipe get off the almost-empty bus and walk to the fence.

Treva and I walk to our spot.

"Felipe," she says, "I'm so sorry about what happened. Is there anything I can do?"

He shakes his head. "You did a lot, Treva. You were quick and brave. Everything you did helped Mamá and Cole get further away."

"What did you do?" I ask her.

"She ran into the kitchen, picked up the spoon Mamá had dropped, and began stirring the soup," says Felipe. "I stalled ICE, saying I was coming, and then I finally unlocked the door or they'd have broken it down. They rushed into the room, shouting '*Verónica Ramirez, step forward.*'"

"Fatima and Salma were backed up into the corner," says Treva. "I could see them from where I stood in front of the stove. ICE turned on them and demanded to know who they were."

Felipe chimes in. "Fatima told ICE she and Salma were U.S. citizens and that ICE had better stay away from them. Treva poked her head from around the kitchen and asked,

'What's going on here? Who are you?' Just like she didn't know. Then ICE turned on her, demanding to know who she was."

"I told them," says Treva, "and I asked them what they were doing in Felipe's house. They said they were there for Verónica Ramirez. I looked behind me, sort of out the window, the opposite direction you had gone, and said she went to the store to get some last minute things for the stuffing."

"That confused them," says Felipe. "They wanted to know which store. Nobody answered. Then they said, 'Which store, Felipe?' They knew my name. I said nothing." Felipe scowls. "Then they searched the house. Went into every room, upstairs and down. Searched the basement. They scared Juliana and Isabella. And Benito, too. I hate them. They're terrorists."

I put a hand on Felipe's shoulder.

"Let's walk somewhere," I tell him and Treva. "I don't feel right talking here. There might be a listening device somewhere."

They look at me as if I'm crazy.

"In the *fence*?" asks Treva.

"I don't know," I say. "Maybe in the trees? ICE has seen us meeting here. Let's talk somewhere else."

They humor me by following me all the way to Euclid Grade School. The streets are empty. Everyone's inside, celebrating Thanksgiving.

We walk onto the playground and sit on the swings that Felipe and I used to swing on. Where Benito, Juliana, and Isabella still swing. Where Nikki Zurlo's kids swing.

Where Mrs. Green's granddaughters play. Where all kinds of neighborhood kids walk to school and go to class and play in the playground and then walk home again. Where more than a thousand people came to hear Dad talk about the importance of keeping schools like Euclid open.

"What's going to happen to Tía?" I ask Felipe as each of us chooses a swing and sits on it. I take a wooden seat, Felipe takes a rubber seat, and Treva takes a tire swing.

"Papá and I talked about it all night." He gives me a quick look and adds, "We turned up loud music and we spoke softly, so it was safe." He stares off into space. "It's possible that Mamá could find sanctuary, like in a church."

"Yeah," I say, "but she couldn't come out. ICE would be waiting for her. I've read about a couple of those cases. One woman stayed inside the church for almost two years. Her family could visit her, but she couldn't go out. When she finally stepped out, ICE grabbed her and deported her to Mexico."

"Sanctuary isn't exactly great," Treva says, swinging on her tire. "It's like removing somebody from their life."

"*Sí.*"

"Where is she now?" asks Treva.

"With somebody," I say. "I don't know where."

Felipe stares off into space. "Papá and I have talked to her on the phone. She gave Papá the address where she is."

"What else?" I ask. "Besides sanctuary."

"We could leave the city. All of us, with Mamá. We could move from town to town, change our name, hide with people, change our jobs. Always be moving."

Nobody says anything for a while. Finally, Treva speaks. "That's horrible."

"*Sí.*"

"You couldn't finish school," she says.

"*Sí.* I could not finish school." Felipe kicks at the dirt under the swings. "Or, Mamá could turn herself in, and ICE would deport her, and we would move to Mexico to be with her."

This is as horrible as hiding out. Felipe has never been to Mexico. Neither have Benito, Juliana, or Isabella.

I would never see him again.

"Or," he continues, "She could turn herself in and we could get a lawyer and fight her deportation. Papá became a citizen just after Benito was born, so she is married to a citizen."

"Isn't that enough?" Treva asks.

Felipe shrugs. "I don't think so. Mamá's afraid that because she ran away, ICE will not treat her kindly. She might not be granted bail. And she might be put on a plane and deported overnight, while we are still appealing her detention."

"Why did Tía run?" I ask. "Why did you tell her to run?"

He thinks about this a while. "Fear," he says at last. "You see ICE hanging around the school. They deported Gi Pak. They deported Hasna. And last year they deported Amani. ICE hates Muslims and Mexicans. I guess Koreans, too."

"Running seems a natural instinct when men with guns come pounding on your door," says Treva.

"*Sí.*"

"But you should at least consult an immigrant rights organization," she adds. "To see what they say."

"*Sí.* Papá will do that tomorrow if they are open. If not, then on Monday. I will go with him."

We sit there a long time without saying anything. Without even swinging.

Treva breaks the silence. "There is another choice."

We look at her.

"Canada," she says. "If your mother can get to Canada, she can seek refuge there, and if they grant her refuge, then you all can move there."

"I don't want to move to Canada," Felipe says.

"I know," says Treva. "But the alternatives aren't good."

I don't want Felipe to move to Canada. It's not the same as moving to Mexico: I could go see him sometimes. But Canada isn't here. It's not where Felipe belongs.

"She couldn't get across the border," says Felipe. "She isn't a citizen, and she doesn't have a Green Card. When the border patrol asks for a passport, Mamá wouldn't have one. They wouldn't let her in. They might even detain her and turn her over to ICE."

"I know somebody who can help," says Treva.

Which stuns us into silence. Felipe and me. We stare at her.

"What do you mean?" I ask at last.

"I know somebody who can help Felipe's mother get across the border."

"Who?" I ask.

"No naming names," she says. "But it's somebody I know. And trust."

Neither Felipe nor I say anything.

"All I'm saying is, I can help." Treva swings way high on the tire, looks down at us, and says, "So if you need my help, just ask me."

She pumps hard for one last high swing, then jumps off the tire. "I've got to go. My mom and uncle asked me to help with dinner."

———

Mom and I and Felipe and his father and brother and sisters, and Bianca, eat our Thanksgiving Day dinner pretty much in silence.

Thanksgiving is supposed to be a family holiday. *Family* is an F word that's supposed to make us think everything's okay. But the people in power, they have no respect for the" family values" they talk about. The people in power send squads of armed men into homes and pull family members apart. They don't care. The people in power don't want organized protest movements, so they put the leaders in jail. Dad's in jail because he spoke up, he organized, he led. Everything the people in power say is false. Another F word.

Nobody eats much.

Nobody even notices that I never made the cranberry sauce. If they do notice, they don't say anything.

I keep thinking of Tía, wondering if she's eating with the people hiding her.

I keep thinking of Dad, wondering what he's eating and whether it's good at all. And whether he's worried why we didn't call last night.

I keep thinking of Treva and the things she said. How does she know somebody who can get Tía across the border? I wonder whether Treva's having a good Thanksgiving with her mom and uncle.

But this is her first Thanksgiving Day without her father.

So it's probably pretty sad.

I miss Dad a whole lot, and I know Mom does too. It's hard to be happy when somebody you love and are with every day is suddenly gone.

But Dad will be home in January.

"I am ashamed of my country," says Tío Carlos as he pushes away his food. "The dark-dressed armed guards who strike terror into our hearts, who break up our families, snatch mothers from their children and snatch children from their mothers. Ashamed."

Nobody says anything. There's nothing to say.

The only things any of us eat heartily are the pies Mom made. We even have seconds. Which we couldn't have if Mom hadn't stayed up baking them.

And then, when dinner's over and heaps of food remain on the table, Tío nods to Mom, to Felipe, and to me. The four of us apologize to Bianca for leaving her with all the work, but she shoos us out and says she'll take care of things. "We should not be seen together much," she tells us. "I will go home when you return."

We put on our coats.

Benito begs to go with us, but Tío tells him his time will come later.

This time we walk to Palmer Square Park instead of to a bus shelter. A few kids and parents wander around. Walking off their dinners, I guess.

We find a bench that will hold all four of us.

"Carlos, have you and Verónica decided what to do?" Mom asks.

He shakes his head. "We cannot decide. We wait."

I want to ask, *Wait for what?* but Mom shakes her head at me.

"I understand," she says. "It's hard."

"Mamá is alone," says Felipe.

"We will wait," says Tío.

"We can only speak to Mamá twice a week. For safety," says Felipe. "She is lonely. She is scared."

"We wait," says Tío. "We do not know what to do, so we wait."

"Wait," I say.

Mom and Tío stare at me. Felipe scowls.

"Wait a minute, I mean. I have an idea that will help Tía. And you."

They wait. Man, there's too much waiting everywhere.

I clear my throat. "Is Tía somewhere nearby?" I ask Tío. "Like, within a three-mile range?"

"*Sí.*"

"Well," I say. "I'm a runner."

Nobody gets it.

"You all write letters to Tía. I go out on my run and drop the letters off. Tía reads them. She writes back and the next day I pick up her letters. And back and forth. Everyone can talk to Tía through letters."

"Juliana and Isabella," says Tio. "And Benito, Felipe, and me."

"And Bianca," says Mom. "And Cole and me."

"How will you drop them off?" asks Felipe. "Who will pick them up? How will you collect them?"

Mom clears her throat. "Bianca has told me where Verónica is. Leave it to Bianca and me. We'll arrange the drop-offs, pickups, and deliveries."

Tío stands. "Let us go home and write letters. Tomorrow Coleto can take them on a run."

CHAPTER 41

SLEEP LATE THE NEXT MORNING, the letters to Tía on my nightstand.

Muffled voices sweep up the stairwell. Who's Mom talking to?

I shower, dress, and head to the kitchen.

There's Benito, finishing breakfast.

The minute I walk in, Mom turns up the music.

Loud. Very loud.

So nobody can hear us, I assume.

"Hey, Benito," I say in a quiet voice close to his ear. "Wa's up? Is something wrong?"

He shakes his head and chews on his toast. Then he reaches inside his shirt and pulls something out, handing it to me.

It's vinyl and mesh, flat and rectangular, with a zipper compartment and a cord.

"Papá's travel wallet." He looks at me, his eyes wide. "It is for you to use."

"For the letters," I say.

"It's called a neck wallet," says Mom. "How many eggs do you want?"

"Three. No, wait. Am I running today?" I look at her. I'm keeping my voice low.

She nods.

"When?"

"Right around lunch time," she says in such a soft voice I almost can't hear her.

"Three eggs, four bacons, four toasts. I can make the toast."

Mom nods and I drop four slices of bread into the toaster. "Want more toast, Benito?" I ask.

"Yes. Please."

"You can have one of these slices when they're done."

I'm thinking that Tío Carlos sent Benito with the neck pouch so that Benito would feel better. Like he's doing something to help his mother.

Last night we all wrote letters to Tía, and then I took the letters home. "The letters are on my nightstand, Benito. Can you get them?"

He doesn't answer, just pushes away from the table and pounds up the stairs. He's back before Mom has even flipped the eggs.

"Good work," I say as he hands me the packet of letters. "Let's see how they fit into the pouch."

Which is all the clue Benito needs. He stacks the letters neatly, then tries to fit them into the pouch. Seeing that doesn't work, he folds the packet of letters in half. They fit. He zips the pouch and hands it to me.

"*Gracias.*" I drape the undercover wallet around my neck. It doesn't feel too bad. But it would definitely be a handicap in cross-country.

"Can I go with you?" he asks.

"No," Mom and I say together.

"Why can't I?"

"Benito, ICE might be following every member of your family," Mom explains. She's still speaking softly, standing very close to Benito. "To see if you have any contact with your mother. She isn't in a sanctuary. If she were, you could go visit her."

"I know what a sanctuary is. And I know which churches are sanctuaries."

I wait, to see if he's going to say anything else, but he doesn't. Mom hands me a plate of bacon and eggs. The toast pops up. I give a slice to Benito and take three for myself.

"How long's my run?" I ask Mom.

"About four miles total. Two out, two back."

"Maybe Benito can run a mile with me, then turn around and run back home?"

Benito sits up. As if we're on starting blocks.

Mom thinks a while. "Okay," she says. "One mile, that's it. Benito, you must promise to turn around and go home when Cole tells you to."

"*Lo prometo,*" he says.

Mom looks at me.

"He promises," I say.

"Where's Felipe?" I ask him.

"Taking care of Juliana and Isabella. It's his turn. Papa said I was the person to deliver the neck wallet."

"How about you call Felipe and tell him you and I are going to hang for a while. Maybe play some video games."

"Doom," says Benito. "Or Hell on Earth."

I laugh at this. Benito knows those are the only two video games I have. "You choose," I say.

"I can beat you," he says.

After we finish breakfast, I clear the table and whisper to Mom. "Where do I go? What do I do?"

She tells me and asks me to repeat it.

Twice.

Then she whispers, "Run in the opposite direction with Benito. And make sure he doesn't follow you after a mile."

A mile in the opposite direction. So four miles becomes six miles. I'll run at a slower pace.

Benito and I play Doom for over an hour. He's better than me at video shooting. Just like Felipe is.

I glance at my watch and see that it's time for me to run. I tell Benito to be ready in ten minutes.

I go to my room, change into a pair of running shorts and shoes and socks. I pull a long-sleeved wicking shirt on over the neck wallet. I stash my cell and key into a super-lightweight running waistpack Dad bought me last year. When I get downstairs, Benito's waiting at the front door.

"Be careful," Mom whispers. "And call me after the drop."

The drop.

I feel like I'm in a TV show.

I run at an easy pace so that Benito can keep up. I'm supposed to be running north, but I run south for half a mile, then west for another half.

"You're a good runner," I tell Benito.

"I'm going to try out for cross-country next year," he says. "In seventh grade."

I'm about to say that's great, when it hits me. Benito probably won't be here next year. Felipe probably won't be here.

I slow down so much that Benito asks me if I'm okay.

"Yeah. Sure." I try to get back into the running rhythm.

After the mile's up I make sure Benito turns toward home, then I veer south, do a quick east turn, then head north, making sure he's not following me.

Which he isn't.

———

As I run, I look around for cars that might be following me. Or people.

Though the people would have to be running pretty fast, and I'd notice them.

Cars, then.

I can't spot any.

But that doesn't mean they aren't there.

I'm not very good at this hiding stuff.

At the halfway point I see a Korean cafe Mom told me would be there. I slow down and walk in.

A server wearing black pants and a black shirt smiles at me. She has a red ribbon tied around her neck, with a raised-fist pendant hanging from it.

"Great day for a run," I say to her.

"He who fights and runs away," she says.

"Lives to fight another day," I finish, looking around to see if anybody's paying attention.

They don't seem to be.

She aims a thumb toward the rear of the cafe. "The washroom's in back."

I walk into the washroom, lock the door, remove my neck wallet, and take out the letters. On the window ledge is a folded copy of the *Tribune*. I take it and place the packet of letters inside. Before I leave, I flush the toilet to make it sound as if I really did use the washroom.

Then I go back to the cafe and order a bottle of water. I leave the *Tribune* on the counter. The woman in black takes the *Trib* and places it under the counter. She hands me a bottle of water, I pay her, drink half the bottle on the spot, then head out, holding the bottle in my hand.

I pull out my phone, hit speed dial, and Mom answers.

"What's for dinner?" I ask.

Which is what Mom told me to say if the drop was successful. She said that if our phones are bugged, the listeners will have heard me ask this question a hundred times—so I may as well keep asking it.

"Turkey-stuffed pasta shells," she says. Which isn't code.

On Saturday morning I make another run, this time to a dry cleaners, to pick up Tía's letters. Assuming she writes back to everyone.

When I pick up the packet, it feels like she's written a book to each of us.

I don't like the way the wallet bounces against my chest, so I flip the thing around. It hangs down my back, where it hardly bounces at all.

I want to run straight to Felipe's and give them Tía's letters. They'll all be home on a Saturday.

But that's not the plan. Instead I run home, shower, get dressed, and wait for Felipe.

Mom takes out the letter addressed to her and hands me the one with *Coleto* written on the outside.

Tía's letter to me is short. She tells me she loves me and is sorry for all the problems and worry.

When Felipe arrives, I give him the packet. I know he wants to turn around and go home with it, but Mom says he's probably being followed and so it should look as if he came for a visit. So Felipe and I go out on the driveway and shoot hoops for an hour. His shots have no energy. Mine don't either.

He says almost nothing the entire time.

On Sunday afternoon Mom and I catch the bus to Cook County Jail.

The afternoon lines are as long as the morning lines. I look for Emerald Jackson but don't see her. And then I remember she said her brother would be out just before Thanksgiving.

> Me: Hey, E—ur brother home? Did U hv gd TDay? We're waiting 2C Dad.
>
> Emerald: He home! Great day! Tell ur Dad he say Hi.
>
> Me: Will do. Thx.

When Dad steps out from behind the steel door, he looks worried. Then he sees us and looks relieved.

"What happened?" he mouths, placing both palms on the glass. "Are you okay?"

Mom puts her hand against one of his, and I put my hand against the other.

Mom sits on the stool and bends down to the grill. "We are okay." She stresses the first word.

Dad sits on the stool on his end. I kneel in front of the grill.

"Not everybody is?" he asks.

"Frozen water everywhere," says Mom. "Easy to slip and fall. And speaking of falling, a roof fell in. Close to us."

I sit there wondering: If I were Dad, could I figure this out? Frozen water = ICE. Roof fell in = invasion?

Dad thinks for a few seconds. "That sounds bad," he says, and I can tell he's trying to sound casual. He bends toward the grill. "Was anybody hurt?" he asks. When he sits back up, he's pressed forward, as if he wants to push himself through the plastic.

A guard steps forward and tells Dad to move back.

Dad does.

The guard steps back. Out of sight. But probably not out of earshot.

I can't tell if Dad knows what Mom's trying to say.

"They got away before the roof fell in," I blurt out.

Dad looks at me. Mom looks at me and nods. I think that means I did okay on the code.

"Good," says Dad. "Ice is dangerous stuff."

"Luckily everyone's safe," says Mom. "So let's talk about other things." She taps the counter twice. If I wasn't looking for those tiny taps, I wouldn't notice them. She makes it seem like a nervous twitch.

"Sure," says Dad, watching us. "What do you want to talk about? How was Thanksgiving, by the way?"

"We missed you," says Mom. "Ever since you've been in jail, I've been reminiscing about all the things we used to do. The three of us. Like, remember when you made Cole a teeter totter? And how you loved hiding from him in hide and seek?"

She stops.

Hide—is that what she's trying to tell Dad? That Tía is hiding?

"Boys are good at hiding," says Dad. Watching.

Mom shakes her head. "You know who's better at hiding? Girls."

Dad looks sad. But also like he wants to jump out and do something.

"Remember when I wanted to build a wooden fence around the back yard?" he asks. "To keep Cole safe?"

Mom nods. "I'm glad I talked you out of that. And look, Cole is safe."

I'm thinking maybe the last word in a sentence is the most important part of what they're saying.

Dad leans back a bit. He takes his hands off the plastic and puts them behind his head, like he's stretching and relaxing.

"I'll be out in thirty-five more days," he says. "And I can't wait for spring. We can go to our favorite camping spot."

Our favorite camping spot is way up in Canada, on Georgian Bay.

I think I get it.

Dad's saying he thinks Tía should go to Canada.

Just like Treva thought.

But I have no idea how.

CHAPTER 42

THE FIRST TWO WEEKS OF December feel like a hundred-pound backpack with no shoulder padding and no sternum strap. Nothing is right and there's no way to make things better.

Felipe and Treva and I meet at the fence like we've been doing all year. But Felipe hardly talks, except to answer Treva when she asks if his mother's okay. His answer is always the same. "No." One day Treva reminds us that she can help. Felipe yells at her. "Nobody can help! Help means doing something. Papá doesn't want to do anything."

Treva steps back. I can see the hurt on her face. "Why not?" she asks after a while. "Why doesn't he want to do anything?"

"BE CAUSE," Felipe hisses, "none of the choices are what we want. We don't want Mamá to live in hiding the rest of her life. We don't want to give up our home and live under false names. We don't want to go live in Mexico. And we don't want to move to you-know-where. ¿*Entiende?*"

He walks away.

Treva and I watch him until he opens the school doors and disappears from sight.

Treva looks like she's going to cry. "Did he ask what my intentions are?"

I move alongside her, take her hand, and hold it. "No. He asked if you understood. He's not angry at you. He's angry at everything. The government."

"Me too," she says. "I'm angry, too."

"Yeah. People who aren't angry are living in oblivion."

She gives a small smile. "Ob-liv-e-on. Good. Just four syllables, though."

The bell rings and we walk into the school.

Every day feels gray and cold. Some days Felipe talks, some days he just stands against the fence and stares at nothing. If ICE or anybody else planted a bug near the fence, they aren't hearing much.

One day Nachman asks me if everything is all right. I tell him it is. He asks if Dad is okay. I say he is.

On another day Coach sees me in the hall and says, "Lookin' good, Cole. How's the running?"

"Good," I say.

Then he stops and puts a hand on my shoulder. He looks me over carefully. "Hmm. Maybe cut back a day or two on the runs. Okay?"

I nod. "Okay. Yeah. Sure."

As if.

"You going out for track again this spring?"

"Yeah."

"Good," he says. "And Felipe will be there to cheer us on."

It's not a question, and even if it was, I couldn't answer.

Coach slaps me on the back and walks to wherever he was going.

I choke up. Try to shake it off.

Felipe's not going to be here. I can feel it deep inside. I rub my eyes and take a deep breath.

When the school day's over, Treva and I have started going to the Crow's Nest and sitting and talking until it's time for me to work. Fatima and Salma come with us a lot of the time. Felipe doesn't. He goes straight home after school. They understand. They were there when it happened.

Mostly, though, I run four miles a day, delivering letters. Somehow or other Mom and Bianca communicate and Mom tells me where to go each day. It's seldom the same person I drop the packet off to. And Mom makes sure it's never the same time of day. Sometimes I run before school even starts. Sometimes before dinner. Sometimes after.

"This was a good idea at first," Mom tells me. "But it can't go on much longer. Every day you run, you increase the chances of being followed. Carlos and Verónica must make a decision."

"I think the letters are helping Tía."

Mom nods. "Yes, I can tell by her replies that they are. But I think we should set a day for you to stop. Maybe deliver letters twice a week instead of seven days." She looks at me to see if I agree.

In my gut, I think Mom's right. When I run, I get the creepy feeling that somebody's watching me. I nod.

Mom gives me a hug.

I find a nice sheet of stationery in Mom's desk and write to Tía.

FAULT

It is not your fault
It is the fault
of the state
that rules
by force

I stuff the poem into the wallet, drape it over my neck and down my back, zip up my nylon windbreaker, and run today's route.

August Mersy's December vacation break is just a few days away. Felipe, Treva, and I are standing at the fence with Fatima and Salma.

Nikki Zurlo walks up. "I'm sorry, Cole. Mrs. Delaney wants to see you. Now."

What?

I haven't done a single thing. I haven't been late for class, I haven't missed a class, I haven't been out in the hallways when

I shouldn't, I haven't done anything Delaney could consider trouble-making.

Not inside the grounds of August Mersy, that is.

"How's Hank doing?" Nikki asks me as I follow her.

"Good," I answer. "He gets out in three weeks. Right after New Year's."

"Everyone will be happy to see him home, Cole. The Save Our Schools committee anticipates another fight this spring or summer."

I'm about to say that Dad always asks about the committee, but we're walking into the principal's office and Ms. Delaney is standing there, in the outer office.

Nikki swings the half-door open and motions for me to go through.

I do.

Nikki goes to her desk.

"Follow me," says Ms. Delaney. She opens the door to her office and waits for me to step into it.

There's somebody already there.

A man. He's a cop of some sort. Close-cropped hair, scrubbed-clean face, suit and tie. And that look. The I-Have-Power-and-I-Will-Use-It look.

I hate him already.

"Please sit down," says Delaney as she goes to her desk and sits.

There's only one of the two old wooden chairs to sit in, because the cop has moved the other one alongside Delaney's desk. He's sitting in it. The two of them face me.

I sit in the remaining chair and wait.

"Cole, this is Agent List. He has some very good news for you."

I think about this. Agent for what? ICE? FBI? CIA? NEA? TSA? Some initials I don't even know?

The two of them look at me. I think they're waiting for me to say something.

But I don't.

List—if that's even his real name—speaks. "Cole, I'm sure you and your mother would love to have your father home for the holidays. So I'm very happy to tell you that your father can be released from jail tomorrow."

My heart jumps.

Waves of happiness flood through me. I can feel a big, happy smile that wants to bust out all over my face.

But I shut it all down. Because "your father *can* be released" means he won't be. They don't need my participation for the *can*. They could have let Dad out this morning.

Or never put him in jail in the first place.

I sit and say nothing.

Agent List and Ms. Delaney make eye contact with each other.

"What do you say to that, Cole?" Delaney asks. "Isn't that wonderful news?"

"It sounds good," I give them.

"I've heard from the principal here that you're an up and coming track star," List says.

"Cross-country," I correct. "And it takes a whole team to win."

"What would you say to a full scholarship at any NCAA Division I school?"

What's he saying? That he'll get me a scholarship? Why? "I hope I can earn one."

He leans forward. "I can guarantee it, Cole. I can guarantee you get a free ride at a Division I school. And I can guarantee that your father will be released tomorrow."

I know these things won't happen, because I know he wants something.

What? What does he want?

"Cole, I think you should show more appreciation for this." That's Delaney. I can't tell if she's being Hard Cop or Soft Cop.

"It's hypothetical," I say. And then, just to rile her, I add. "That means it hasn't happened yet."

"I know what hypothetical means!" she snaps at me.

Score one for me.

But something bad is coming, I know it. I notice List staring at my knees.

They're bouncing up and down.

I make my legs go still.

For maybe twenty seconds we're all silent.

Then List speaks. "All we need, Cole, is for you to tell us where Mrs. Ramirez is hiding."

I go cold. Like all the fluids have left my stomach, and if I don't do something quick, I'm going to start shaking all over.

I jam my hands down on each side of the chair and press hard. That doesn't work, so I slide my fingers under my legs, trying to keep warm.

They're watching me.

They can see I'm upset.

I stop with the hands and fingers and just sit there, saying nothing. It takes all my energy to sit there without shaking.

"Your father would love to come home," says Delaney.

"How do you know? Have you been to see him?"

"You know I haven't," she says.

"Because he's a troublemaker and you don't like trouble-makers."

Delaney looks at List, who looks at me.

"Is Mrs. Ramirez a troublemaker?" I ask.

"She's in violation of the laws of the land," List says. "She could have become a citizen but chose not to. If she can get away with this, so can others."

Man.

I sit there.

They sit there.

Finally List stands up. "If I were you, Cole, I'd tell us where she is. A lot can happen to a man in jail between now and the time of his release."

I jump up so fast the chair crashes behind me. "Is that a threat?" I shout. "Are you threatening to hurt my father?" I'm shouting. Screaming. Screaming so loud my ears hurt.

He moves close to me, almost bumping me in the chest.

I'm not afraid of him.

The door opens.

"Is everything okay in here?" Nikki asks.

"Go back to your desk," orders Delaney. "And don't open this door again without knocking first."

Nikki looks at Delaney. She looks at List. She looks at me. All very slowly. Like she's committing our faces to memory. "Are you okay, Cole?"

"No, I'm not okay." I point at List, almost stabbing him in the face with my finger. He doesn't flinch.

"He wants me to tell him where Mrs. Ramirez is. If I don't, he'll have Dad hurt while he's in jail."

"Leave this office at once," Delaney tells Nikki.

"We're done here," says List, brushing by me, nearly knocking Nikki over as he goes out the door.

"I don't know where she is!" I shout after him. "And if I did, I'd never tell you! Never!"

I turn to Delaney.

"What you did is foul." I'm still shouting. "Foul! I don't see how you can live with yourself."

I pick up my backpack and ease past Nikki, who's still standing there holding the door open.

I don't go to history class. I spend the whole first period in one of the boys' rooms, pacing back and forth. Kicking at the stalls.

Pounding on the walls.

Dunking my head under cold running water.

Toweling it dry.

Tossing the paper towels anywhere and everywhere.

I know I did the right thing.

I couldn't have done anything else.

But will Dad be safe?

Nikki helped, she really helped. She's a witness. In case…
I don't want to think about it.

I go to second period class.

"Are you okay?" Treva whispers. "Your hair's wet. So's
your shirt. What happened?"

I shake my head. "Later. I'll tell you later."

I must be sending off waves of Help Me, because
Nachman comes back to my desk. "Cole, do you need help?"
he asks.

I take a deep breath. Two of them. "Thanks," I say, "but
I'm okay."

He keeps looking at me, like he doesn't believe me.

"I'll write about it," I tell him.

He gives a small smile and pats me on the back. "I'm
eager to read it. Or should I be anxious to read it?"

Nachman.

Always the teacher.

"Eager," I say. "Anxious isn't necessary."

CHAPTER 43

FOES

Foul
fiends
everywhere

flint
where hearts
should beat

fangs
behind
their smirks.

I long
to knock
them flat,
topple them from
their thrones.

I long
to flush
them down
the toilets
which they
inhabit.

CHAPTER 44

T LUNCH TIME I HURRY to meet Felipe and Treva at the fence. The hallways are almost empty. Everyone's in the cafeteria or study hall. Or, like me, skipping lunch to go outdoors, even though it's December.

August Mersy's built in the shape of a giant X. I don't know if that's meant to locate the spot, or to say that education inside these hallways is a mystery. I'm hurrying along on one leg of the X, ready to make a left-hand turn, when out of the corner of my eye I see two people at the far end of the right-hand leg.

Jillian and Jared.

Their backs are to me, and their heads are close together.

Sort of the way that Treva and Felipe and I put our heads close together if we don't want anybody else to hear what we're saying.

Are Jillian and Jared back together?

I'm standing there, staring at them, thinking that I'll never know if it was one of them who told ICE to check out the Ramirez house and deport somebody.

It could have been Delaney.

It could have been a stranger.

Or nobody.

I must be giving off waves of something because Jillian and Jared both turn in my direction.

They stare at me.

And then, even though it's hard to tell from such a distance, I swear they both smirk.

I glare at them and their smirks fade. F word, *fade*.

I wish Jared and Jillian and people like them would fade away.

But that's not going to happen. They have to be fought against.

I turn and continue down the left leg of the X and through the doors and meet Felipe and Treva at the fence. We move away from it to a new spot. Every day we pick a new spot to talk. Just in case.

I tell them what happened in Delaney's office.

They're so shocked they're silent.

"Why do they want Mamá so bad?" Felipe asks in a low voice. "She is one of millions. What is it about her?"

I want to say that it isn't about Tía, it's about Felipe. He's the one Delaney thinks is a troublemaker. He unites kids. But I don't want to say that because it will make him feel even worse.

And maybe it's not about Felipe. Maybe it's about Bianca. The work she does to defend immigrant rights.

Felipe looks at me, then away. Then back at me. "Tío Hank," he says in the same low voice. "Are you worried?"

I feel my fist clench. Treva reaches out a hand and puts it on my fist, lightly.

I unclench.

I nod. "I am."

"I don't think you should worry too much about your father," says Treva. "What Nikki Zurlo did will help him"

"How?"

"Because she saw the federal agent or cop or whatever he was in Delaney's office. Because she heard you yell so loud that she came in to see if there was a problem. Because when she asked if you were okay, you told her they were threatening your father. And the agent got up and left. So she's a witness."

I don't like the way that sounds, *witness*. As if somebody's going to hurt Dad and then we'll call witnesses to testify. I'm afraid.

Suddenly Felipe steps forward and wraps his arms around me. "I thank you for this. Papá and Mamá thank you." He lets me go and looks me in the eye. "And Tío Hank will be very proud of you."

Treva clears her throat. We turn to look at her.

"Felipe," she says, "I know you don't want to make a decision. I understand *why* you don't want to make one. No matter what you choose, you are choosing an injustice."

He nods. I nod.

There's more coming.

"But," she says, "the signs are saying you have to make one."

"What signs?" he demands.

"Delaney. The agent. It's as if they've thrown a net around your mother, and they're drawing it tighter."

He doesn't say anything.

I think Treva's right, but this is hard on Felipe, and I'm not going to make it harder.

The bell rings and we walk back into the school.

For the next few days nothing happens. Nothing except my running letters back and forth. Our December holiday break finally comes.

Two days before Christmas I'm down in the basement, looking at Dad's weights, when there's a pounding on the back door.

I see it's Felipe, and I let him in.

"Bianca! She has been taken in for questioning!" He paces around the kitchen table.

"When? By who? The cops?"

"No. ICE. They came to her apartment. I was just leaving when I saw them go in. I followed them and saw them taking Bianca. She told me to call a lawyer."

"Did you call Ms. Kazarian?"

"*Sí. Inmediatamente.*"

He sits at the table. "I have not called Papá. I will wait until he gets home from work."

I don't know what to say. Or do. I sit down across from Felipe. "What did you go see Bianca about?"

He stands, removes his backpack, reaches into it, and removes a bundle of papers. "Her letter," he says, sitting down. "We each enclosed a small present for Mamá. But I think everything will still fit into the wallet."

He looks so lost I know that I'll make the bundle fit, no matter how large it is. I heft it in my hand. "I think it'll work."

I go to the coat rack, remove the hanging wallet, and bring it to the table.

Felipe and I take turns smoothing letters out and carefully fitting them into the wallet compartment.

The gifts feel like thin pieces of jewelry, maybe something to hang from a bracelet or necklace. One is larger than the others, kind of thick and clunky feeling.

"That is from Isabella. She made it out of clay. Isabella does not yet understand *tiny*." Felipe smiles at this.

Somehow or other we manage to squeeze everything into the packet. Felipe zips it closed, tamps it down, and hands it to me. *"Gracias, hermano. Mi más profundo agradacimiento."*

I put up my hand and Felipe presses his against it.

He follows me up to my room and waits as I gear up in running shorts and shoes. I stash my phone into my thin waistpack. I pull on a long-sleeved wicking t-shirt, drape the packet of letters around my neck so that they're hanging down my back, and pull on a lightweight running jacket.

We go out the door together. I lock it behind me and do a few stretches alongside the house. It's 4:30 p.m. and practically dark. My jacket's neon green and reflective, so cars can see me.

Felipe and I fist-bump and I take off. At the end of the block I glance back. He's still standing there. Worried about Bianca. Worried about his mother.

By the end of a mile I'm hot, so I unzip my jacket and let the winter temperatures cool me off.

Today's drop-off is different from the others. It's also a pickup, so that Tía can send gifts back home. I don't know how she was able to buy gifts. Maybe Gretchen—if she's still with Gretchen—took her out shopping. More likely, somebody bought the gifts for her.

Before I enter the drugstore, I move the wallet so it hangs down my chest. I unzip it, enter the store, find the customer with the Milwaukee Brewers baseball cap and walk by, saying "Great day for a run," and he answers "He who fights and runs away," and we finish each part of the whole code, then he drops a magazine and I bend down to pick it up. First I slip Tía's letters out of the magazine. Then I slip the packet for her into the magazine, straighten up, and hand him the magazine. He stays where he is and I buy a bottle of water, drink it down, and head out the door. I slip into the nearest alley and stuff Tía's letters into the hanging wallet, zip it, and drop it down my back, between my shirt and jacket.

As I run back home I realize I'm not paying much attention to my running form. Not as much as Coach wants me to. And then I realize I haven't been writing any poems in form, either, like Nachman suggested. My poems have been angry ones, spilling out all over the page. I don't think I'm ready for form poems, not the way I feel.

The only thing I pay attention to is my zigs and zags. Running zigs and zags, not poetic ones. Down one street, across another, down an alley, down another. Street, alley, street, alley. I feel like one of those dogs that runs obstacle courses: fastest time through the obstacles wins.

I turn a corner into another alley and right away my peripheral vision sees two dark shapes standing alongside a garage door. They're in the darkest spot, under an overhang.

My stomach goes cold.

The shapes step forward. I see the silhouette of holstered guns on their belts. I see three large capital letters across their jackets.

ICE.

I pivot as fast as I can, doing a u-ey in my tracks.

But one of them rushes forward and pushes. I fly chest-first across the cinders, cutting my palms, knees, and legs. My brain shoves everything aside. *Run!* it screams. I scramble up, ready to push off.

Boot. Coming my way. I twist away from the kick.

My butt takes some of the impact and I go sprawling again.

Push! Starting block! Run!

I'm thinking I'll make it.

But ICE must know about starting blocks, too—one of the men grabs me to spin me around. I see a garbage can as I'm being spun, and I reach out, grabbing its lid.

My heart is pounding hard. Do these guys want to kill me? Or beat me so bad I'll never run again?

I swing the lid with all my force. I hear an awful sound. Like bone crunching. Whoever I hit screams.

I turn and run like hell.

One of them's chasing me.

I hear the feet. Feel heaving breathing behind me.

He grabs me.

But I'm gone.

I'm out of there, leaving my windbreaker behind, in the hands of whoever it was.

They're going to shoot me in the back, that's all I can think of. My heart's pounding like it never has, not even for the last cross-country race. I race out of the alley and into the middle of Western Avenue. I run down the center of the street, cars honking their horns at me, veering left and right.

As soon as I see a chance, I run across an intersection, down another street, down an alley, and then down another street.

I keep looking behind me.

There's nobody following me.

Not as far as I can tell.

I keep running south and west until I'm at Palmer Square Park. I want to collapse on one of its benches.

But home is just half a mile ahead.

My butt hurts so bad I can barely jog.

I limp along, moaning out loud, holding my butt with my hand. Trying to make the pain go away.

Somehow I make it back home and climb the stairs. I sit on the stoop, just to recover.

I reach for the packet of letters.

The cord's not there.

The packet is gone.

CHAPTER 45

TEXT FELIPE.

Me: @home. Emergency.

Felipe: On way.

He's there in ten minutes.

"What happened?!" He looks at my cuts and scrapes.

I put music on and turn up the volume. Louder than I've ever had it. I tell him what happened. The attack, and that Tía's letters are gone. In the hands of ICE.

We're trying to decide what to do when Mom gets home from work. She takes one look at us, comes up close, and asks what happened. It's hard to hear her because of the loud music. I put my mouth close to her ear and tell her.

She runs up the stairs and comes back down with a bunch of my clothes. Sweatpants and sweatshirt and fleece hoodie. She also has rubbing alcohol and cotton swabs and gauze.

"Clean up all your cuts," she says, "and put on these warm

clothes. You're shaking."

I go into the bathroom. The rubbing alcohol stings. I'm shaking from being so cold, which makes me spill the alcohol over the cuts more than once. I get out of my running clothes and into the warm ones.

Mom has a couple of blankets ready. She tells me to lie down on the couch. Which sounds like the best idea I've heard all year. She covers me up. She and Felipe talk about what to do. I hear them talking and I want to say something, too. But they sound far away.

Felipe sits on the couch and every once in a while pats my foot. Which hurts when he does it. But feels good, too, because my best friend is there and he wants to make me feel better.

Under the blankets, I wrap my arms around myself to stay warm.

I think I fall asleep, 'cause the next thing I know, Mom's telling me to sit up. I manage to do that. She hands me a bowl of hot chicken noodle soup. It feels good in my hands. And in my stomach.

The loud music is still on. I slept through this?

"Where's Felipe?" I ask.

Mom sits down close to me and talks almost directly into my ear. She tells me Felipe went home and that he and Tío Carlos will return within an hour, so that we can all go outside, find another bus stop, and talk.

"I wanted to go to Felipe's," says Mom, "and let you sleep. But he said you needed to be there when we talk."

Felipe's right.

"I hope we can find a nearby bus stop."

"We can," she says. "Would you like more soup? And crackers?"

"Yeah."

***

By the time Tío and Felipe arrive, I'm starting to feel stiff all over. Still, nothing feels broken.

Not that I would know what broken feels like.

Sharp pain, probably.

I put on a jacket and the four of us go down the outside steps. Some of us more quickly than others.

We walk to a nearby bus stop that has a bench.

Tío Carlos speaks first. "The time has come to act."

We nod.

"No choice is good," he says. "But of all the choices, Canada seems best. Stacey, do you know anybody who could get Verónica into Canada?"

Mom shakes her head. "I don't," she says. "I'm sorry."

"Bianca cannot risk doing anything," says Tío. "It is like a hungry hawk is watching her."

"She's home again?" I ask.

"*Sí*. Bianca is a citizen. ICE cannot keep her."

Mom keeps shaking her head. "I'm so sorry, Carlos. I could ask around, but I'd have to be super cautious. And it could take weeks. The situation is fraught with danger." She sighs.

Fraught? I make a mental note to look up that word.

Tío nods. "This is what we thought. But there may be another way."

"What way?" asks Mom.

Tío looks at Felipe, who continues where Tío left off. "Treva," he says. "She says she can help. She says she knows somebody."

"Who does she know?" Mom demands.

"We don't know," I say. "She said it's best to not name names."

"She's right about that. But I don't know about this. I just don't know. Carlos?"

Tío shakes his head. "We have no choice. I have talked to Verónica. She is willing to take the chance."

Mom looks at me. "Cole, do you trust Treva?"

I nod. "Yes. I do trust her."

"I do, too," Felipe adds. "So I went to her house before we came here."

Mom and I stare at him. "You did?" I ask.

"We went outside and I told her what happened. We can meet the person she knows."

"That's good," says Mom. "I want to evaluate this person."

"*Sí,*" says Tío Carlos.

"Six o'clock tomorrow morning," says Felipe. "We'll meet him. Or her."

CHAPTER 46

NOW IS FALLING, SPARKLING IN the streetlights when Mom and I leave the house. Felipe's walking toward us, brushing a few snowflakes off his hair.

"Where's your dad?" Mom asks.

Felipe shakes his head. "He cannot come. This is a very busy day at work." Felipe's shoulders pull back. He stands taller. "Papá trusts me to decide."

Mom nods.

"With your help," Felipe adds. "He trusts the three of us."

By the time the three of us reach the Crow's Nest, the snow's packed into the treads of my boots. I'm limping a bit, but not much.

Mom goes in first, then Felipe, then me.

I stop.

Treva's there.

But so's Nachman.

I forgot. He eats at the Crow's Nest every morning at 6:00.

But why's she sitting with him?

Mom and Felipe have also stopped. But Treva and Nachman both wave us over to their table.

So we go.

Treva stands. "Mrs. Renner, this is Wyatt Nachman. Wyatt, this is Stacey Renner. Cole's mother." Treva smiles.

Wyatt? She calls Nachman by his first name??

Mom and Nachman shake hands. Felipe and I look at each other. Confused.

"Let's get settled," says Nachman, "and order breakfast." He motions for us to sit. I notice that the table has six chairs.

Treva clears her throat. "Wyatt is my uncle. He can help."

Uncle?

Uncle??!!

"You never told me Nachman's your *uncle*," I blurt out. A bit too loud.

"You never told me you spray-painted the school," she says.

I shoot a glare at Nachman. He holds up his hands and shakes his head. Not him.

I look at Felipe. He gives me a *don't-even-think-it* scowl.

"It was me," Mom announces. "I told Treva." She looks at me and shakes her head. "I assumed you had already told her."

Everybody's looking at me. Nachman's amused. So's Felipe. Mom has her eyebrows raised.

I take a deep breath. Look at Treva. "I don't know why I didn't tell you. I just didn't want to talk about it. It was…"

"Anarchistic?" she asks.

I see Nachman hide a grin.

"It was a poor tactic."

"Okay," she says. "The reason I didn't tell anybody that Wyatt's my uncle is that I didn't want anybody thinking he was favoring me in class. I should have told you and Felipe."

"Good," says Mom. "Now that we have that settled, let's talk about what to do." She looks right at Nachman. "Is this a safe place to talk?"

Before he can answer, a server comes to take our order. She looks about as awake as I feel. We all turn our coffee mugs up and she fills each one, then takes our orders.

After she leaves Nachman answers. "Safe as can be. The owner's an Iraqi War vet. Intelligence. Surveillance."

"He makes sure there are no bugs?" Mom asks.

Nachman nods.

I'm having a hard time processing this. Nachman as a... revolutionary? I glance at Felipe. He looks as confused as I feel.

"And he's trustworthy?" asks Mom.

Nachman nods.

"And *you're* trustworthy?" she asks.

"Yes. I've done this twice before."

We stare at him.

"Helped people get across the border," he explains.

"How?" Felipe and I ask almost at the same time.

"I drive them to Lansing. Somebody from Canada takes them the rest of the way."

"Who?" asks Felipe. "Who takes her? How do they get her across the border?" He's whispering.

"It's best to not name names," Nachman answers. "But I've worked with her twice before. She speaks Spanish. She will be kind to your mother."

"What about the documentation?" asks Mom. "How will Verónica get across?"

"That's what the Canadian friend does. The documentation. She'll need a photo of your mother, Felipe."

Felipe nods, but I can't tell if he's agreeing or not.

Our food arrives. Other people come into the diner and sit at tables and start talking. We're silent. Just eating.

And thinking.

I trust Treva and I trust Nachman. Man, he has a whole new side to him. Not new, I guess. Who knows how long it's been there. But he keeps it hidden in school.

Not that I blame him.

If Delaney knew, she'd expel him.

Nachman looks directly at Felipe. "If you decide to do this, we should act fast. From what Treva tells me, ICE really wants to find and deport your mother."

"Yes. I want to do it." Felipe turns to Mom. "Tía?"

Mom nods. "Yes. This is Verónica's best chance."

Felipe looks at me. I nod.

"When?" he asks.

"Tomorrow morning, four o'clock," says Nachman.

We sit there in silence. Maybe shock.

"Tomorrow's Christmas Day," Felipe manages.

"Good time to move," Nachman says. "I'll need a photo right away. You can meet Treva somewhere and give it to her."

"Okay with me," says Treva.

Felipe sighs. Then sighs again. "Yes. I will get the photo. And I will be ready at 4:00 a.m. to go with you to Lansing."

"Me, too," I say without thinking.

"No." Mom and Nachman say it together. Then they say it again. "No."

"She is my mother," argues Felipe. "I haven't seen her for a month! She will be afraid."

Nachman shakes his head. Mom shakes hers.

"My presence will help her," Felipe argues. "I'll be helping *you*. Mother and son and family friend. Out to visit friends in Lansing. I won't go with her all the way. Just to Lansing."

"No way," says Nachman, drinking a big gulp of coffee. "You," he says, pointing at Felipe, "and you," he continues, pointing at me, "and you," he finishes, pointing at Treva, "are all minors. Just going on sixteen years old. Haven't graduated from high school. If anything goes wrong, I don't want it on my conscience that I involved you."

"We're already involved," says Treva.

I guess she wants to come, too.

Mom speaks up. "But you haven't done anything that might be considered a crime. Like helping somebody across the border might be. Wyatt is right. You can't go. Not until you're eighteen and out of high school," she adds with a grin.

Sometimes Mom thinks she's so funny.

CHAPTER 47

FINDING IS BINDING

I find myself
through writing

I find my father
in jail unjustly

I find my mother
strong and steady

I find love
by surprise

I find my best friend
driven into exile

I find my world
owned by monsters

I find
unexpected goodness
in the hearts
of others.

CHAPTER 48

HRISTMAS DAY IS GLUM.
Mom and I are at Felipe's, sitting around with him, Tío Carlos, Benito, Juliana and Isabella. And Bianca, who looks the glummest of all. Presents sit under the tree, unopened.

My phone pings.

Suddenly we're all alert.

Treva: Delicious dinner waiting.

"It's Treva," I say. "Nachman's on his way back."

Felipe looks over my shoulder at the pre-arranged message which means Tía's heading to Canada and Nachman's heading home. He reads it to everyone.

Tío Carlos breathes deeply. "*Bueno*. We will eat. Then we will play some music. Then cards, perhaps. And before we know it, the second message will arrive."

I hope the second message is from Tía, telling us she's in Canada. Not from some border guard.

Bianca and Mom start getting the food ready. Juliana and Isabella help set the table. I know I should get up and help, but dread is pushing me down.

Yes, I want Tía Verónica to make it safely to Canada.

No, I don't want Felipe to move away.

The two are mutually exclusive. She wins, he moves. She loses, he moves. It's a lose-lose situation.

Felipe sits, staring into space. Maybe he's thinking the same things.

Benito goes over to the tree and picks up a present.

"Benito!" warns Tío. "Not until we hear from Mamá."

Benito sighs.

Bianca calls us to the table.

This whole meal reminds me of Thanksgiving. We pick at our food. Even Dad is probably happier than we are right now.

Mom apologizes to everyone that she never had a chance to bake anything. Tío and Bianca wave away her explanations.

"I made dessert," announces Benito.

I stare at Felipe. *Benito cooks?* Felipe shrugs.

"Let us see what you've made," says Bianca.

Benito goes to the refrigerator and opens the freezer door. He comes back with two quarts of ice cream. "It is Cherry Garcia. Mamá's favorite."

"*Gracias* Benito," says Tío. "In Mamá's honor, we will all have some."

And we do.

Then it's back into the living room and more anxious waiting.

Darkness comes. Bianca turns on lights.

Felipe asks if he can light a fire. I can just hear Treva saying, "I don't know—*can* you?" I smile to myself. Tío says yes. Felipe builds a fire and lights it.

The room seems a bit more cheerful.

Finally, Tío's phone rings. We all jump, the sound we've been waiting for is so unexpected.

He picks it up. *"Hola."*

But he's picked up the wrong phone. The burner phone. It's his regular cell that's ringing.

He tries again. *"¿Hola?"*

He listens, and then, phone pressed to his ear, he turns away from us. He listens some more, making occasional answers I can't hear. He turns to us. He's crying. But he's smiling at the same time. He gives a thumbs up to us, then turns away.

We make a lot of sounds. Sighs. Cheers. Laughs. Cries. Gasps.

Finally, Tío Carlos hangs up. He stands there before us. "She is in Toronto at an immigration center. They have assured her she is welcome. The rest of us will join her next week."

Dead silence.

Next. Week.

I glance at Felipe. He looks the way I feel. Dazed.

This can't be happening.

Felipe's phone pings.

"Mamá!" he shouts. "She is texting."

He opens his text. I'm looking over his shoulder. It's a photo of Tía, standing at a counter. There's a maple leaf logo on the counter. She looks like she's trying to smile.

Felipe shows the picture all around. Juliana and Isabella want to keep the phone so they can stare at the picture. Felipe lets them.

Everyone's mood grows a little lighter. The dread of knowing what would happen is gone.

But what looms ahead…

I feel forlorn. Way deep inside is where I feel it. Which is how I know it must be an Anglo-Saxon word.

Mom is saying something about how she and I should get going. My phone pings. Probably Treva.

I look.

It's Tía Verónica.

"It's from Tía," I tell everyone. Tía has never texted me before. Phone calls, yes. Texts, no.

They wait while I read it.

Veronica: Coleto, you were a small boy who did not want to be cabbage. But who was happy to be a jacket. You have been my jacket, Coleto. Please come stay with us all summer long, so you and Felipe can be together.

I feel tears rushing down my face. Felipe takes the phone from my hand and reads the text. Then he reads it out loud.

"*Victoria.*" he says to all of us. "*Tengamos coraje.*"

"Victory," I translate for Mom. "Be brave."

She takes my hand and squeezes it. Just like she did the morning Dad went to jail.

CHAPTER 49

TIO'S CAR AND THE RENTED trailer are stuffed so full their sides are bulging. Felipe and I helped load all day yesterday.

One by one, Mom and I hug Juliana, Isabella, Benito, and Tío Carlos. One by one, Felipe hugs and kisses them.

Tío puts both arms on Felipe's shoulders. "Be well, my son. Do what Tía Stacey and Tío Hank ask you to. Be a good *hermano* to Coleto. And be a good class president." Tío is trying not to cry. We're all trying not to cry.

"You will come home to Canada the day after school ends."

"We'll drive him there, Carlos," Mom says, wiping her eyes.

Tío nods. "Please tell Hank I am sorry the government would not allow us to visit. We wanted to see him."

"I know," says Mom. "He'll miss you deeply. I will miss you deeply."

Tío swallows hard. "*Quizás*... perhaps we can return one day."

We nod.

I have no idea if they can return one day.

Tío steps into the car and backs out of the driveway. The car windows are down. Benito, Juliana, and Isabella wave. And wave and wave, until the car turns the corner and we can't see them anymore.

It's New Year's Day.

Mom, Felipe, and I slowly walk back to our house. Somehow Felipe managed to convince Tío to let him stay and finish out the school year. And Mom insisted Felipe stay with us. Tío and Felipe brought his bed and dresser over yesterday.

Felipe and I climb the stairs to our room.

Last night Mom stenciled Felipe's name above mine, so the wall outside my bedroom door now says FELIPE'S ROOM & COLE'S ROOM. I asked Mom to put his name on top: I thought it might make him feel better.

That's the first thing Felipe sees when we reach the top of the stairs. He stops in front of the letters. Touches them. "This is the proper order," he says. "The class president is always listed first."

"The first name's responsible for room cleanup," I tell him.

We walk into the room and stare at his unassembled bed.

I lean against the headboard, which is leaning against a wall. "Which corner do you want?"

He looks around, then points to the corner opposite my bed. We set up his bed so that the two of us will be facing each other.

The room's a bit crowded, but not too bad.

Felipe looks around. I don't know what he's looking at, he's been in my room thousands of times.

"Anything wrong?" I ask.

"Colors."

I look at my walls, which are the same shade of gray as August Mersy school colors. With touches of crimson. "You want a different color? We can do it."

"Colors," he repeats. "How about turquoise and yellow."

I look at him. "Stripes?"

He stands on his toes and starts sparring with me. We go back and forth, around and around the small space in the room. My reach is longer, but Felipe makes up for it by constantly ducking under my arms and pretending to hit my stomach. I hope he doesn't slip.

"Okay," I say as we circle each other. "Not stripes. Polka dots?"

He backs away, grabs a pillow off his bed, and throws it at me. I deflect it just in time.

"Two walls turquoise," he says, "two walls yellow."

"I get turquoise."

"*No hay problema*. I like yellow."

"When should we paint them? School starts in two days."

"What about today?" he asks.

"You think any hardware stores are open?"

"Somebody's always open," he says. "Home Depot. Target. Somebody."

We go downstairs, where Mom's staring at the refrigerator. "Can't figure out what to make for dinner tonight," she says. "Dad's coming home Saturday and I want to serve a holiday meal for him. I thought I'd make turkey and stuffing and mashed potatoes and pumpkin pie, plus ham and wild rice and lots of pastries—Thanksgiving and Christmas and New Year's all in one meal."

"I am ready!" Felipe tells her. "I will help Tío Hank eat everything in sight."

"Mom. We want to paint our room. Me and Felipe. Like, today. Is that okay?"

She closes the refrigerator door and stares at us. "I taught you both how to paint interior walls. But that was three years ago."

"I remember how," Felipe assures her. "I will make certain Cole remembers."

Mom smiles at this. "Where will you get the paint?"

"I think the hardware store's open for three or four hours today," I say.

"What colors?" she asks.

"Turquoise and yellow," Felipe says without hesitation.

Mom nods. She understands. He wants to feel the presence of his family.

"Let me get you some cash. If the hardware store isn't open, you can take the bus to Home Depot."

The hardware store is open, and the owner seems happy to see us. Nobody else is around. "What can I help you boys with?"

"Interior paint," I say. "We're looking for two gallons of deep turquoise and two gallons of sunshine yellow."

He points to where the paint chips are. Felipe and I study them. Finally, we make our choices and give them to the owner, who goes to mix the paints.

He puts the four cans on the counter, along with a couple of mixing sticks.

"I haven't seen you in a while," he says to me. "Not since you bought the poster board a few months ago."

"Wow! How did you remember what I bought?"

"If I recall, you were particular about the size I should cut the board."

I was pretty exact about the size so I could keep the poster board in my backpack, between my books. *Fa mi lia.* F word.

"I've never seen any school project that needed such small posters," he says. "What was it for?"

"Our class election. Felipe was running for class president."

He looks at Felipe. "Did you win?"

For a second or two Felipe doesn't say anything. Finally, he does. "Yes. I won the election."

The owner looks at him. "You don't sound too happy about it."

"I won the election, but I lost the battle."

"That doesn't sound good," says the owner.

"Losing a battle doesn't mean losing a war," I say. "We haven't lost the war."

"That's good to know," says the owner, handing me the change. "Happy painting."

CHAPTER 50

"**WHY AREN'T WE STANDING CLOSER** to the door? We're, like, twenty feet away."

"Because," says Mom, "it's none of the guards' business what we say to each other when Dad comes out that door."

Mom, Felipe, and I are standing outside Cook County Jail, near the door they told us Dad would come out. It's a Saturday. Mom's holding one of Dad's winter jackets for him. It was a hot day in September when he went to jail.

We hear the creak of a heavy metal door and look up.

It's not Dad.

This goes on for maybe fifteen minutes. *Creak. Exit. Creak. Exit.* No Dad.

But then, suddenly, it *is* Dad!

He sees us.

Grins.

And covers the distance in no time. Not running. Just walking tall and steady. With a purpose.

The first person he hugs is Felipe.

"I'm so sorry this has happened to your family, Felipe." Dad pulls back to look Felipe in the face. "How are you holding up?"

Felipe nods. Swallows. "I will be brave, Tío. Like you."

"You have a home with us as long as you need it. You know that," says Dad.

He hugs Felipe a while longer.

Then it's my turn.

Dad and I squeeze each other tight. It feels good.

"I'm glad you're out, Dad. I'm glad you're safe."

He pulls back, his arms on my shoulders. "You've grown an inch."

I want to say something, but I'm too choked up.

Then Dad hugs Mom.

A long time.

She drops his jacket. I pick it up.

Finally, Dad steps back. "Brrrrr!"

I hand him his jacket. He shrugs into it and zips it up.

The four of us link arms and walk away from Cook County Jail.

Mom, Felipe, and I tell Dad everything that's happened since he's been in jail. We talk at the same time, sometimes finishing another person's sentence, sometimes veering to another subject. We all pull out our cells to show Dad different pictures: Felipe's election campaign, his celebration party, my cross country win at the last meet, everything we've recorded for him to see.

Dad listens and looks. "You did what?" he asks several times. Or: "Whoa, whoa! Back up a minute! Explain that."

We walk all the way to the el stop, talking the whole time.

We talk all the way to the Logan Square el stop, where we get off. Dad says he'd rather walk home than catch a bus, so we walk south on Kedzie.

Dad says to Mom, "I could use some good food. How about we all grab a bite somewhere?"

Felipe and I look at each other.

"How about we do that tomorrow?" Mom asks as she puts her arm around Dad's waist. "There's something special waiting at home."

"Oh. Okay. What is it?" Dad asks.

"It's a surprise," says Mom.

"I hope there's beer involved."

"There is."

Felipe and I are walking behind, letting Mom and Dad take the lead. When they get to our street, they turn the corner.

Our block is full of people. Maybe four or five hundred. They see Dad and cheer. *"Welcome home, Hank!"*

Dad stops in his tracks.

A banner spans the whole street, held up by lampposts on each side. WELCOME HOME HANK RENNER!

People cheer and whistle. They stomp their feet and clap their hands.

The smell of food fills the air. Brats. Tacos. Barbecue.

Mrs. Green and Nikki Zurlo worked together to get a block party permit from the city. Felipe and Bianca coordinated the food and drinks. Mr. Cafasso, our school janitor, somehow found out about the party and said he wanted to paint the banners.

Each year there must be thousands of block parties in the neighborhoods of Chicago. But I wonder if any besides this one have ever taken place in January.

Dad rubs his face. Then he steps forward.

People rush up to greet him.

He grabs Mom's hand and pretty soon I can't see either of them any more. They're swallowed up by the people.

"We may as well eat now," says Felipe. "Tío Hank will not stop until he has spoken to every single person."

"Like somebody else I know."

"*Sí.*"

I look around for Treva and spot her standing on the stairs of my house. I make my way over to her while Felipe goes off to sample the foods.

Treva is standing with two other people. Nachman and somebody I don't know. But she looks a lot like Nachman.

"Mom, this is Cole Renner," says Treva. "Cole, this is my mother, Winona Soldat."

I shake hands with her mother, who has sad eyes.

"Your father is a hero of Treva's," says Mrs. Soldat. "She read about him when we lived in Portland. The things he was doing inspired her to be part of the student boycott of standardized testing."

Treva smiles. "I was hoping to meet him today, but it looks like he's never going to come out of this crowd."

I climb up a step so I'm standing with Treva and Nachman. "He'll make his way here," I tell them. "He wants to meet all of you. It's really good of you to come."

I see Felipe making his way toward us. He's not holding a plate of food after all. He's bringing a bunch of tenth graders our way. Emerald. Fatima. Ethan. Salma. Ricardo. He texted them all and asked them to come.

Nachman looks at me. "This might be a good occasion for a poem, Cole."

I think about that.

Then I pull out my phone and write.

I know the F word I want. The F word we all need to learn if we're going to survive.

FIGHT

We will fight back
Against those who would keep us down
We will fight back
For bread and butter that we lack
Your laws are framed to keep us bound
You will not sink us to the ground
In every school and every town
We will fight back

Treva's reading the poem over one of my shoulders, Felipe over the other.

Felipe goes into the house and comes back quickly.

He hands me Dad's megaphone.

Our megaphone.

I turn it on. I read my poem to the crowd.

DISCUSS

THIS BOOK

1. *Friendship* is an F word, and Cole and Felipe have been friends since first grade. How does Cole and Felipe's friendship compare to your idea of friendship? Discuss the ways in which they count on each other and trust each other completely. What is your favorite Cole-and-Felipe scene? Why?

2. Discuss the cross-country scenes. What do they show about teamwork? What do they show about Cole? How does Cole's cross-country running help shape who he is?

3. A stranger coming to town is a common plot element in fiction. In *The F Words* Treva is the stranger who comes to Cole's school. How do things change because of Treva? What might have been different if Treva hadn't come to town? What other examples can you think of from books or film in which a stranger comes to town and affects the course of the story?

4. Discuss the parallels between Cole's experiences in school and his father's experiences in jail. In what ways are they similar? In what ways are they different? What do you think these parallels say about our society?

5. Which is your favorite F-word poem in the book? Why? Think of an F-word that says something about your life. What is it? If you wrote a poem about that word, would you try to write the poem in free verse? Or would you try some sort of syllable-count? Or would you try writing the poem in a form, such as a sonnet? Why?

6. On the first page of *The F Word*s Cole is communicating with the world. On the last page of *The F Words* Cole is communicating with the world. In what ways has his communication changed? Consider media, content, audience. By the end of the story, in what ways has Cole stayed the same? In what ways has he changed?

PRAISE FOR THE F WORDS

"I have wondered for a long time where the YA stories with young-person-as-activist have been hiding, or waiting to be written. Wait no more. I love the way this book captures the advice out there to think globally by acting locally. Cole is a model character for our time, and for readers of all ages."

—CHRIS TEBBETTS, CO-AUTHOR OF THE #1 NYTIMES BESTSELLING *MIDDLE SCHOOL SERIES* WITH JAMES PATTERSON

"In The F Words, *Gregorich's beautifully crafted, diverse characters use the power of words to fight racism and injustice. They tackle today's issues in a take-your-breath-away page turner that teens will want to read in one sitting. I hope this finds its way into every high school classroom."*

—ROXANNE F. OWENS, PhD, CHAIR, TEACHER EDUCATION DEPAUL UNIVERSITY COLLEGE OF EDUCATION; EDITOR, *ILLINOIS READING COUNCIL JOURNAL*

"The F Words powerfully and cleverly highlights how injustice, both personal and political, becomes a catalyst for high-schooler Cole Renner to change his own life—and that of his fellow students. What a great notion—to make the writing of poetry a tool for growth and finding one's voice! This book will capture the interest of any young reader and may very well change lives."

—ROBERT BURLEIGH, AWARD-WINNING AUTHOR OF MORE THAN 50 BOOKS INCLUDING *FLIGHT: THE JOURNEY OF CHARLES LINDBERG, HOOPS* AND *ABRAHAM LINCOLN COMES HOME,* A PRAIRIE STATE AWARD WINNER

"Barbara Gregorich has given us a politically admirable story about young people fighting injustice. It is not only inspirational; it is also an entertaining, gripping read. Smoothly and clearly written, lively, clever, believable, and witty. The F Words *is a genuine page-turner."*

—BRUCE LEVINE, AUTHOR OF *THE FALL OF THE HOUSE OF DIXIE*

OTHER BOOKS BY

BARBARA GREGORICH

She's on First

Women at Play: The Story of Women in Baseball

Sound Proof

Jack and Larry

Charlie Chan's Poppa: Earl Derr Biggers

Cookie the Cockatoo: Everything Changes

ABOUT THE
AUTHOR

ARBARA GREGORICH HAS DESIGNED, BUILT, carried, and shared protest signs. On the street, not in books. Now, because the world needs people to protest injustice, she has written *The F Words* — in which she brings the importance of those signs into a story which honors the powerful role that young people have always played in movements for social change.